The Good Bride

The Good Bride

A Novel

JEN MARIE WIGGINS

CROOKED
LANE

NEW YORK

Copyright © 2024 by Jen Marie Wiggins

Published in the United States by Crooked Lane Books, an imprint of The Quick Brown Fox & Company LLC.

Crooked Lane Books and its logo are trademarks of The Quick Brown Fox & Company LLC.

Library of Congress Catalog-in-Publication data available upon request.

ISBN (hardcover): 979-8-89242-004-4
ISBN (ebook): 979-8-89242-005-1

Cover design by Heather VenHuizen

Printed in the United States.

www.crookedlanebooks.com

Crooked Lane Books
34 West 27th St., 10th Floor
New York, NY 10001

First Edition: December 2024

10 9 8 7 6 5 4 3 2 1

*For the people of Mexico Beach, Florida,
and for Travis.
Both whose quiet resilience is beautiful.*

PART 1

Chapter One

Ruth

❧

The road to hell is paved with secrets.

It's a strange thought for Ruth Bancroft to have as she pulls up to the Reid Street boutique, Two Be Wed. She always did that. Let her student's work creep in even after she left the classroom.

The assignment—rewrite a common expression—was designed to spur critical thinking skills, and the response from a soft-spoken 11th grader had taken her by surprise.

Good intentions and secrets are cut from the same cloth, she thinks, pausing to admire the shop's window, its mannequin in a playful avant-garde ball gown made of seer sucker and lace. It was the kind of quirky teacher comment she usually liked to include along with a student's grade and might be suiting too many scenarios lately.

Ruth pushes open the boutique's door and a bell chimes, the familiar smell of fresh paint and industrial glue everywhere since Hurricane Kerry. Her sister, Sophia, and mother, Caroline, are perched on the settee in front of the sales floor's three-way mirror, two glasses of champagne fizzing between them. Ruth can see from the set of her mother's mouth and the pinched appraisal of the plastic flute in her hand that she won't be drinking it.

Sophia looks up, blonde waves slipping over her shoulders as she shuts the binder in her lap. It's only 84 degrees outside, mild for October in the Florida panhandle, but Ruth is already sweating. Her bushel of too-thick hair is spurring a four-alarm fire against her neck. As usual, her sister looks impossibly put-together, her linen tunic unwrinkled, fresh lipstick. Every bit of her permeating the Instagram Influencer she is.

Sophia stands, phone in her hand and smooths her outfit. "Jo's running behind—maybe grab some pics now?"

"Well, hello to you too, big sis—it's nice to see you this morning . . ."

There's a quick hug, a set of air kisses along with her sister's flippant laugh, and Ruth pastes on a smile, willing herself again not to count all the ways her "little beach wedding" isn't going as planned. In the twelve months since she'd pitched the idea to her fiancé, the town had nearly been leveled. The now famous category four storm barreled through Blue Compass on the same day their engagement announcement hit the Savannah Morning News. Kerry's last-minute turn had taken everyone by surprise—especially Blue Compass residents who never evacuated for any storm and certainly hadn't batted an eyelash at earlier predictions of a softer brush to the east.

From the comfort of her fiancé's couch, they'd watched as the storm made direct landfall, the clarity of Teo's absurdly big television unsettling as roads cracked like wet spackle in front of them and whole homes washed away in real time. Six weeks later, when the National Guard let people return, she'd been inconsolable, stammering over and over that a bomb had gone off. Kerry had sheared the entire beach district. Every plant and tree, business and home ripped up by the root. Even Blue Compass's famous sugar white sand was gone. In its place was a gritty dirt landscape dotted only by driveways—the parking slabs like gravestones while mountains of debris lined every curb.

Once the shock wore off, Ruth dug in. Blue Compass needed her more than ever. Teo said he would marry her anywhere. Her family was a much harder sell.

So now here she was—a year later, Blue Compass's reluctant poster bride in front of the camera again. Another painful round of forced smiles, more craning and contorting. Hips back. Chest up. Always in that way that everyone knows looks good in photos but feels ridiculous in the moment. She didn't need another reminder that the publicity was a good thing.

Two Be Wed was lucky to be open at all. One block to the left, the roof was still caved in on a consignment shop with an identical store front. Blue Compass's little version of Main Street, once lined in pots of mums and marked by an American flag, was nowhere near restored. Since her sister's account, @sophiasez, began featuring the wedding, donations to the city's recovery fund had tripled.

"Lord, let me do it." Sophia jams her head into Ruth's, and she yelps as her sister snaps a few artfully arranged selfies in front of the shop's etched glass logo. As Ruth peels herself away, the clicks continue.

"There's my *bride* . . ." The voice comes from a tiny office in the back as Kayla Jennings appears, the young owner strapping a pin cushion to her wrist.

Ruth smiles and squelches the urge to do a double take, her eyes shooting to the floor as Kayla tosses back hair that should be coarse and black—yet suddenly isn't. Since their last visit, her wedding planner has colored and straightened her tight curls, a surprise bubblegum pink now peeking from the bottom layer.

"It's so cute." Sophia's squeal is cloying as she reaches out to touch a pink strand before going in for a full hug.

Kayla is about to say something when the front door flies open. A burst of noise and a dirty Ked propping it in place as Ruth's niece and nephew toddle in. Behind them, Jo Bancroft-Hunt, teeters in the doorframe. Her sister is sweaty and balancing on one foot, a death grip on the wrist of each of her twins. A menagerie of backpacks and diaper bags look ready to topple her.

"The sitter still hasn't shown, and Daddy's out too far fishing." Jo rolls her green eyes on the word *fishing* as she sheds the bags on the satin chair next to Caroline, who slides over. Jo turns, catching a glimpse of herself in the mirror. A sinister looking brown stain streaks her white Henley. "Well, that's *new*." She licks her thumb and rubs at it aggressively before rolling her eyes again and giving up.

"There's the most beautiful flower girl in the world." Ruth runs over to scoop up her four-year-old niece.

"Champagne?" Kayla holds up the bottle as she looks at Jo, bending to pick up one of the twin's bags and hang it on a hook.

Jo nods emphatically, "Sweet angel from heaven—yes."

The twins plop down next to Caroline on the settee as her eyes go wide. "Beauregard Frankford Hunt, what's in your pocket?" Caroline leans over to examine her grandson's hand as he reaches into his shorts. Her voice jumps three octaves as he lifts his palm toward her face. "Is that a dead frog?"

Caroline recoils as Jo grabs for a trashcan by the counter. When she's finished shaking Beau's hands out over the gold bin, she wipes her own on her jeans before searching through a unicorn backpack until she unearths matching iPads. Handing them over to the twins, she sighs, "Yesterday, I found one of those snake skin molts in his backpack. I swear I miss the nanny more than I do the firm, hands down."

Rhea wiggles free from Ruth to grab at the tablet then looks back up at her aunt. Her emerald eyes pinched in a serious expression. "Dere's a man in our window."

"What?" Sophia laughs.

"I told Mommy. I don't like dat scary man."

Jo suppresses another eye roll. "*Daddy* let them watch a Halloween movie marathon last night . . . obviously, we're crushing this parenting thing."

Kayla hands the sisters their bridesmaid dresses in heavy plastic bags, and Ruth follows them into the tiny fitting room, relieved her own Alexander McQueen gown hadn't needed much alteration. The strapless bodice sat perfectly at her waist, the simple neckline chosen to accent where Caroline's necklace hit just at her collar bone. The diamond choker with its intricate filigree was something she was still wrapping her mind around wearing. The center stone alone was six carats. It was a family heirloom, and Ruth knew that if she so much as nicked a filigree, she would be disowned.

"I'm so glad this is the last of the errands." Ruth zips up Sophia's dress. "I just want as little drama as possible for the rest of the week."

Sophia lets out a snort. "*Umm*—says the girl who waited till this morning to drop the bomb that dear ol' Dad is walking you down the aisle."

"Come on, you know how hard that was for me—but Dad really wants to . . . and at least he's trying—"

"Seriously, I'm shocked Mom is here at all—or that she's even talking to you." Jo steps out of her jeans and into her dress. "It's like this wedding is mellowing her out."

The bridesmaid designs were pale pink and made of a soft shantung silk. Ruth had been mindful with their selection, each tailored to work with the sister's body type. With the help of Kayla, Sophia's skimmed the lines of her waif-like figure offering the illusion of curves. A few skillfully placed darts cinched Jo's dress in all the right places. The results were better than Ruth could've imagined.

"The dresses are perfect. Caroline is going to die." Stepping aside, she clears a path so they can squeeze by and get the final nod of approval, which is waiting—as always—from their mother.

Chapter Two

Kayla

❧

Outside the dressing room curtain, Kayla's relieved to hear the oldest sister and the mother are finally happy with the dresses. Bizarre requests and prewedding jitters are nothing new—though it is usually coming from the bride. Seven hundred thousand followers or not, "Insta-zilla" was definitely a new wedding hybrid—and one that was working her last nerve.

Last week, that sister had actually sent her an email wondering if they could "find a way to lure the area's sea manatees and make them swim near the reception?"

Who knew what fresh hell she might have today?

Sophia parts the garnet velvet curtain that divides the dressing area, and scoops up Rhea who is still sitting quietly with her iPad. She fishes two patterned headbands from her purse and arranges them on the child's white blonde head, then her own. Angling her phone, she snaps a few shots of them together.

Sophia's eyes meet Kayla's, and she says, "Don't worry. These have nothing to do with today—just grabbing for later. I love

9

the light in here." Sophia adjusts the curls around the girl's gingham band. "I just became Bella Headbands' newest brand ambassador. The company's algorithm tells me the best time to post, and I like to have a few options ready for them. After dinner is usually peak shopping."

Kayla offers her a tight smile. For the thousandth time reminding herself of all the reasons she's doing this. Though it isn't just for the money, she tosses in a mental tabulation of her commission for good measure.

Ruth Bancroft's wedding is definitely the biggest she's ever planned, and the fanciest the town has ever seen. Two hundred plus out-of-town guests and first-class everything. The Bancroft name carries enough weight to have people streaming in from all over Georgia. There isn't a small business the wedding hasn't touched. From Reid Street Coffee locals to a million faceless strangers on the Internet, no one can seem to get enough of the "Gulf Coast's Wedding of the Year." Though she'd take all the free press she could get for Two Be Wed, the glamor of it was long ago lost on her. Putting together an event post-Charlie meant outsourcing everything from the wedding invitation's 100-pound linen cardstock to every platinum rimmed place setting for the reception. Her only saving grace was that Blue Compass's crazy celebrity chef had agreed to cater the wedding—which definitely wasn't saying much.

Jo steps out of the dressing area, hanging her dress as she touches her forehead. "I'm suddenly not feeling the greatest. I'm gonna get out of here before the twins break something—Kayla, you're a magician."

There's a round of hugs, and the sister is gathering the children when the doorbell chimes again. Kayla turns to find familiar faces in the doorway, both men sunburned and carrying picket signs.

"Guys, there's got to be other places to go on Reid Street." She shoots them a glare even as she reaches behind the counter and hands them a key to the restroom.

Caroline turns, setting down her still-full glass of champagne as she sizes up the two visitors. "Oh—I thought we closed the store for today's fitting?"

Kayla shrugs, "The perks of being so close to City Hall. It's either them or trick-or-treaters all week."

In fishing hats and flip flops, Jeff and Randy-Jo Markson are old classmates of Kayla's. They nod at the family before leaning their signs against the wall and ducking into the restroom. The words "Vote No on Building Ordinance 23" sprout upside down on the carpet. The other sign, "No High Rise Hell" sits upright, the words struck through in red like they're bleeding.

"I'm just glad somebody's holding City Council's feet to the fire." Ruth scrunches up her nose. "Can you imagine this place turning into Myrtle Beach?"

The stories were practically folklore now. Anyone connected to Blue Compass knew about real estate developers with deep pockets salivating at the doorsteps of traumatized beach owners. They arrived before Kerry's flood waters had fully receded, before some owner's loved ones were cold in the ground. But Blue Compass had always been an untamed beach bum, its charm carved out of pure stubbornness and a generations-long distaste for progress. It was one of the reasons Kayla never left. This was a place where someone still answered the phone at City Hall, and people didn't feel the need to paint things weathered by salt air. Her father was the chief of police here, and though she might have her issues with him, they had both worked hard to put down roots. No building higher than four stories strangled Blue Compass's skyline, and she hoped it never did. Now, the heady combination of desperation and easy money coupled with the cities' mounting seven-figure shortfall had begun to reprioritize some people's thinking.

Fresh meat.

Was that what the yummy fiancé had called it? At one of their meetings, the groom, who worked for some law firm in Savannah, had mentioned experience with these types of developers—and it had not been good. Kayla heard he was doing pro-bono work for a few of the locals, and he seemed to know what he was talking about. Sadly, and just as the fiancé had predicted, there'd been some initial resistance, but a vote to amend the city's building ordinance was on the docket for next week. Now, the city's fate—and its soul—rested in the hands of the new City Council and its newly re-elected mayor.

Sophia takes out her lipstick as the front door closes behind Jo and the twins. "I think it's great what they're doing—the protestors. It's why what *we* are doing—the wedding is so important." She reapplies using the big mirror, making a duck face as she closes the tube. "I'll check the Go Fund Me when I have time and make sure to post about it—my readers have been so crazy generous already . . ."

Kayla forces a smile. "There are still a ton of last-minute details to get through. Let me grab my checklist from the back."

In her office, she finds her clipboard where she left it. The counter and cabinets along the back wall meant to serve as her kitchen and breakroom were completed last week. For months, she'd been bookmarking stone and interesting veined countertops, but when it came time to install, her budget only allowed for a cheap speckled Formica. God, even Mother Nature seemed to give preferential treatment to the rich.

The Bancroft's vacation home, "Summerhouse," had fared better than most of the town. The lucky one-mile difference of their neighborhood, Nautilus Cove, had set the sole strip of estate homes just inside the storm's eye wall. The Bancroft's sprawling beach property was slated for the rehearsal dinner's planned oyster roast. Next to it, the neighborhood clubhouse and pool complex would host the ceremony and reception. For the next four days, she was in charge of both.

Kayla takes a deep inhale through her nose as she returns to the sales floor. When she gets there, she catches Sophia crooning something about "crowd control" and when she realizes the women are discussing the weekend's security, she feels her face get hot.

They'd only needed one security guard to obtain the necessary permits, she explains.

"And there's no reason to think we need more?" asks Ruth.

The mother finally looks up from her phone, freeing herself from some serious texting. Her face is flushed, and for a moment, Caroline Bancroft could be the bride's sister. Ruth has the same bee-stung lips, the same bird-like features. Rumors of a youth spent on the pageant circuit explains the mother's ramrod straight posture.

"I agree." Sophia scribbles something in the massive bridal notebook. "We don't want a bunch of 'looky-loos' everywhere."

Kayla shoves down a pang of guilt. It's mostly a lie of omission. Twenty-four hours ago she'd come in to find Two Be Wed's back door ajar. Nothing gone. Nothing out of place. The police had gotten there in minutes. (The perks of a small town—especially when your father's the police chief.) After they searched the store and came up empty-handed, Kayla attempted to start the day's business in her office, finding the room still tidy, the Bancroft wedding folder still neat on her desk. Yet, she wasn't fully convinced the open door was the carelessness of the janitor. The old man never forgot to lock up.

"Three valets and one security guard is perfect," Kayla says. She closes her eyes and pictures the metal stakes around the pool and clubhouse. Painted white and designed to mimic beach pickets, they offered a natural and picturesque barrier that under normal circumstances would be more than adequate. *If her father thought it was best not to worry the family—who was she to argue?*

* * *

Thirty minutes later, Kayla is still feeling guilty as she locks up behind them. The three women had left in a hurry, eager to get ready for the bachelorette party later that evening. She'd just flipped the sign to "closed" when she hears it. A scream—high-pitched and sharp enough to make her drop her keys. The sound comes from beyond the display window, her view blocked by the puff of her bridal mannequin's skirt. Kayla, who always prided herself on staying calm, goes cold. Grabbing for her keys, she kicks open the door and runs.

Chapter Three

Teo

~

Weddings make people crazy.

Teo Vargas takes a sip of beer, thinking it's clearly having that effect on his fiancée. Ruth had just phoned, talking too fast. There'd been something about a Halloween prank? A flat tire and a fake bloody eyeball? He'd tried not to laugh as she described it—the rubber decoration sitting in a pool of fake blood. Ruth must've picked up a nail somewhere, and her tire had gone flat outside the bridal shop. Then some kind of early Halloween prankster had taken the opportunity to leave a fake eye there. For a second, the girls had mistaken the red ooze seeping down the wheel as real. He could almost see it—Ruth's doey eyes going wide, Sophia screaming till people came running out of the stores.

So, you got slimed? Sounds like a memento for the wedding scrapbook? Sarcasm was always his go-to. Toss it in like a grenade and you could disarm any situation.

Let's keep the eyeball. Someday we'll let our babies play with it. She had laughed, and that seemed to snap her back to herself. *Or you could always call the tow truck and leave it in the driver's glove box.* After a moment, even Caroline was laughing.

Teo takes another swig of his Blue Moon and looks around the dingy beach rental. Pushing back a pair of stiff curtains, he peers out at the gutted backside of the Sailfish Motel, wondering if maybe it's his own wedding decisions he should be second guessing. Two small bedrooms, one bathroom. He knew Ruth's father had tried—that the pickings for rentals were slim—but one thing was certain, no matter how the bachelor party went tonight, someone was sleeping on the floor.

When Ruth's father, Thaddeus Hargrove, resurfaced six weeks ago—contrite and flashing a one-year sobriety chip—everyone else had been skeptical. Everyone, except Teo's fiancée.

Ruth saw him without hesitation, somehow forgetting that his presence in her life had always been like a game of reverse whack-a-mole, his last re-emergence culminating with a no-show at her college graduation. The details were hazy, but from what Teo could glean, Thad was like most addicts: sporadic, unreliable, and mean when he didn't get his way. The family's first semblance of stability came later with Caroline's second marriage to Blake Bancroft, the original owner of Summerhouse.

Still, this *new* Thad had been nothing but an open book. He had a job managing some restaurant and hadn't asked anyone for anything. There'd been a handful of dinners and outings, a day trip from his place in Atlanta to Savannah. Though Teo didn't like that the old man was still playing poker—an admission he'd offered freely with an elbow to Teo's gut and that same god-awful wink (*"One vice at a time, Big T. One vice at a time . . ."*)

It wasn't that Teo minded the sparse conditions, but he'd have been just as happy to stay with his mother in the Bancrofts' carriage house. He already felt bad leaving her alone with Ruth's family, but his fiancé had pleaded, "Boys in one place, girls in another—one last time."

Usually, he found Ruth's old-fashioned tendencies a little more charming. Still, they were almost to the finish line. *You only get married once,* everyone keeps telling him.

Teo's phone buzzes, and he's checking his texts when there's a sound at the door. His soon to be father-in-law is in the entry-way, sport coat and jeans, his arms loaded with grocery bags and a suitcase.

"There's the man of the hour." Thad drops everything on the floor, and the two shake hands and slap shoulders before he puts his things in the bigger of the two bedrooms. "Boy, this place sure looked better in photos." Thad scratches at his chin and wipes sweat from a silver, over-gelled hairline, the part unflinching. "I had to scramble after the other one fell through . . . something about termites but—yikes, maybe I can call somebody . . ."

Teo shakes his head and says that it's fine, as a car peels into the driveway. He looks through the window, knowing it has to be the one he's been waiting for. Even as kids, Nicholas Finley had always known how to make an entrance. Gravel flying, radio at full blast, Teo watches as his best man cuts off the engine, presses a button to shut the automatic top of a red Mustang convertible. His pale skin is freckled from the drive, and unruly ginger hair tumbles from a straw cowboy hat, yet Nick hasn't aged at all. There's that same pummeled nose—broken too many times to count—thin lips turned up in a smirk, an awful pink flamingo button-up only he could make work. Two years of medical school on the other side of the country clearly hadn't changed him at all.

"Only you would rent a Mustang . . ." Teo smiles and rolls his eyes as he steps off the porch. Teo has three inches of height on Nick, but when Nick gets to him, he picks him up and spins him around.

"Come here, you sexy Latin lover! You know you're the only guy in the whole universe I bring out my *good* hat for." He sets Teo down, wrestling the groom into a playful headlock before he yanks off his thatched yellow Stetson and smashes it onto Teo's head.

After introductions, the three men are in the kitchen, easily talking. Teo offers Nicholas a beer as the two catch up, and they both try not to watch as Thad examines the contents of the fridge over and over. With each open and shut, stale air fills the kitchen.

"You sure you don't mind us going to a bar?"

"Not at all." Thad twists off the top of a nonalcoholic beer. "Trust me. There's no worries—it's *your* night. Besides, I heard the karaoke at this place is epic. Now, where is JD? Surely, Jo has let him off his leash by now?"

Teo finishes his beer and feels the tension leave his shoulders. The last few times he'd been here, he'd been buried in piles of paperwork for his probono Blue Compass clients. He'd promised himself and Ruth nothing too wild tonight, but maybe he can stand to let loose a little.

A few minutes later, Teo's soon-to-be brother-in-law, John David Hunt pulls in. JD drops his overnight bag on the already cluttered counter. "Man, I gotta tell you about this monster *'Red'* I reeled in today. He was a fighter."

It was one of things Teo loved about JD, about Blue Compass as a whole. With the quintessential sunburnt neck and fishing oxford pulled tight over a soft midsection, JD could be any of a hundred anglers crowding the docks of Blue Compass. There was always some long passionate oration about wrestling a fish or the best coordinates to find grouper or snapper, strong opinions about which jigs and gaffs to use or the optimal type of bait depending upon whatever fishing season it was or was about to be. In Blue Compass, the passion was always as palpable as the humidity, but with JD it was downright manic.

Teo tosses his empty bottle at the trashcan and looks at the three of them, thinking suddenly of his own father, that he was the missing piece right now. A pang of sadness washes over him, and he pushes it away, unearthing a flippant comment about JD and his fish smell instead. Maybe some guy time was just the thing. One night at a rundown oyster joint . . . what could possibly go wrong?

* * *

The LookSee Lounge is the only bar up and running in Blue Compass since Hurricane Kerry. Situated across from the beach district on the business side of Highway 98, the half-biker joint, half-oyster house had never been much to look at, or its view much to see. Still, the gravel lot is already packed as the four men arrive in Nick's Mustang.

They step inside, and Teo inhales the same dank smell of fish and cigarettes, relieved to find the owners haven't gone overboard with repairs. There's a new roof, new bathrooms, a fresh coat of shellac on the cement floors, but the walls remain exposed, the decaying karaoke stage is untouched. The only other addition is a three-foot high water line that spans the ancient driftwood bar, "Fuck You Kerry" scrawled across it in thick black Sharpie.

They are all starving, and the four men order buckets of beer, wings, and fried crab claws as well as four dozen of the LookSee's famous salty oysters. By the time the baskets of greasy food arrive, they've burned through two buckets of beer and are busy swapping fishing stories. On stage, a leathery woman Teo knows as Mabel performs a raspy mike check as she yanks at her thigh-high sequin skirt. As she adjusts the microphone, Teo tries to recall her exact age. She was in a record book somewhere. Skirting at least 80 years old, she wasn't just the oldest and only karaoke DJ in Blue Compass, she and her pink cowboy boots were known all over this side of the Mason Dixon line thanks to her massive social media following.

Teo leans back in his chair as the warmth of alcohol swirls in his stomach. "This place is great—I love it here."

"Seriously, you should've had the whole wedding here." Nick licks two fingers. "You could do the ceremony right there on the karaoke stage, oysters instead of hors d'oeuvres, Mabel could officiate . . ."

JD rolls his eyes. "Sophia is already making my wife—*everybody*—nuts. She would've loved that." He scrapes at the shell of an oyster, guiding its plump body onto a saltine. "Jo about lost it today because I was six miles out when the babysitter canceled. How am I supposed to know the girl was gonna flake for the whole week?"

Nick scoots back his chair and crosses his hands over his heart like it hurts. "I don't dare claim to understand the heart of the finer sex—but you're about to find that out ol' boy—" Nick stands up and slaps Teo on the back as he challenges JD to a game of darts. The pair disappear to the back of the bar, and when they're gone, Thad looks up from his food.

"By the way, please thank your mom for me—she gave me a—" Thad lowers his voice "—she gave me a referral for—ya know, for a guy to see—a therapist, and he's great."

Teo shifts in his chair, surprised that Thad's bringing it up. "Oh yeah?—glad to hear it." He takes a bite. "You know, some people feel weird about that kinda stuff, but I grew up with it. My mom helps a lot of people—everyone needs someone to listen to them . . ."

Thad looks down then starts to peel the label from one of the bottles of beer on the table. "Yeah well, so far so good—thank her, will ya?" They eat in silence for a moment before Thad launches into another long story, this one about his days as a high school swimmer. Teo feigns interest as he turns his attention to JD and Nick who are choosing a karaoke song across the room. A second later, daylight seeps in over his shoulder from the fire exit. A man slides in, head down.

The newcomer takes a seat at the bar. His neck, his build, an elaborate tattoo creeping up from his collarbone, are all thick. Though in a bar full of fisherman and burly bikers, it fits the aesthetic.

But his jacket doesn't.

In all his visits to Blue Compass—even in January—Teo has never seen a man wearing that kind of expensive designer jacket—and for some reason, it makes him stop. He might not know labels like Ruth's family did, but that kind of smooth leather was high end. This guy definitely wasn't Blue Compass's usual brand of tourist.

The stranger catches him staring, and Teo pretends to be looking at the list of draft beers on the chalkboard behind the bar.

As the music starts up in front of them, Teo tries to return to his food, a hint of paranoia hovering around the fuzzy edges of his fifth beer. This person is watching him back. *Teo feels it.* From the far end of the bar, he's daring him to look.

A second later, Teo chances another glance. The man cranes his neck to the bartender, and the tattoo on his throat comes into full view. Teo's skin prickles as he places it, an unsettling shaded scene that sends him reeling back to his Catholic school days. There, peeking from the coat's creme neckline is Beelzebub, the Fallen Angel. The demon of gluttony crouched, yielding a bloody sword, and poised for attack.

Teo's still taking it in when their waitress interrupts him. She's balancing a round tray full of shots. Someone from the bar who seems to know him, or maybe JD, waves and shouts congrats. Everyone waves back.

"You only get married once, right?" Thad picks up his sweet tea from the table as the rest of them reach for the plastic cups.

"To your beautiful daughter!" The table cheers, and they all throw back their drinks.

Three more shots and thirty minutes later, Teo, JD, and Nick are on the karaoke stage. Sharing the same microphone, they sway in unison to a rendition of TLC's "Waterfall," which in their current state they're all certain is pure genius.

From the platform, Teo's wobbly focus scans the room. He spots the same stranger at the far end of the bar, still alone, still giving him the creeps. The bar is L-shaped and at the shorter end, Thad is talking to someone. A heavy man who looks vaguely familiar. The man is leaning against a bar stool, his posture aggressive as he pokes a finger at Thad.

The edges soften as the song ends, and Teo takes a careful step down from the stage. A second later, the ground goes soggy, and Nick catches him like a football, two feet from the concrete.

The men are still laughing as they carry each other back to the table. They throw back one final shot. The burn at the back of Teo's throat is the last thing he remembers.

* * *

The next morning, there are only pieces. The smell of something rancid. A sound like a truck above him. Teo's eyes fly open. He is facedown, the buzzsaw above him is Nick snoring on the pea-green couch.

His head screams as he racks his memory: *Loud music. A spinning room. Sips from a silver flask. Slow motion jelly steps. Sweat and fists.*

An aching hand shoots to his left eye, which is tender. As he strains to sit up, the full picture emerges like a train out of the pitch black of his memory.

They'd been in a fight.

There are more flashes. Overturned tables. Nick tossed to the floor. The body odor of a bouncer hurling them out the door. Had they started it?

Teo looks for his phone and finds it next to his pants, which are sprawled across a knocked over chair. There are seven text messages and four missed calls, all from Ruth. As he skims their content, panic collects in his chest, the surprise like a punch as he reads the last few, each a single word set in its own text bubble.

What.

The.

Hell?

Chapter Four

Ruth

❧

Four hours earlier

It's almost two in the morning when the Uber pulls up in front of Summerhouse, and the three sisters stumble into the driveway in a tequila-fueled jumble of snickers and shushes. Though they'd spent the hour-long trip home from the Panama City Bar Club in a heated and hardy dissection of their waitress's boob job, a consensus had yet to be achieved.

"I'm not tryna be a hater. I don't like to judge—" Jo opens the car's back door for Ruth. "I'm just saying it looked like somebody pumped those things full of air. I mean look at Mom's . . . you gonna go there, keep it classy, *Philadelphia*."

"Speaking of Caroline, since when does Mom stay out later than we do—at a bar, no less?" Ruth crawls out from the backseat, linking an unsteady arm through Sophia's as her sister unearths a wad of cash from her purse, thanking the Uber driver whose eyes widen at his massive tip.

"*Yeah*—and since when does she pay so much attention to—what is it, Mayor Williams? Bob—*ha* . . . what about Bob? Do people really still call him that—*Mayor Bob*? It's really weird that he showed up. What's he doing all that way out of town anyway?"

"It's not exactly easy to get a decent bottle of wine around here." Sophia stoops to take off her high heels before they turn to begin a careful scale of Summerhouse's porch stairs. "It's been like two years since Blake—she deserves some fun."

Jo leans into the railing. "Hey—I'm proud of *us*. It's waaaay late." She turns to look out at the bay then buries her head in her hands. "I can't believe the babysitter bagged out for the whole week. Ruth, your mother-in-law's a saint."

"She definitely took one for the team tonight—but I feel bad."

Sophia snorts, "I still can't get over the fact that you're gonna have a mother-in-law who's a therapist—like an actual *psychotherapist*. Considering our own mother—it's either the craziest thing I've ever heard or makes perfect sense . . ."

At the top of the stairs, Ruth finds her keys then pauses to take in the sound of the cresting waves floating up from the beach. She'd only really ever had her sisters at Summerhouse. In most of her memories, her sisters were already gone. Either in high school or off and graduated, living their lives everywhere but Savannah. This had always been the place where the eight years between her and her two older sisters (born a year apart) mattered less. The days spent hanging out on the beach or bickering, braiding each other's hair or arguing over the television were her favorite—it didn't matter what it was. She loved any of the things Ruth imagined sisters did and she'd missed out on.

The thought stops her again, and she's so absorbed in the rhythm of the rolling waves and her sisters' laughter that she almost misses it. As she scales the last step—cool air from inside the house. The front door is open, *wide open*.

They all see it at the same time and freeze. The first floor of Summerhouse is one long great room, its open concept offering sight lines to the kitchen, dining and living room areas. The door to the downstairs master is shut, but Caroline's Tiffany lamp is shattered on the floor by the sofa, shards of crystal glinting. Ruth's eyes dart to the open drawers under the TV credenza, the magazines and pillows on the floor. The book she left on the kitchen island has fallen to the wood floor, the dog-eared pages of *Madame Bovary* stirring as the scent of ocean blows in from another set of doors.

Ruth turns to the porch's double doors, her stomach seizing. They are open too. Heavy, made of hurricane glass, their handles are too cumbersome for little hands.

This wasn't the work of Rhea and Beau.

Jo has the same idea. Her eyes widen, and she bolts up the stairs. Ruth and Sophia follow as she slams open the door to the twin's room. Their bunk beds are empty; each one still neatly made. She takes off at a sprint. Down the stairs, out the kitchen door and across the back galley to the carriage house, her thick runner's legs at full sprint.

When she gets to the door, Jo flings her body against it, banging with both fists. Two seconds pass like an eternity before she bangs again. "Maya. *Maya*—tell me you have Rhea and Beau?"

The light over the door flickers on and Maya is there, the mother of the groom wearing pajamas and a confused expression. Her salt and pepper hair is loosened from its usual braid, and her thick curls are wild. In the oversized doorway, she seems even smaller than her five feet stature, and the juxtaposition is strange, making Ruth think of a lion.

"What time is it?"

Jo pushes past Maya and into the garage apartment. It's a tight space, designed originally for the help. With only a single bedroom, she finds the twins in an instance. They are snuggled under the covers, their heads on the same pillow. Rhea is snoring.

"We fell asleep watching that cartoon dragon movie."

The room seems to fill with oxygen again, and Sophia whips out her phone. "So you didn't leave the front door open?"

Maya's eyes go wide. "What—why would I leave it open?"

Sophia steps away from the bedroom and into the adjoining bathroom. Eyeing the twins, she eases the sliding door closed, her voice a hard whisper. "I'm calling the police—and security too. Lock the door."

Ruth obeys, going first to the kitchen wall and shivering as she draws a butcher knife from the block before latching the carriage house door. Ten feet away, they are all paralyzed, listening as Sophia quietly barks instructions at a 911 operator, and Ruth is suddenly grateful someone else is taking charge.

She finds her cell and dials Teo, cursing as the line trills twice then goes straight to voicemail. She'd made Teo promise not to take her drunken calls tonight—to turn off his phone and enjoy his own party. She'd also insisted JD stay with the boys at the rental house, selfishly wanting both her sisters to herself.

The one damn time someone actually listened to her.

"Did you see? They—*whoever*—left by the beach. The patio was open." Jo eyes Ruth's trembling hand and reaches for the knife, easing it from her before she sets it on the table.

Ruth pictures the long screened porch that overlooks the bay. Like most of Blue Compass, Summerhouse's exterior lights on the beach side had been replaced with red bulbs. The "sea-turtle safe" fixtures were a requirement during nesting season. The light they gave off was negligible and eerie, especially on their lone stretch of beach. There'd been more turtle tracks than usual this year, and Ruth was sure she'd flicked off all the porch lights before leaving for the bachelorette party. With the empty lot next door and their dark quiet beach, it made for an easy get-away.

* * *

From the window, they watch as retired cop Bart Brinson peels himself from Nautilus Cove's security vehicle, a white Toyota Prius. Ruth exhales, suddenly grateful for the twenty four-hour security she'd always thought of as frivolous. His round stomach emerging first, he looks as if they'd woken him from a nap.

"Somebody go get him."

Sophia and Maya head outside. The two huddle in the spot-light of the car's high beams as the older man walks the perimeter of the property, a flashlight in one hand, a stun gun in the other. Inside the main house, he flips on lights, and the tall windows flood the beach in a blinding reassurance. They're all still huddled in the window watching, and they jump when Bart knocks at their door.

"Whoever was there is long gone now. One bedroom is torn apart. You can go in. Just don't touch anything."

Jo stays with the twins and promises to reach Caroline, who is hopefully already in an Uber on her way home. With Maya leading, the rest of them make their way to the house, all of them tiptoeing and bumping into each other.

When they get inside, Bart turns to Ruth. "Check around and see what's missing."

Ruth's heart stops. "No—you don't? . . . oh God, no—"

Panic balloons in her chest as she tears up the stairs. Her room is exactly as she feared. Torn apart. The drawers pulled out. Her suitcase knocked from its luggage rack, the contents everywhere.

"No. No. No." She rifles through the pile of clothes on the floor, her stomach curdling as her mind reels back to the morning. "I didn't leave it out. I didn't leave it out . . ."

The necklace, that giant exquisite diamond, was sitting right there on her dresser. She'd been drinking coffee and had picked it up, fingering the intricate platinum filigree, marveling at the center stone when Rhea had opened the door. Her niece's eyes going wide at the "pretty" in her hand. She'd crawled into her aunt's lap, and Ruth had taken the heavy piece and fastened it around her niece's tiny neck, thinking, *a small fortune between pigtails.*

Ruth's heart sinks as she looks at the tattered bed, the mattress askew in one corner. After Rhea had left, she'd put it back on the dresser.

"It's not here." She says to no one, falling onto a pile of clothes. The necklace had been a gift from Blake to Caroline on their wedding day, an heirloom he'd meant to be handed down. Ruth is already racking her brain, scouring it for all the people, all the ways in which someone might have known about the necklace—about its whereabouts and value. There was the *Brides of Savannah* magazine cover she'd let Sophia talk her into. A fitting at Two Be Wed where they'd brought it with them for the dress. She couldn't remember if Sophia had mentioned it specifically on her Instagram. It was one of the many things that had fallen through the cracks lately.

A while ago, Ruth had stopped checking on her sister's social media. She couldn't keep up. There were too many posts. She thought she remembered them deciding against mentioning it specifically.

*   *   *

The next hour is a blur of questions, a female officer glaring at her. The words "contaminated crime scene" roiling her stomach as she dusts for prints, the policewoman's eyes pinched at her under a pair of eyebrow rings. The other officers were more casual, one seemingly star struck by Sophia. Still, Ruth couldn't seem to stop shaking, wincing every time a camera flashed. At some point, Marcus Jennings arrived and the mood shifted—his appearance changing the chatter, officers standing straighter, shoulders back. When Caroline had revealed what the necklace was worth, the murmurs returned and a second round of pictures and fingerprints were taken.

Around 5:00 AM, the house empties and Ruth struggles up to her room. She downs a bottle of water then dials Teo's phone again, knowing he won't answer. When she crawls under the covers, she's still spiraling, regretting the last few texts she's fired off to Teo. As she finally drifts off, the faintest hope lingers that it's all just a bad dream.

Chapter Five

Marcus

❧

The sun is almost up as Marcus Jennings backs his cruiser down the long driveway of the Bancroft estate. At the street, he glances down at the fourteen waiting text messages on his cell phone—all of them work-related, and decides his need for coffee supersedes anything else.

The line in front of Katie's Sunny Side Up Cafe is crawling as usual. The original building, which had been situated just across the beach on Highway 98, was torn to pieces by Kerry. Two months ago, the owners had opened a food truck in the same spot, and it's no surprise the place is slammed, everyone hungry for the faintest sign of something familiar.

The line snakes around the red metal structure into the parking lot, and as Marcus waits, a collection of handshakes and "morning, chief's" greet him. Someone offers to let him jump the line, and he declines, pecking at his phone as he waits. In front of him, cars whiz down Highway 98, the steady stream of taillights oblivious to the suddenly unobstructed million-dollar views around them.

When Marcus gets his food, he heads to his cruiser, gathering his thoughts as he eats from the Styrofoam container.

It must've been a full moon last night.

When he got the Bancroft call, he'd just fallen asleep after a marathon call with one of his deputies, a veteran cop he'd been talking off the proverbial ledge—and not the first one that week. The city council' last meeting had amped up the rumors. No one was saying it out loud, but all his deputies felt it.

Hell, he felt it.

Blue Compass was broke. The whole department was on the chopping block. Consolidation with the Bay County police department was a terrifying probability. The city had just completed the final tally for the hurricane debris removal. The city was looking at a sixty million dollar bill.

Marcus exhales and takes a sip of coffee. There was supposed to be federal and state aid and, of course, FEMA. The city had gone hat in hand to every door stoop it could find. So far, those funds were only trickling in, and while the Mayor wasn't exactly forthcoming with numbers, he knew it would only cover a fraction of the losses. Last year's entire operating budget was only two million dollars, a drop in the bucket.

So when his phone buzzed last night, taking him to the Bancrofts' monstrosity of a mansion, he'd understood the implications right away. He went way back with that family.

Usually he knew where to start. On the surface, the whole thing seemed like a regular B and E. All the home's locks were intact, but something about the scene seemed off.

Everyone in that neighborhood in Nautilus Cove labored under the same false idea that their little enclave was untouchable. Certainly Caroline Bancroft couldn't be bothered to lock her doors. The security gate at the front of the neighborhood was a bit of a joke too. Still with their full time rent-a-cop and security vehicle roving around, there were easier places to steal from. Especially when most of the year, there were plenty of tourists and out-of-towners leaving their beach rentals unlocked. Most of his boys spent their summers responding to car burglaries, stolen purses and wallets—always the tourists, reluctantly admitting they'd left their keys sitting on the dashboard. All those old homes with their thirty-year-old locks and ancient sliding doors were practically an invitation.

The two biker gangs in town were relatively harmless, though they'd seen their share of petty crime. Since Kerry, the town had seen an uptick in meth. It was cheaper than the prescription stuff a lot of them had started with and tended to make people more sporadic, more violent too. Still, the addicts kept to the outskirts, and didn't generally venture to Nautilus Cove.

But these days, lots of people were hurting. And all this construction going on? Blue Compass had contractors and crews from all over the Southeast. Most people weren't exactly doing background checks. He'd heard the sister was some kind of internet famous too. His jaw clenches as he pictures one of his younger officers at the scene, all sweaty and stuttering like a teenage boy asking out the prom queen. He was glad his crime tech, Jade, had taken it upon herself to be the one to interrogate Ruth. He'd had to take the kid outside, talk some sense into him so he could go back in and do his job.

Marcus rubs his temples. There were too many possibilities and too many eyes watching. He drains the last of his coffee, knowing he can't put it off any longer. His daughter is probably just waking up, brewing that weird tea she drank. Her apartment was a casualty of Hurricane Kerry, and so Kayla had been in her childhood bedroom for almost a year now. Though lately, she'd been talking about adding a second floor to Two Be Wed, turning it into a loft. He was in no hurry for that to happen. It was nice having a second dirty plate in the sink.

Marcus wipes his chin with a napkin then dials Kayla.

"You up?"

"Just."

Her voice is groggy, and Marcus tries to hide the worry in his own. "It's not a big thing, Sweetie. I got some news you're gonna need to hear. That bride of yours has had a bit of bad luck. Something that might throw a wrench in your plans."

Chapter Six

Ruth

Ruth wakes to the sound of banging in the kitchen. Light streams in from the tall windows, and the promise of coffee and bacon sifts up. She peels back the sheets, the realization creeping in slowly then smacking against her as her feet hit the wood floor.

Someone had been in their house.

Downstairs, she's surprised to find Sophia at the stove. Her sister's hair in a messy knot, her head slanted as she stares out at the quiet bay in front of her.

"You awake already?"

Sophia exhales then looks down, as if she suddenly remembers the pan in front of her. "I couldn't sleep so I'm cooking." She scrapes hard at the skillet with her spatula.

Ruth pours herself coffee and rubs her temples. Her mouth is sawdust. Today's hangover would be a doozy. "You don't make breakfast. You microwave. You take-out. You Uber-eats."

"I've been telling Mom to upgrade that security system for years—or at least use it. Jo tried to get her to buy one of those

Ring door things last year and she *refused*. And of course, the neighborhood's front gate is broken again. Mom said someone plowed through the automatic arm last week—like that stops anyone anyway. You literally can just get out of your car and walk around it . . ." Sophia turns off the stove, grabs her coffee and strides to the screened porch. When she gets there, she chooses the rocking chair closest to the door and curls up like a cat.

Ruth takes the seat next to her and studies her sister from the side. Her lips are pursed but open, eyes twitchy, it's a facial expression she's not familiar with.

"You know this Instagram thing has been a lot for me. Right? That it's important . . . that I see it as a real job?"

Ruth sighs, "Sophia, you heard the police. We can't talk—you can't post about this."

"I know that," she snaps. "I wasn't planning to—what I mean is, it's been pretty crazy—but it's good, too. Me and my own thing." Sophia sits up, looking off into the distance. "You know that I'm so happy for you and Teo—that I've spent a lot—I mean, *a lot* of time on the wedding."

Ruth nods and peers into her coffee cup, wondering how they even got to this place. At first, she'd been happy to have Sophia's help. Her sister was so much better at things like this, but it had all gotten so out of control.

Sophia turns to her and sucks in her breath. "Listen. Umm. There's been a few threats on my feed."

The story comes out in rushed pieces, Sophia's words darting around like fish. Ruth hears her whisper "death threats . . . and the 'C word' . . . something about 'wackos and Instagram trolls' . . . lots of bitch and whore."

Sophia pauses like she's calculating something then adds, "I'm pretty sure that one photo of the necklace didn't get significantly more traffic than the rest?" She looks away as a seagull dive bombs from the sky into the water in front of them. "It got worse a few weeks ago. And there were more of them. One wrote: 'Those slutty sisters would be easy to find.' And there were creepier ones . . . more explicit. Some people get off on hate. I swear I never thought it was real or that it was a big deal or—"

Ruth presses her hands to her chest, pushing against the ball of rage that's forming there. "You just said someone wrote, 'Those slutty sisters would be easy to find'—and that's not a big deal?"

"I meant I didn't think it was *real*."

Ruth opens and clenches her fists, her fingernails digging into her palms. "So this is a thing? Like a *real* thing? People making threats—threats against our family and what—you just deleted them—blocked them—what?"

She jumps up from her rocker, suddenly needing to be far away from Sophia, from this reality. But her sister is two steps behind her. "Ruthie, I'm sorry. I really am. I'm sick about this. I just thought it was part of it—ya know, like people knowing your name—and I think we mentioned the necklace like once, maybe twice—tops. I'm going right to the police, right now. It just didn't occur to me *last night*."

Ruth whips around, hardly able to believe her sister's nerve when the doorbell rings. They both freeze, staring at it. Finally, Ruth says, "This *discussion* is not over—not even close," before she goes to open the door.

On the landing, a face from their childhood stares back at them, and Ruth feels her emotions collide, trip over each other as she takes in Colt Thistle. He is taller than in her memory, a pink bakery box under his arm. His Coastal Catering polo is rumpled, jeans low on his hips. "Hope it's not too early. They said you were waiting for this."

"No way," Sophia says. "It's like seeing a ghost. Get in here." She tugs him into the kitchen and gives him a giant hug.

Not wanting to be rude, Ruth joins the embrace and a wistfulness washes over her, momentarily overriding the potential danger Sophia could have put them all in. "It *is* good to see you." Colt Thistle was a staple of every sunburned memory the three sisters had in Blue Compass. He was thinner somehow, smelled of the same Camel cigarettes. Even his posture hadn't changed. Colt's mom, Deena Thistle, had been Summerhouse's estate manager and summer maid even before Blake met Caroline. Colt was a few years older than Ruth and had grown up fishing off the Nautilus Cove pier. After their mother's wedding, he'd quickly become family to them too. It wasn't until Ruth was almost fifteen that she'd begun to think of him as a boy.

"God, how are you doing? Every time I walk down the street, I wanna cry. This place is breaking my heart."

Colt's smile disappears. "Can't complain. It's great seeing you, great of you to be here—to celebrate your wedding and publicize the town like this."

"What have you been doing with yourself, boy? Tell us everything." Sophia sits down at the kitchen table and pulls out a chair.

Ruth had kept in touch with Colt through the occasional text and email. He'd gone to Colorado for a few years, but he came back before the storm to care for his mother who was fighting Alzheimer's disease. A few weeks before Hurricane Kerry,

Colt had reluctantly moved her to a memory-care facility in Panama City. A move which—in a strange twist of fate—saved his mother's life. Kerry had washed Colt's family home clear across Highway 98. Ruth had already filled Sophia in on all this, though other people's personal tragedies weren't always the kind of thing her sister tended to remember.

"How's your mamma doing? I'd like to get over there to see her before we take off for the honeymoon."

Colt's face goes still. "She's doing OK—we're keeping busy. I'm working a few jobs here and there." He shoves the cake box toward Ruth. "Well, you can see that—" He breaks out in a smile. "It's really good to see you."

Ruth opens the box and finds a round miniature cake inside.

"It's not decorated and fancy iced like the 'real one' but Justin wanted to make sure he got the recipe right. You know, Justin—Mr. America's Star Chef. I guess his pastry guy up and quit, and he's gonna do it himself."

"Well, we already did this once but, *yay* for us." Ruth pinches off a corner full of frosting and pops it in her mouth. She closes her eyes and whispers yum. Sophia had chosen the cake recipe. The champagne berry wedding cake with a champagne preserve was in some online magazine. As usual, her sister was right. The infused butter cake layered in strawberries was even more spectacular the second time. "Colt, tell Justin it's amazing—I still can't believe how lucky we are to have a celebrity chef doing our wedding."

Colt fidgets with his hat then puts it on backwards. "Blue Compass's one claim to fame. No one ever said the man didn't know his way around a kitchen."

"It's sad that his restaurant in Atlanta didn't make it." Sophia takes the elastic band out of her hair and shakes out her blonde waves. "I still say he shoulda let my PR firm do their marketing—our Atlanta office is so talented."

"I hear he got some bad advice—a bad agent or something. Though I imagine Justin was glad he got some time with his momma . . . before the storm." Colt looks out at the bay. "After the last year, I think we all see things a lot differently . . ."

Sophia pops a piece of cake in her mouth. "Not to change the subject—but, you know there's this ratty boy who used to follow me around all summer, and I still haven't gotten his RSVP for the wedding."

"Umm. I'm actually *working* the wedding . . . and the rehearsal dinner. The catering company really needs people. I'm the head waiter—and already committed." He straightens up. "But I am looking forward to meeting your husband . . . I see you on the internet—follow you on Instagram or whatever. From the looks of things, you're just leading one hot mess of a life."

Sophia giggles and shoves him playfully as Ruth shoots her a sidelong glance, a twinge of tangible embarrassment that their friend is *working* the wedding—a fact which her sister seems to completely miss.

"Sam is tied up with work right now. His partner's ill, and the practice is so busy—but he should be here by then . . ."

"Sophia just made breakfast. Why don't you sit and eat with us?"

"I got one more delivery, but a cup of coffee couldn't hurt."

They sit at the table and catch up. Ruth and Colt swapping anecdotes before and after the storm. Sophia peppers their memories with the awkwardness of their middle school years then the rebellious phase of Colt's high school. As they talk,

Ruth's emotions sway, alternating between her frustration with the randomness of Mother Nature, the unfairness of the hurricane. *Summerhouse wasn't just still standing; it was perfect again.* Caroline's money and insistence had jumped the line. Gotten them the best contractors. There were lifelong locals still sitting in trailers and motel rooms. Ruth's stomach twists as Colt's voice pulls her back to their conversation.

"I remember that first summer y'all came—all those dead fish washed up on the shoreline, and we were all convinced the pier was haunted. God—that smell. Your mom about lost it."

"If memory serves *me*—" A smile sneaks across Sophia's face. "You two brace faces had your first kiss *under* that pier too."

"Sophia, how come I always ended up on the *dare* end of your bad ideas? The things you convinced your baby sister to do . . ."

"Hey, now. It wasn't my first kiss—exactly." Colt traces his finger over the rim of his coffee cup. "If memory serves *me*, Sophia. *You* were pretty busy wearing out half this town under that pier—and you didn't need anybody daring you to do nothing . . ."

Sophia giggles and pours more coffee, artfully switching subjects. She launches into the events of the night before, swearing Colt to secrecy before offering an embellished version of the break-in where she stars as Summerhouse's savior. Her version highlights how she'd found the front door open, she'd found the twins, she'd called the cops. As Ruth listens, her head starts to throb. It suddenly feels like it might explode—like all of her might.

"Jesus, Sophia. There were *other* people there last night, too—what is with you? I—"

The sound of a key in the door makes her stop. They all turn to see Teo stepping inside. He beelines over to Ruth. Still in yesterday's clothes, he is panting and pasty white. "Everybody's good? Everybody's alright?" He plucks her from her chair, checking Ruth up and down before engulfing her in a hug. "I can't believe I wasn't here—well, I got someone coming now to check that alarm system. Is anything missing?"

No one answers, and there's an awkward silence before he notices the third person at the table. Colt pushes back his chair.

"Teo, this is Colt. He brought over some cake samples." She offers a weak smile and runs her hand through her hair, thinking how awful her fiancé looks. "He's an old family friend—I've told you about him before."

Teo takes a breath then wipes his hands on his pants. "Oh, hey man—nice to meet you." He reaches out his hand to Colt's. "Sorry. I'm a little amped up about last night."

They shake hands as Ruth tries to read Teo's face. For most women, it was her fiancé's dimple, his square jaw that made him so attractive. He was the kind of tall and broad shouldered that brought up jokes about cartoon superheroes. Though she'd long ago gotten used to the way women stared at him, it had always been something else about Teo for her. When they first met, he'd listened with his eyes. There was a vulnerability she couldn't place but wanted to have as part of her life. At the moment, it was plastered all over his face.

Colt stands up and heads to the door. "Nice to meet you—ladies, it was so great to see you. Say hi to Jo for me. And sorry 'bout . . . all your trouble—probably is a good idea getting that alarm fixed. Strange characters around here these days . . ."

As they say their goodbyes, Teo fiddles with the alarm system, the pad spitting out different sounds with each number punched.

When the door closes, Sophia escapes to the porch as Ruth goes to Teo. "I missed you—" He smells awful, an acidic mixture of sweat and what she assumes was last night's good time. She hugs him tighter than she means to and when she finally releases him, she cocks back her head. "What in the world happened to your face?"

Teo's about to answer when she reaches up with one finger to shush him. She has to stand on her toes to kiss the swelling yellow and purple mass under his eye before she whispers, "You better hope you're OK 'cause when Sophia realizes what that thing's gonna do to the pictures, she's gonna give you a second one to match."

Chapter Seven

Kayla

~

Kayla strums her fingers on the oak kitchen table. Was this whole thing a bad idea? She'd been so focused lately, with Two Be Wed's business picking up again and the unfathomable to-do lists for the Bancroft wedding, she'd been deep in thought, feeling better about her master plan when her father called.

God, that *sick* necklace. It wasn't exactly the kind of attention the wedding needed—that *she* needed. Though maybe it wasn't as bad as it seemed? Ruth could probably find something to wear from Caroline's other jewelry—not that Alexander McQueen generally needed much accessorizing. The family had long ago forgotten this was a beach wedding. She still shuddered every time she thought of Ruth sweating through that enormous ball gown, the sand stuck between layers of designer tulle. She guessed Sophia was probably already in some sort of full jewelry meltdown mode. Still, that girl could spin anything. Lord knew, Ruth probably wouldn't have much of an opinion. She was always checking in with everyone else, always making sure they were happy with her choices. It would be a shock to hear her speak up about something for once.

Wanting something to distract her, Kayla reaches up to the old transistor radio on the kitchen shelf and flips it on. She still missed her little two-bedroom apartment, though privacy wasn't the issue it was when she was younger. Her dad never seemed to be around anymore.

Her parents had bought this three-bedroom bungalow fully furnished when she was in elementary school, never imagining it as more than a little summer haven three blocks from Blue Compass's white sandy beaches. Back then, the sturdy and out-dated furniture, a mix of mid-century modern was part of its charm. After her father had taken the job in Blue Compass, they'd moved in permanently, and her mother had upgraded all the beds and mattresses and not much else. The dark kitchen was still begging to be put out of its misery with its Harvest Gold appliances and chocolate wood paneling, the orange lino-leum floors and sailboat wallpaper curling in the corners.

Her mom was just broaching the subject of a major remodel when the bottom dropped out. Somewhere around here there was still a thick scrapbook of magazine clippings and renovation sketches Kayla and her mom had collected, both of them sure that despite Marcus's penchant for penny-pinching, his two girls would win him over. After the accident, it had all gone in a box in the back of the closet, the house a time warp—as stuck as they were.

The thought makes Kayla's stomach turn, and she puts on the teakettle. On the phone, her father had mentioned he thought he could keep the Bancrofts' break-in out of the media, though as she opens her laptop and waits for the kettle to boil, she finds he's wrong. There are already several mentions on her Instagram feed, though she notes that @sophiasez is peculiarly silent. The sister's last post was a group photo from Ruth's bachelorette party. A nauseatingly perfect shot with the bride at the center, the brigade of shiny blonde heads and hands on nonexistent hips. Underneath the caption read *Sip Sip Hooray–It's Almost the Big Day,* the amount of corresponding unnecessary hashtags just as gag-worthy. Still, for a moment Kayla finds herself transfixed by the screen. Sophia is looking right at the camera, her jade eyes fixed like they are staring right into Kayla's.

What have I gotten myself into?

As much as she hates to admit it, she knew her father was downplaying things from last night—his voice lowered to a baritone when he was hiding something. He always did that, tried to fix everything for her, sanitize the world. It was maddening, though for once it might actually be necessary. They both knew there were things that needed to stay quiet. What was that saying about the frog and boiling water on the stove? From the beginning, the heat on this whole event had been creeping up so slowly, the inching pressure meaning something was bound to give. She stands up and heads to the kettle to turn it off, then returns to the table, reaching out to study the photo on the screen once more.

Chapter Eight

Ruth

❧

Ruth needed a run. Her head was swimming, and her body itched for motion. She and Teo had planned to run together every morning until the wedding, both of them imagining it might be the only time they might get together alone the whole week. She finishes relacing her shoes, and it strikes her that she's actually glad to go alone today. She never minded a good jog with Teo, but like most things he did, Teo ran because he should. Because it kept him lean and because the surgeon general recommended sixty minutes of physical activity a day. It wasn't like that for her. Running kept her in one piece, kept her sane, and at that moment, she needed to work some things out. Right now, she was dying for distance.

She first started running at age eleven. In those days, the signs of her father's binges were as familiar as family. The way the engine cut off at a certain hour. The odd angle his headlights would arrange themselves in the driveway. Her sisters sometimes slept in headphones, usually in the same bed. When the side door slammed, Caroline's petite frame was already bracing for that first furious accusation, her father's venom was the most consistent thing about him.

She's still not sure what was different about that night, that particular brawl. Broken dishes weren't anything new. He'd hardly been around that week. But Ruth fled. Out the back door, down the street and up the hill in front of their house, her sandals mere hangers on as some dormant preservation instinct propelled her forward. Even as her lungs began to scream and her body protested. Long after she'd cleared her block. Every step, a little rebellion. She ran until there was nothing else, till there was only sweat and ache. Chest burning, searing pain down both shins. When she collapsed behind the FoodMart, she was almost three miles from home, the flesh between her legs rubbed raw from her flannel pajamas. Drenched and gasping for air, everything had been both empty and clear for the first time. Her mind, a perfect blank oblivion.

The next day, that feeling was all she could think about. She didn't need to wait for another fight to start. She took off again. A shorter run, which her body seemed to tolerate better. Soon, she was experimenting with distance. Always outside, always chasing the after. The summer her father left, she joined the cross-country team, the first fifth grader in the history of their public elementary to be allowed to compete "up" in middle school sports.

It was the end of sixth grade when their new stepdad, Blake, had brought them to Summerhouse, and she'd fallen in love with this running path. The trail ran parallel to Highway 98 and all the way through Blue Compass. She knew every pothole and crack, the silhouette of every house and tree. Now the signs and buildings were gone, once-green landscapes were dead or rotting. The homes and tiny strip malls mostly gone, a few in different states of disrepair. Nothing looked the same.

The morning's hangover is still hovering at the back of her head as she takes off, and she knows the next few miles will be grueling. There's been a lot more drinking than she is used to, but it will burn off.

To her left, the bay peeked out between the backsides of Nautilus Cove's massive homes. Behind them the tide is coming in, the palette of soft blues swirling like a Monet painting as it rushes at the shore. Many of the bay front homeowners had already renourished their lots, the truckloads of fresh beach sand adding a creamy white backdrop to the water, though a mile further down, it's a stark contrast to the rest of the beach district. She turns and looks to her right across the two-lane highway, the view so different she thinks of her students—of their favorite word. The one she often begged them not to use in term papers: *Cringy*. The strange, mauled woods that ran perpendicular to the neighborhood were definitely cringy. Once-lush forests of green pines slated for Phase 2 of Nautilus Cove was now an arid landscape of dying trees, the acres like the scene from a sci-fi novel. Not a single leaf clung to the black branches, the rows of fragile trunks all snapped in half at perfect right angles.

Ruth looked away as the sun frees itself from a cloud, and she adds speed. A few seconds later, the running path takes a slight Y, and the bay view turns into ocean. The sea has churned up suddenly, and white caps crash at the shoreline as blue water reaches out indefinitely past the St. Andrew's Peninsula. As Ruth takes it all in, she knows she can't ignore it any longer—what she'd run here to think through, what she couldn't run from anymore.

That bizarre text.

Six days ago, it had meant nothing. Now she wasn't so sure.

She'd been in her classroom, finishing up some lesson plans for the substitute teacher. Her printer buzzing out copies when her cell phone pinged.

don't trust the people around u

The text was from a blocked number, and Ruth had actually laughed out loud. Despite herself, looking around the empty classroom. Last week, all the teachers in the teacher's lounge had spent their lunch laughing at a recent barrage of strange texts and scams that they'd all been receiving. From Saudi Princes who wanted to give them free money to weird photos and memes from strange numbers. The librarian had told a story about some lewd texts that would have made a teenage boy blush.

At the time, there'd been so many other things taking up the space in Ruth's brain. She had a wedding to plan, a substitute who would need a lesson plan for the next two weeks. It still seemed sort of silly but as she looked out at the ocean, her stomach did a flip flop. Could the text somehow be related to the break-in? And her bizarre flat tire?

As the last turn of the street comes into view, she tries again to remember if she'd blocked the number on her cell. Had she deleted the text at all? She'd meant to. But with all the wedding stuff, too many things were falling through the cracks. She honestly had no idea.

As she approached Summerhouse, it was the first time ever she could remember feeling less clear after a run. She was still angry with Sophia—that much she was sure of. Everything else was muddled.

Grabbing a water from the beach-level garage fridge, Ruth wipes off her sweat with a beach towel. Her eyes fall on the little cubby door beneath the stairs. The arched wooden entrance was ajar. The "Keebler Elf door," named by Rhea because she thought it looked like the cartoon one in the cookie commercials. Full of sand and cobwebs, it housed a dank storage space that Caroline had learned the hard way rusted anything that went inside it. Ruth put her weight onto the door, forcing it shut as voices from above carried down. Everyone she cared about in the world was chattering one floor up from her, their laughter floating down from the big driftwood dining table.

Of course, she knew what she would do.

She would be better than Sophia at protecting her family. She would see if she could find the text. She would tell Teo.

At 3:00 PM, they had to get their marriage license, then they would go see the chief of police. It's probably nothing, she tells herself. She just hoped the police would let her keep her phone.

Chapter Nine

Marcus

~

The precinct is quiet for a Thursday afternoon, and Marcus is at the front desk dealing with Janice, the world's most forgetful reception clerk, when the sky outside goes gray through the double doors.

The waiting room is almost empty, and though he tried not to think about it, this whole year had been eerily somber. Construction was still eking by at a snail's pace, and since there was no basic infrastructure to support tourists, there had been no vacationers or festivals, fishing tournaments or Fourth of July fireworks show. Hell, he even missed the biker rallies revving their engines and clogging up Highway 98 at all hours of the night. Sometimes, he still came in, half expecting to see the drunk tank full, the usual handful of rowdy tourists sleeping it off or inebriated teenagers sobbing until their parents picked them up. Blue Compass had always shared the same complicated relationship between its visitors and summer people he imagined all tourist communities struggled with. It was a push and pull he suddenly missed with a passion. This last year, the only fresh faces he'd seen were those of forlorn homeowners, the part-timers saddled up next to the locals at the LookSee Lounge, everyone moaning about the same battle with insurance companies and contractors.

He looks through the glass doors and sees Teo Vargus and Ruth Bancroft walking arm-in-arm toward the precinct. The groom phoned earlier, offering some vague reason he needed to stop by, and insisting it couldn't wait. Marcus had been knee-deep in the fingerprint analysis of Summerhouse at the time, mulling over everyone's prints—the families, their help, even Kayla's was there—but no intruder.

A soft roll of thunder rumbles outside, and he holds open the door and shouts, "Come on, it's gonna open up."

The couple rushes inside, narrowly missing the first drops of rain.

"I was surprised to get your call—thanks for coming down." As the door inches closed behind him, Marcus runs a hand over his stout bald head before he reaches out to shake their hands. The pair are flush and panting and though he generally tries not to worry what people think, he suddenly does. Being a Black cop in a Southern town is not the easiest of endeavors, and he had worked hard so that everything about him—his wide shoulders and solid hand-shake, his pressed uniform and gleaming shoes, commanded respect.

"We just got our marriage license." Teo smiles. "Pretty convenient that you're right next door."

"Oh yeah, how's our boys outside—they let you through OK?" Marcus turns to look out the front door. The wall of angry faces and picketers spilling down toward City Hall are on the move to get out of the rain. As long as there's good weather and government workers in the building, the sidewalk is clogged with the protestors' lawn chairs and coolers, angry sunburnt faces chanting, "Don't sell our souls." Marcus guesses there is twice the number as yesterday. He should have one of his boys work crowd control, add some extra shifts. It was an idea that didn't hold much appeal for him. He was already short-staffed.

"I don't know where they're all coming from?" Ruth says. "Town's not that big—but I get why they're so riled up."

"I heard a group from DC came down to throw their hat in with the protesters," Teo adds, "An environmental activist lobbying organization or something . . ."

Ruth scrunches up her nose. "Can you imagine Highway 98 full of outlet malls and all-you-can-eat seafood buffets, wall-to-wall putt-putt golf places?"

Marcus has the urge to nod, but says nothing. Earlier, one of his beat cops had mentioned that Cyus LaCroix, a Blue Compass city council member, had joined the picket line too. He'd been glad to hear it but offered no opinion. With the current political landscape—and everything else bubbling under the surface—he knew the less he said, the better.

They follow him down the hallway as overhead a clap of thunder rumbles the low ceiling. A sheet of rain unleashes against the windows. Lightning flashes. Once. Then twice, though inside the disturbance hardly seems to register. The lobby receptionist doesn't look up, everyone goes about their business. Pop-up storms were nothing new for Blue Compass. The sudden intense bouts of wind and rain or thunder and lightning usually came out of nowhere, often disappearing just as quickly.

The three are almost to Marcus's office when a louder clap of thunder makes the lights flicker. The station goes dark. Teo and Ruth freeze. Only a few seconds before the fluorescent lights return and the low hum of a generator kicks on in the background.

"Gotta love this town. Sometimes electricity feels more like a suggestion than a *given*." He steps into his office. "Kerry sure didn't help matters. Power grid's a mess . . ."

Teo and Ruth follow him in, and he watches as the two take in the eclectic surroundings. Kayla liked to say that he'd choked his office in fish decor. On the walls, there were too many photos to count, fish taxidermy and decorative fishing rods mounted between them. The dozens of colored picture frames all held some version of the same photo—Marcus and his catch, the fish strung through the mouth and displayed like a proud parent.

Teo's eyes shoot to the arched window behind his desk. A massive marbled blue and green tarpon hovers above it, its shiny body at least three feet long. It curves over the newly installed window molding like it's been plucked from the ocean mid-leap.

"Took over two hours to reel that one in." Marcus's face lights up with the memory. "I've fished in a lot of places and Blue Compass still has the best fishing, hands down."

The room goes silent and Teo's eyes linger on the fish. A minute that seems much longer, his face is twisted in concentration like he's trying to memorize the tarpon's dead eyes. Finally, he whispers, "My father was a fisherman too. He would've loved this place." His eyes mist and he clears his throat. "Every time I come here, I always think how much he would've loved it here. He liked small towns . . ." He stops, wiping at one eye. "I'm sorry, I lost him a while back . . . I don't know where that came from—"

Ruth reaches over and threads her hand in Teo's while Marcus looks away. When his cell buzzes, it's the excuse he's looking for to step out and give them a moment. Easing the door closed, he heads into the hall. Once there, he finds a media alert has popped up. Marcus still didn't understand how all that stuff works, but Kayla had set it up after the Summerhouse burglary, and as he skims the local article, he's glad she did. The story is another reiteration of what the Panama City News had published that morning. Frustratingly, both had included the Summerhouse police report.

It was another reminder how careful he had to be. Everyone had an opinion about the identity of the Summerhouse thief, and now it wasn't just the locals eating this stuff up. He knows if people got wind of the fingerprints—or lack thereof—it would only add fuel to the fire. Things were precarious enough. Even the slightest hints of incompetence could torpedo his department. He'd heard that awful true crime blogger from a couple towns over—Tania Something-or-Other—was already covering the break in. There were even rumors of a Facebook page where people were exchanging theories.

Marcus taps his phone, trying to remember how to set a reminder to check the social media stuff for tomorrow. He waits one more second, then re-enters his office, apologizing to the couple as he scoots into his desk again. Outside, the rain is already waning. "OK. Now, what can I do for you two—did you find something else missing?"

Chapter Ten

Teo

~

Forty minutes later, Teo and Ruth pull into Summerhouse, just in time for dinner.

"Are you sure you're OK?"

It's the second time she's asked, and Teo nods, his hands choking the steering wheel. "I said I'm fine. Can we please drop it?" He knows she can't help herself, but whatever that emotional outburst was in Marcus's office had caught him by surprise. His mother's dinner was tonight, and it was a big deal to her. He needed to be all smiles. Not embarrassing himself by falling apart in front of strangers. Right now, he didn't have the time or the bandwidth to deal with whatever this wedding was suddenly dredging up.

Ruth looks out the window. "I'm sorry. I just want you to be alright—for *things* to be alright." She sucks in a hard breath. "Nothing is going like we planned."

Teo puts the car in park and turns to her. "I'm sorry too. I was just surprised—and annoyed. I would think the chief of police would take that text message more seriously."

He'd also hoped to have time to mine for specifics on the investigation. He was no stranger to a deposition and after the requisite small talk, he'd never gotten around to asking about the outcome of the fingerprints or where they were leaning with viable suspects. He knew Sophia had gone in that morning, offering up her password and a print-out of those awful Instagram posts—or at least, the ones she hadn't already deleted. But Marcus seemed distracted by the alerts on his phone. He'd just taken down some information, asked a few questions, then given Ruth's phone to the crime scene tech in the next office. He might as well have patted them on the back and given them a lollipop.

Teo had met Jade Marshall a few times through his pro bono work in Blue Compass, wrongly assuming the crime scene tech was ex-military. The twenty-something was stout with thick hands and a pair of eyebrow piercings over mahogany eyes, a black cropped cut that was anything but the traditional Blue Compass cop aesthetic. Still, her reputation preceded her, and she'd certainly won Ruth over when she'd emerged fifteen minutes later and handed back her phone.

Now they were supposed to just sit around and wait. *Wait and worry.* He slams the front door and goes to the kitchen, pouring himself two fingers of Scotch. His mother is standing at Summerhouse's giant island, mixing something in a stainless-steel bowl.

"Oh my—going for the big guns?" Maya raises an eyebrow, moving the reading glasses perched on her head to rest on the bridge of her nose. "Everything good?"

Teo exhales, glad to see his mother knee-deep in what she's been referring to as The Big Dinner. She'd been planning it for months—ever since it had become apparent that Caroline was hosting the rehearsal dinner. The home-cooked dinner party was a compromise that had taken a lot of finessing. At the time, he'd been slammed at work and just trying to keep the peace, part of him laboring under some misguided idea that weddings were really for the bride anyway. Seeing how meticulously his mother planned for this one meal and now navigating his own flood of emotions, he was realizing how wrong that was.

"I hope you guys are hungry." Maya's voice is sing-songy as she set down her bowl to give Teo a hug. Teo inhales, a few noisy breaths then turns toward the bay. The first hints of a sunset are already emerging, and he takes another gulp letting the booze churn in his stomach along with a pang of guilt. Against his better judgment, he'd let Ruth convince him not to tell anyone about the text message—for now. Though he made it a practice to never lie to mother—and for good reason.

Teo drains his glass, the memory washing over him with the alcohol.

It was his first high school party ever. Always the dutiful son, he'd felt like someone else, sneaking out and drinking flat keg beer. Somehow, he'd managed to get back into his house without getting caught. The next morning, both guilty and giddy, he'd gone downstairs for breakfast to find both his parents waiting at the kitchen table. Their arms crossed. Food untouched. For a split second, he was sure he'd been caught.

We're afraid there's some bad news. To this day, he could still feel the words in his gut, taste the bile in his throat. He'd never even heard of colon cancer. Six months later, they'd buried his father at Bonaventure Cemetery.

Now, no matter how irrational it was—and how logically he knew that the two incidents were in no way related, Teo never lied to his mother. She was all he had.

"No, Ma—it's just . . . everything. There's a lot swirling around in my brain right now. *Tengo hambre.*"

"I still can't believe you got in a bar fight." Maya shakes her head, flipping her long braid off one shoulder and onto the other. "I am gonna give Nicky a spanking when I see him. Now go set the table. The guys should be here in a minute."

When Maya invited everyone to The Big Dinner, Teo had neglected to explain to his mother the precariousness of the Bancrofts' family dynamics. By the time he'd realized, it had been too late, and Thad had already accepted his invitation. Now Caroline was in her bedroom pouting, the prospect of breaking bread with her ex spurring her to change outfits twice.

Teo is still setting the table with brightly colored china and an oversized vase of fresh daisies—Ruth's favorite—when there's a knock at the door. The twins make it there first. They open it to reveal Nick and Thad. The pair look freshly showered in khakis and oxfords, Nick's button up du jour is a loud sunflower print. Under Thad's arm is a bakery box. He shoots the box over his head, telling Rhea and Beau the cupcakes are for after dinner as they jump at the treats like puppies.

Teo's hand instinctively goes to his eye, still a little swollen and yellow. He has yet to decipher his own feelings about Ruth's father. When he went to the rental house to shower before heading to city hall, it was like Thad was waiting there to debrief.

The conversation was odd. Thad—the guy in AA—found the bachelor party hilarious. He'd laughed, peppering Teo with questions about his memory loss as if a bar brawl with strangers was completely normal. Or better yet, hilarious. Teo was still trying to scrape together most of the night and was mortified. It was the one and only time he'd ever blacked out from drinking.

"Alright, let's do this, for better or worse—let's *eat*." Caroline races out of her bedroom, her brow furrowed, her caftan flowing behind her as a wrist full of bracelets clink together. Eyes on her Manolo Blahniks, she charges to the dining room table as Thad, who is chatting with Nick, flips around, both of them reaching for the same chair at the same moment. The room goes quiet as Thad's eyes slide from Caroline's hand to her face, Thad's grin widening with a "nice to see you again, C."

Caroline eyes flick up and down him, her lips pursing to form a "hmph" though no sound escapes. She spins on her heels and finds a seat across the table, whipping out her phone before aggressively pecking at the keys.

A few seconds later, they are all at the long driftwood table. Ruth leads them in a quick prayer then they all dig in. Maya's love language has always been food, and tonight's menu includes all of Teo's favorites. There are steaming plates of *tortilla española*, *shrimp paella*, *mofongo* and for dessert, her famous *arroz con dulce*.

As they sit and eat, the conversation is a mishmash of awkward chitchat, the weather report for the weekend and the progress of Blue Compass's rebuilding. Teo is on his second helping of *mofongo* when Rhea scoots back in her chair suddenly. She's across from Thad and toddles to the banquet of windows behind him, checking the closest one for a moment before she turns to him, yanks off her bib and climbs into his lap.

"Mr. Thad—I like you—are you my grandpa?"

Jo's eyes go wide, and Caroline stops chewing.

Thad shifts in his chair. "Well—as a matter of fact, I am, hun—ain't I lucky?"

"How come now?"

Thad's eyebrow arches, "Well, I've always been your grandpa—"

"Ha!" Everyone's eyes shoot to Caroline, whose hands are flanking the table, her posture like a panther about to pounce. "You've got to be kidding—"

Ruth looks terrified, her eyes darting to her mother. Her face pleads for her to stop. Caroline looks around, inhales and then pinches the bridge of her nose. "I mean—I suppose it comes down to priorities, *Rhea*. I guess, some grandparents are just around more than others . . ."

"Ri-or–it–ies?" Rhea narrows her eyes, her giant pink hair bow hanging crooked over her forehead as she tilts her head at Thad.

"Boy, Maya, this is—wow—more wine?" Nick scoots back his chair, his voice loud as he pats his stomach before reaching across the table. Everyone stops—the obvious distraction tactic working until he adds, "I mean—I know we have a celebrity chef for the *actual* rehearsal dinner, but I think you coulda beaten him on that reality show. It's hard to imagine better food . . ."

Teo stiffens as his eyes shoot to his mother, Maya's body flinching on the word *actual*. Nick couldn't know his complement was more salt in the wound. *God, how had he gotten so many things wrong?*

"Thank you, Nicky. Glad you're enjoying it." Maya sighs, picking at her food for a second before she refills her wine and clears her throat. She scoots back her chair and stands up. "I want to thank everyone for being here for dinner tonight, and I want to thank our host, Caroline, for letting me cook in that amazing kitchen. Weddings bring up a lot of emotion in people, and I am just so glad to be here." Maya looks around at each of them, her eyes welling up as they land on Teo. "I am also so happy that Teo has found such a beautiful and good girl. Your father would be so proud. He would have loved this one right here." She puts a hand on Ruth's shoulder. "I know you will have a long and happy marriage filled with—"

"You're so very welcome! It really is about love—isn't it . . . and *family*—" Caroline is on her feet as she raises her own glass, the cut-off so blunt that Maya's mouth falls open. "I'm just so happy you could all be here to share my home, to share this momentous occasion—I mean what a week—" She coughs out a fake laugh. "I mean—with my necklace going missing—God, I still just can't believe it—that priceless family heirloom gone— and the police moving at a snail's pace . . ." She huffs and shakes her head, "But anyway, I'm so looking forward to our ladies' brunch tomorrow . . ."

There is a noise at the door, and Caroline turns toward it as if on cue, her face brightening with the recognition of who's there. She takes a deep breath and clears her throat. "In that spirit of love and romance, there's something—someone else—a little surprise I want to introduce."

Teo turns, following Caroline's gaze to Mayor Bob who, to everyone's confusion, is standing in the entryway. Caroline rushes over to him, kissing him full on the mouth.

Mayor Bob waves timidly, a cloud of eye-watering musk entering the room with him as Ruth quietly stutters her mother's name. When Caroline returns to her spot at the head of the table, she lifts her glass again. "Well, you all know Mayor Williams. He's a smidge early but—well, we just wanted to—I dunno—it sounds silly but introduce ourselves . . . that we're together."

The mayor stands between the door and the table closest to Caroline, a mouthful of giant teeth fixed in a catlike grin. For a few awkward seconds, the pair stare at each other like the rest of the room doesn't exist, two dopey-eyed teenagers in middle-aged bodies.

"We've been keeping it under wraps since Bob was running for re-election. I mean he was always a shoe-in—and we didn't want to steal Ruth and Teo's thunder either . . ." Caroline's voice trails off as the two lock eyes. There is a moment of frozen queasy horror as they inch toward each other, their faces drawn together like magnets before they steal another kiss, then turn back to the room like nothing happened.

The twins burst out in giggles at the sight of their grandmother smacking lips, and Ruth's eyes become saucers. She opens her mouth to say something then presses her lips together. Maya slides back into her chair, hands wringing a napkin. *His mother is pissed.* Teo can see in the set of her mouth, the barely perceptible grit of her teeth. But Caroline is droning on about how the break-in at Summerhouse made them realize how precious time was, that they shouldn't put off "coming out" as a couple any longer. At some point, Ruth's mother finally brings the speech back around to Teo and Ruth so no one can accuse her of overlooking the real reason everyone is gathered. When they all lift their glasses, Nick adds an uncomfortable "and to Caroline and Bob too . . ." before Maya saves them all by offering dessert.

After dinner, Nicholas, Teo, and JD are getting ready to take the twins sand-crab hunting. Beau and Rhea stand at the ready on the porch with their buckets. According to JD, this long-standing Summerhouse tradition, part hide-and-go-seek, part catch and release, is older than the town. At sunset, the beach fills with tiny silvery white crabs—really, sand fleas—that freeze like deer in headlights under the beam of a flashlight. It was a common sight in Blue Compass to see children squealing and running down the shore with flashlights and tiny nets, their buckets emptied back into the sand before the tourists retired to their rentals for the evening.

The porch darkens suddenly as a thick gray veil of weather casts its dismal ambience into the house. Jo says, "Sorry, Beau—it looks like tonight's entertainment is gonna be indoors" as Ruth procures a Scrabble set from a chest in the living room amid a chorus of groans and moaning. Caroline purses her lips as the first drops of rain pelt the tin roof above them, the pings echoing like firecrackers.

"Blake picked out that roof specifically for that sound." She rolls her eyes. "It was all about porches and that roof when he designed this place. He loved it, but it's the one thing I hate. We know it's raining, we don't need to *hear* every drop. The beach is so dark already, and it looks eerie enough when it storms."

"I've never known this house not to creak and groan," Sophia says. "I swear it's worse since Kerry."

The wind picks up into a low howl, and Teo closes his eyes as a wet breeze blows through the screen, misting everyone.

"Wow—look at that pier. Wouldn't want to be in that water." Nick cranes his head as furious white caps sling themselves against the rocks at the bottom of Nautilus Pier. The howl outside seems to get louder as the room gets quiet. Sophia is just about to place a triple letter score when the power flickers and darkness closes in around them. The moon is gone and with nothing to blunt it, no street lights or stars, the inky abyss reaches out endlessly. Behind him, the twins whimper, and Teo twists toward the sound as the hair on his arms stands up.

A second later, light floods the porch once again. Around him, they all exhale. Ruth sits up, much less affected. "Didn't even need the generator that time." She shrugs and picks up her glass. "Who wants a refill?"

There is a chorus of "me's" except for Jo who mumbles something about fitting into her bridesmaid dress. As Teo finishes the last of his beer, it happens. Something much more frightening than the darkness from a moment earlier. Ruth is complaining about her lack of scrabble letters when her phone pings. Still talking, she picks it up and reads the screen, stopping mid-sentence as the color drains from her face. A second later, she returns it to the same spot, this time facedown before she pushes back her chair and quits the game, taking her phone with her.

Teo waits as long as he can before he leaves to follow her.

The light in her room is off, her dim silhouette is at the foot of the bed. Her shoulders collapsed, the overhead in the hallway backlights her in a diaphanous glow as she twists at her engagement ring. The sound of thunder rumbles above them. Ruth looks up as she reaches her phone out to him. One hand to her lips and the other trembling. The text app is still open. A single bubble on the screen.

silly spoiled Ruth cant see the truth your next

Chapter Eleven

Ruth

⌒

The next morning, Ruth opens her eyes to find her jaw sore. At best, she'd slept three fitful hours, this new text swirling around in her brain all night. She kicks back the sheets, thinking the last time she ground her teeth like this, she'd been in braces. All night, she'd worked at convincing herself this latest text wasn't related to Sophia's Instagram. There was no doubt that her sister's posts made her—*all of them*—look spoiled. But she wasn't sure the tone matched the Instagram threats. The online messages were filled with vile obscenities, pornography and violence. This was more direct and more threatening.

Your next?

Bad grammar aside—the English teacher in her had caught that right away—someone planned to come after her. Why?

She was a public-school teacher from Savannah. She'd stop taking money from Caroline after college. As far as anyone was concerned, the only thing of value in her two-bedroom condo

71

might be that necklace—though Caroline had always kept it under lock and key at the bank.

She'd been so worked up that, against her better judgment, she'd had Teo stay over. When they'd finally fallen asleep, he'd mumbled something about enlisting the HOA's security. His side of the bed is already empty when she opens her eyes, and as she opens the curtains, she finds he's made good on that promise. The Nautilus Cove's security Prius is parked squarely in front of their curb.

An alarm buzzes on Ruth's phone alerting her she's late, and as Ruth tries to click into her routine, to make herself get excited for the bridal brunch, she finds she's stomping around in a funk instead. It takes a moment to place it. As she picks through her outfits—pulling out the Balenciaga dress she's supposed to wear, the one that is too low cut but that her mother insisted on—she finds it.

She's furious with Caroline. That interruption at dinner. Mayor Bob.

Ruth grits her sore jaw. It wasn't enough that Teo's mother stepped in and became the twins' unpaid nanny the last few days, she'd also spent the whole day cooking. Her mother couldn't play nice for one night? She had hijacked that beautiful meal, reduced it, dismissed it in the same careless way she did so many other things.

Running a brush through her hair, Ruth recalls how her mother scooted her food around her plate, not really eating anything. The only person at the table who had not offered a compliment to the chef. The two times she'd spoken were to insult her father and interrupt Maya's toast.

"It's not OK," Ruth says out loud to no one. She is tired of her own complicated relationship with her mother, tired of the fact that her entire childhood was a first-hand account of Caroline's rigid standards and penchant for withholding praise—except when it came to her love life, of course. Then all bets were off.

She knew she should've stepped in last night. Though she'd learned the hard way that her mother didn't acknowledge any kind of wrongdoing, didn't believe it could even exist.

For the first time, a thought washes over Ruth and though it seems crazy, she wonders if maybe her mother has something to do with all the bad things that are happening around the wedding? Maybe Blue Compass's residents aren't as thrilled with this event as she imagined? Outside her social circles, it was no secret her mother could be an acquired taste. And Mayor Bob? He may have won his election in a landslide, but Ruth had heard the reviews about him personally were mixed. As she finds her purse, she thinks of Colt Thistle, and resolves to ask him about this later. He was definitely in the know when it came to Blue Compass.

Ruth's phone pings again, and she grabs it. Just Sophia asking if she's on her way yet. Good. She doesn't have time for any more major life revelations. She's glad to be headed to brunch. She really needs a drink.

* * *

Three hours later, the family is seated around a table on the veranda of Franco's Beach Bistro. The bridal lunch has lasted longer than Ruth anticipated, the morning a dizzying blur of the same story over and over. Everyone asking some form of the same question: *How did you meet? Can I see the ring? How'd he propose?*

In the jumble of food, gifts, and polite conversation, people appeared happy to have her be the center of attention, thrilled to celebrate how lucky she was to be marrying Teo—all of it a welcome distraction.

The restaurant had reopened two weeks earlier and though the brunch started out as something for Ruth to do with her sisters and girlfriends, she hadn't counted on how hard it would be for most of them—who were also teachers—to take time off. Only one of her coworkers, Jane, was making the trip down for the wedding, and she'd texted that something had come up, and she wouldn't get there until tomorrow.

So instead, Ruth had spent the bulk of the morning trying to remember the names of her mother's friends. At some point, they'd begun to blur together, and she'd internally started calling them the "Presidents Club." There was the Junior League president, the Savannah Bridge Club president, the wife of the Dental Association president, the Savannah Yacht Club president. So much Aqua Net and expensive shoes.

They had rented out Franco's ocean view patio for the rest of the afternoon, and as Ruth watches the last guest drive out of the parking lot, relief washes over her. Now they had the expansive veranda—and its spectacular views—free of Caroline's hangers on.

"Ruth, did you hear me?" Jo smacks her on the shoulder. Her sister's face has a happy slack to it, and she lets out a hooting laugh. A half hour earlier, Maya took the twins home, and Jo began kicking back mimosas. Even Sophia, who usually nursed a single cocktail, was keeping up.

Jo signals the waitress and orders another pitcher. She props a single foot up on the empty chair next to her, declaring, "Now—as I was saying—since all the old biddies have gone home. I pronounce this the last single sister's brunch."

Jo holds up her glass, and Caroline makes a huffing sound as she rolls her eyes.

"Today, Ruthie dear—I am going to give you the toast that I should give you at your reception—the one you *really* need but Mom would never let me give."

Scooting back her chair, Jo stands up, commanding the attention of the empty patio and toasting the air. "Ruthie dear, a good marriage is a lot like a memory foam mattress." She pauses. "Now personally, I know I wasted way too much time '*shopping*' for my mattress." She air quotes with her fingers, sending orange liquid sloshing from her champagne flute. "But that's what we Southern women do: We obsess. We agonize. We scour the internet." She pauses again. "Now, Lord knows I probably '*lay*' in one too many 'mattresses.'"

Her fingers form more air quotes as Sophia laughs and adds a sidelong eye roll. "Amen to that."

"Then one day you find one—*the one*—and, God, you're so relieved." Jo starts to pace in her tall wedges, back and forth on the cobblestone patio. Arms flailing, the kind of exaggerated movements Ruth imagines she used in the courtroom. "And it's a whole new world. Some days you roll over and think '*What have I done?* This will never work. I should have gone with the more attractive mattress or the more practical one.'"

Ruth giggles and takes a drink of her own Bloody Mary.

"But life is always moving, and you're usually catching up. Sometimes it's great. Sometimes you get the crap beat out of you. But at the end of the day, you come home and there it is—*your* mattress." Jo turns to meet Ruth's eyes. "In that moment—when you truly need it, it's *everything*. Not too hard. Not too soft. The edges line up. You fall in and a hundred thousand impressions cradle you exactly where you need it."

Jo flops back into her chair, arms clasped behind her head as she props her feet back on the table then crosses her legs. "Worn to perfection, my dear Ruthie—that, my dear, is a good marriage."

The table is quiet for a second, and Ruth resists the temptation to clap. "I love it—except if I had my way, the wedding toasting would be with really fantastic *coffee*—not champagne. I still can't believe how much we are spending on that stuff." She looks out at the ocean, hugging herself. "I can't wait to be Teo's lumpy mattress."

"That was quite a speech there, sister of the bride . . . Hello ladies." Coastal Catering's owner, Justin Sellars, is behind Sophia's chair, the smell of vodka making Ruth twist in her seat. His round face is red, and wetness peeks from his underarms as he balances a manilla folder, a clipboard and a Bloody Mary, the tall glass sweating too.

Caroline sits up in her chair and crosses her arms. "Well, if it isn't our favorite star caterer—enjoying a little R and R before the big weekend?"

"Well, actually—" Justin scratches at the scraggly day-old scruff on his chin as he gazes out toward the ocean, wrinkling his nose at something unseen. "Actually, I'm here because I'm considering buying this place—gonna do it my way this time."

Caroline raises an eyebrow. "That's amazing. I didn't know it was for sale."

"The owners have decided not to rebuild their house. I guess after what it took to get this place back in shape, they didn't have it in them—wanna be near their grandkids or something." He puts everything down on the table and reaches in his pocket, pulling a round peppermint from its wrapper before popping it in his mouth.

Ruth smiles, "Well, they did an awesome job with the remodel, and your food's obviously the best. Sounds like a match made in heaven."

Justin picks up his glass and takes a healthy gulp. "How did you like that cake I sent over—much better than the first version I bet?"

"It was fantastic, but you didn't have to do that. Teo and I have total faith in you."

"I appreciate that—it just needs to be right—it *all* needs to be right. Anyway, I'll let you ladies get back at it. Obviously, I've still got a lotta things to do . . ."

"That's right—it's a *big* week for you, I keep forgetting you're on the city council now too." Ruth widens her grin, all teeth and enthusiasm, hoping it's enough to distract him from the daggers her mother is shooting at him. "With the ordinance vote next week and the wedding, you *do* have your hands full."

"Nothing I can't handle—though I've got big shoes to fill. Mom held that seat for twenty-five years, and I'm already making plans to honor her memory." He looks at Ruth then Sophia. "I make it my job to watch out for things that need helping. By the way, bride—you look stunning today—a rose between thorns." He coughs out a strange guffaw as he looks around the table, his eyes pausing on Caroline. As he turns to leave, he adds, "Don't you worry, I got it all under control."

When he's out of earshot, Sophia whispers, "That guy's so weird."

Caroline huffs, "*Please,* tell me our caterer is not out day-drinking the afternoon before your rehearsal dinner?"

Jo hiccups, "Hey—we don't *judge.*"

Caroline shoots Jo a look. "God, what a week—first my necklace, now—" She inhales, fingering the thick gold chain currently around her neck. "I swear I don't care how famous he once was—if he doesn't come through . . ."

"Come on—the guy won a whole reality show. He's—like an artist—an eccentric." Jo takes a sip of her drink. "Don't you remember on the show how he thrived on the pressure—he probably gets off on it . . ."

Ruth takes out her phone. "If it makes you feel better, we can order a backup cake from somewhere and Sophia can have Sam pick it up on his way in—it can always be a groom's cake."

Ruth looks at Sophia who's staring at the floor. She picks at her manicure. "Sam isn't on his way. He's not coming tonight."

Jo nods, "The morning is probably better anyway."

There is another long silence. "He's not coming at all—he's leaving me."

Caroline blinks hard like the light is suddenly too bright. "Your husband? What are you talking about? Of course he's—"

Sophia's body seems to collapse. She buries her face in her hands, and her tiny frame erupts into sobs. A few seconds pass before she croaks, "I think he's fucking a CRNA. He's leaving me."

Ruth and Jo shoot up in their seats as Caroline's eyes go wide. She declares, "*Your* Sam with someone else—a divorce? I don't believe it."

"It's true, Mom. It's why—" Sophia's voice cracks. "It's why I've been working so hard on my . . . my Insta—God . . . I'm such an *effing* cliché."

Sophia sits up and rubs her temples then bends in half, bringing her head between her knees. She inhales and sits up, the remains of a Chanel smokey eye smeared in joker-like circles, her lipstick smudged up one cheek.

Caroline whips out a mirror from her bag. "Sweetie, *fix* yourself."

Sophia grabs the compact and opens it. Her shoulders collapse again at her reflection. "Look at me." She tugs at the black smears under one eye. "They said this stuff was waterproof—is there *nothing* you can count on anymore?"

Jo is out of her chair, arms around their sister as her chest rises and falls. Ruth wants to get up, but she's frozen, her stomach twisting as she realizes her wedding had added to her sister's pain. All those hateful messages, all that effort, sometimes it was hard to tell what was real with Sophia. Ruth looks beyond her sister's heaving shoulders, taking in that breathtaking beach view, her favorite place in the world that felt nothing like it should.

Chapter Twelve

Kayla

～

There's no food at the house, and Kayla's stomach is growling. Her father is working late at the precint again, and she decides to drive the few blocks to the Piggly Wiggly. The small store anchors a hollowed out strip mall and is the only grocer open for business. A few minutes later, she's in the cereal aisle overwhelmed by all the choices when her phone pings. As she tugs it from her purse, she scrolls her texts to find it's from Sydney Raines. The Bancrofts' wedding florist was a portly New York transplant who had moved south and rebranded himself as Panama City's "exclusive floral glam engineer." It was one of his many quirks that he texted Kayla in full sentences replete with periods and semicolons and even the occasional em dash, and though it generally amused her, as she skims his message her stomach drops.

Hello Darling! I hope you aren't too crazy busy. There's some kinda nutty blog post from that Tania blogger person who keeps talking about the wedding. You might wanna check it out . . .

Kayla holds her breath as she clicks on the link.

The sight loads quickly, familiar shades of hot pink and neon yellow as a giant photo of the biracial blogger, Tania T, pops up. The photo is taken from above her and the twentysomething gazes up at the camera in a suggestive pose, arms cupping an ample chest as red glasses slide down her nose. Her persona is meant to be something like a Gen Z version of the sexy secretary, but to Kayla it reads media sycophant more than anything else. In the last few months Tania T had become wildly popular rehashing well-known true crime cases, and had recently expanded her blog to include a podcast and thriving TikTok account where she would "go live" and hypothesize about everything from blind items to murder trials. Unfortunately, since the theft of Caroline Bancroft's necklace, she'd also taken a sudden interest in the wedding, sometimes sprinkling cryptic comments into her more recent live shows that made it sound like she had an insider source. Kayla holds her breath as she starts to read.

Hey All You Out There,

Tania's here with the latest 'T' and though today we will be primarily focusing on the Ribman Murders, I just wanted to highlight some juicy bits on the Blue Compass B&E. Now, we all know and love that bride, Ruth Bancroft, and since her yummy mummy's diamond necklace disappeared, we hear there may be even more looming on the horizon—like which Blue Compass native close to the family is keeping a few secrets of her own?

Let's just file it under more to come and things that make you go Hmmmm . . .

"Shit." Kayla rests her head on the plastic handle of her shopping cart. When she lifts her head, she sees a client whose daughter's pageant dress she is altering. Hardly in the mood for small talk, she straightens up and turns the corner, so consumed with getting away that she bumps headfirst into Jo Hargrove.

"Whoa nelly—" Jo laughs. "Hey there, lady." Jo's cart is piled high with diapers and goldfish, Cheerios, and apple juice. The twins are strapped into its metal front, their dimpled legs dangling side by side. They seem unaffected by the surprise collision, each sucking on a lollipop. Beau doesn't look up, too enthralled with a new plastic flashlight he's already ripped from its packaging.

Kayla apologizes and shoves her phone into her purse, zipping it up like someone trying to hide a national secret.

"I swear I run into everybody here—an outing at the 'Pig' is always a social occasion. I was—" Jo stops, cocks her head back and gives Kayla a puzzled stare like she's remembering something. The sudden shift in demeanor is palpable, and Kayla's cheeks go hot.

"Momma, here's the toe-nin." The little girl twin hands Jo a plastic container of purple vitamin gummies she can reach from her lofted perch in the cart.

"Yes—*Mel-a-tonin,* thank you, Rhea." Jo takes the sleep aid from her daughter's sticky hands before shuffling something around in the cart, and tossing two boxes of Q-tips in. "Both of them are having trouble going down at night, which is weird. They usually sleep like rocks at the beach."

"Well, they're getting big—they can't sleep like babies forever." It's a bad fake laugh, and Jo looks at her again—tilting her head in a rote concentration like she's working something out. Kayla fixes her eyes on the end cap behind her, a pyramid of stacked pink Pepto Bismol boxes with a sign that reads "Keep

Calm and Carry On." The sister couldn't know, she tells herself, couldn't possibly have put it together.

"Hey, I know we owe you a check—I forgot to give it to you at the fitting the other day. You've been working so hard, and it's just ridiculous that your commission is late—*ugh*." Jo rakes her fingers through her hair. "Mom isn't the best at taking care of that stuff, and now she's just all over the place with the break-in and her necklace being stolen." Jo looks away, pushing the packed shopping cart back and forth in a rhythm like she's trying to rock the twins to sleep.

"Oh yeah—the check." Kayla spits out a relieved sigh. "Yes—that would be great—whenever." Her eyes dart down the aisle toward the cashier. "Between you and me, I never thought that dress needed anything anyway—I mean unless she's decided to do some other necklace, which is great, too . . ." She knows she's rambling, hears herself but can't stop. "You know anything Sophia and Ruth would pick would be totally on point. Sophia's style is always amazing . . ." She finally takes a breath before asking if there are any good leads on the theft. There's an uncomfortable laugh before she adds, "My dad doesn't tell me anything—obviously."

Jo stops rocking the cart. "No—the police have been pretty quiet so far—great—but quiet . . . And I think Ruth is gonna bare-chest it for the wedding—ha."

"Well that's great too—so good to see you." As Kayla peels herself away, she waves to the twins, thinking Jo was really looking at her weird. As she spins on her foot and heads to the wine aisle, she grabs the first bottle she sees then runs straight to the door.

Chapter Thirteen

Ruth

~

It's still dark when Ruth wakes up. She's managed four hours of hard sleep and rolls over, telling herself to be grateful for them. Part of her still wants to call off the rehearsal dinner.

She and Teo had decided she would call Kayla and get extra security for the oyster roast.

Everyone would be vigilant. Everything would be fine. Ruth rubs her temples, repeats it again to herself, almost believing it when her phone pings on the bedside table. It's the first of a thousand reminders and alerts she's set for today. The weather app pops up first, and it's no surprise. Today's forecast is partly cloudy, a 30 percent chance of rain and scattered thunderstorms. It's basically the forecast year-round in Blue Compass. Tomorrow's forecast is identical. Her stomach does a flip-flop.

Tomorrow, she will be married.

With the break-in and all the planning, it was easy to lose track of what the weekend was really about, bogged down in seating arrangements and practicing makeup instead of thinking about her life with Teo forever. She could honestly say he was the best person she knew. They made sense in all the right ways. She trusted him completely, and trust wasn't something she gave away freely. Her father had seen to that. Teo was the only person, other than her sisters, who'd managed a crack in the otherwise impenetrable windshield from behind which she navigated her careful life.

Even before she'd met him, she'd had that feeling. The one you get when you know something big is going to happen, when you know you're on the verge of something important, and there's a hint of a precipice everywhere you look. Though she'd been dreading the actual date with him. (Blind dates weren't really her thing, but *thank you very much*, Principal Milken.)

She'd walked into that rundown hibachi restaurant, and there he was—stupid handsome, sitting on a bar stool in the lounge. One dimple on full display and an intense concentration on the chopstick tee-pee he was building. He looked like a kid who'd snuck in and was suddenly unsure what to do now that he'd managed to pull off a seat at the bar. He spotted her with a questioning wave, that dimple tripling in size. Later, she would realize that something inside her had already said yes. She didn't want to call it "soulmates," but when Teo kissed her for the first time, her heart rolled over and something released. After that, there'd only ever been one word: *Yes*.

Still—as sure as she was about Teo—it was the "till death do us part" that sometimes made her queasy. In the last few years, she was the only "good" Catholic left in the family, but going to regular Mass didn't automatically wash away all your reservations. She wanted to believe what the Church taught about marriage. What her elementary school rearing said about it being a permanent holy order, an irrevocable gift from God. She needed to believe it.

Still, sometimes she couldn't help but wonder how anyone could spend their whole lives together without regret? Without wanting to kill each other? Even roommates wanted to murder each other sometimes—toss in love and sex and (hopefully) kids. Was the idea that one person could be your everything forever archaic or just insane?

Ruth's phone pings again, and rather than a to-do reminder, she looks down, surprised to see it's a message from her father.

couldn't sleep. want to see u before all the fuss. any time 4 ur dad and a walk

Twenty minutes later, she is waiting for Thad outside Summerhouse, her stomach full of knots. Thad appears by the stairs, his hands full with two giant coffees and a pink gift bag. She hasn't seen her father in sweatpants in twenty years and without the usual heavy-handed hair gel, his thick hair billows in the breeze. At the edge of the sea oats, they kick off their shoes and for a second, he looks strange to her somehow, soft in a way he isn't.

"The best coffee I could find for the best daughter—and *bride*—a dad could have." He reaches in, going for a full hug, and she flinches. There's a flash of another father. Thad, younger and red faced, late at night, booze and rage oozing from his pores.

She stiffens against the memory, and as he lets go, she exhales, reminding herself that so much of what happened feels like it happened to someone else. Over time, her memory had become fickle, the parts that cut too deeply gone. It was fascinating the way the brain could do that—block things out. Wash away trauma like soap. It was the body's way of helping you cope. But there were things that never left her. The sound of glass shattering. The smell of exposed drywall before a hole had been patched. She didn't know if the small moments of remembering were better or worse, Mother Nature's mercy or her detriment.

"Hey—you, cold?" Thad rubs his arms up and down Ruth's shoulders before he turns, his gaze running up and down Summerhouse. "I gotta admit. I still feel kinda weird here." His eyes slide around Summerhouse's tall architecture, the connecting porches and landings, and he shudders with a mock exaggeration. "If your mother was a house, she would be this place. I know she doesn't want me in the wedding—that if she had her way she would ban me from this giant creepy McMansion."

"Regardless of popular belief, it is *my* day. Besides, you know how Caroline is about her beauty sleep. Nothing wakes her up . . ."

"I always forget that you girls still call your mother by her first name—does it make her crazy?"

"One of life's little pleasures."

"I bet you girls got a name for *me* when I'm not around . . ."

Ruth shoulder checks him playfully, not sure what to say. As they come to the shore's edge, water laps at their bare feet, and they step around the roped-off footprint of tonight's tent. The stakes are already driven and the square is massive. Next to it, a tall stack of firewood has been delivered, the skeleton for tonight's bonfire already assembled and waiting.

"I'm just glad that everything's OK. *Everyone's* OK. That was so scary—the other night—do the police have any leads on who mighta broke into the house?"

Ruth looks out toward the ocean, hoping he can see from her expression that she doesn't want to talk about that. There were too many emotions, too many moving parts to include him. She and Teo had settled on only telling the police chief about this latest text, and she was still second guessing that decision.

They walk in silence for a minute, and as they head toward the pier, the sun finishes its rise to the east. Overhead soft smears of peach and gray disappear, and they each try to fill the silence with different versions of small talk, the attempts strained like acquaintances riding in an elevator. When she tries to ask him about the bachelor party, he bats away her question with a dismissive wink, his frustrating, "What happens at the Looksee *stays* at the Looksee . . ." answer riling something in her stomach.

They are almost to the Club House when they stop to watch workers milling in and out of the pool area. An awning of twinkle lights is being strung across the Nautilus Cove's pool deck, and they both agree that it will look amazing.

The gift bag still hangs from Thad's wrist, thumping against his thigh as they walk. He hands Ruth the gift bag, his expression sheepish. "I know I shoulda been around more—that I ain't always been—" He clears his throat. "That my drinking used to—well, that's why I'm here. Clean and sober . . ."

Ruth puts her hand on her father's chest, then turns away and looks out to the ocean. "I know it can't be easy. Everyone hasn't exactly rolled out the welcome wagon. I think it takes a lot of courage—well, I'm just happy you're here."

As the words leave her mouth, Ruth chides herself. *She always did that—gave people a pass, filled in the uncomfortable spaces for them.* She wonders if she's wrong to do it again here.

In college, she sometimes felt different from the other girls on campus. They always seemed so riled up. Full of teeth and passion, always on the lookout for one injustice or another. Like everyone, she'd gone to college to expand herself, to meet people and gain new experiences. Certainly not to get her "MRS" as she'd heard her classmates laugh one too many times. But she could see the other girls didn't believe her, could feel how they took her in, studying her pearls and pastel sweater sets with both an incredulous fascination and a pious pity. Their dismissal of her was always quiet, the slightest eyeroll, backs turned, like clustering with like, unspoken but absolute.

Ruth knew she was conventional, agreeable. She couldn't help if it just seemed logical that her version of Barbie's Dreamhouse was situated down the path of least resistance. Lately, she'd started to feel a certain annoyance for having to apologize for who she was. By her estimation, weren't romantics actually the more evolved species? The world was ugly, damn it. Cynicism was easy. It took real strength to find the good in people no matter what.

Her father kneels to pick up two rocks at their feet, handing one to Ruth, the motion pulling her from her thoughts. "I just wish your sisters gave me a chance—got things like you do. Forgive and forget isn't exactly in their vocabulary." He turns over his rock, rolling it back and forth over his knuckles like a poker chip trick. He motions with his hand for her to try it, and her attempt with the rock is clumsy. It falls to the sand. He scoops it up before sending it skipping into the waves.

"Enough of this mushy crap. Open your present."

Inside the wrinkled bag, Ruth finds a little glass sea turtle and a bottle of vintage champagne. She shifts from one foot to the other, knowing he couldn't know she never drank champagne. He hadn't been around much since she was old enough to develop opinions about alcohol. She and Sophia had a heated debate about the need to serve champagne at the wedding. The bubbles always guaranteed Ruth a stomachache. The fact that Teo didn't like champagne either had swayed no one.

Thad stares down at his feet. "I knew you had a bunch of them stuffed turtles around your room when you was little. Figured you and that fiancé could have the champagne on your honeymoon—it's the good stuff."

The champagne is Caroline's favorite brand. At that moment, two bottles with the same gold label sit at the counter at Summerhouse. She flips the little sea turtle in her hand, the swirls of pink and blue-opal iridescent in her palm. It was the kind of knickknack found in a thousand coastal gift shops down the beach.

Ruth's phone pings with another wedding reminder, and she's saved from having to say more. They walk in silence as she checks reminders until they get to her father's car. She tells him again she's glad he's here. As he backs out, she rolls the little turtle in her palm. He's different in a way she can't place. The bluster is missing, his big voice almost vulnerable when he said, "Me too."

Two simple words tossed off as he hurried down the driveway, uttered without any real thought, but for the first time ever, her heart rolls over and she thinks he might mean what he says.

Chapter Fourteen

Kayla

Minus eight hours to the reception, Kayla pulls into Summer-house with a stomach full of butterflies. A month ago, the house's exterior had received a fresh coat of cobalt blue paint, the same color chosen originally by Blake Bancroft to rival the bay's blue waters. It was the way she preferred to remember Summer-house. Years before Caroline and her daughters, her father's late best friend and once stubbornly single town dentist, had built this mansion on the sea to commemorate his tenth and final franchise opening.

Most people either have sense in their head or money in their wallets—very few get both. Her father liked to say this about Blake. It was a regret of hers that she hadn't bothered to get to know him before he got sick. Her father was so fond of him, and the designer in her had always enjoyed getting the blow-by-blows from her father as Blake dreamed into reality the biggest house Blue Compass had ever seen. Like everything the dentist did, the result had been neat and carefully executed. Built a half a story higher than the homes around it, she doubted he could have ever imagined its arrogant stature saving it from the wrath of Hurricane Kerry.

Kayla parks her Honda in an out of the way spot and grabs her iPad and a Tupperware bin she'd coined the "give me box." Full of fabric tape and stain stick, deodorant and ibuprofen, vendor contracts, and any other thing she'd ever needed and forgotten at an event, she steps inside Summerhouse and sets the plastic tub on the floor. The house is even neater than usual, every inch of it the show palace created with the help of one of the Panhandle's most expensive designers.

Of course, no one will see a stitch of it tonight. Caroline wasn't even allowing the caterers inside—God forbid her guests dent the fibers of her ten thousand dollar rugs or crease the plush chenille fabrics that seemed to Kayla so out of place on the beach.

At least the weather was cooperating. Ruth's family had scoffed about getting married so close to Halloween, but tonight would be warm, not too hot. Autumn in Florida was always a crapshoot and though she'd planned for all contingencies, by cocktail hour the weather would be the kind of breezy perfection that felt decadent.

Four hundred yards down the beach, there was only one flaw in tonight's perfect aesthetic. Kayla looked out the row of Summerhouse's tall windows to Nautilus Pier, still a giant eyesore. The pier was once a one-of-a-kind optical design, the combination of its angles and furthest end tapering allowed the pier to fade into the bay like an infinity pool.

Now, what was left was a twisted spine of gnarled wood, the surviving planks sticking out at odd angles. Its rails were jagged and missing whole sections. Beneath them, rocks once intended to fight erosion now cradled crooked pilings. Despite Caroline and the mayor's heavy intervention, no string had been pulled hard enough to get it repaired in time. A run of bad luck and federal red tape prohibited the necessary permits. This weekend, they weren't allowed to even touch the pier's entrance. It was the one bit of real life in this whole spectacle.

The tablet in Kayla's hand buzzes with an email: the final check through from the rental company. The struggle had been real when it came to tonight's décor, too. Finding a way to balance the casual feel that made sense for a beach dinner with Caroline's over-the-top tastes had taken months. In the end, they'd landed on a palette of soft white against touches of gold and burlap. The tables covered in custom burlap runners, specially ordered for the thin gold velum woven through them. The center pieces of white roses, hydrangeas, and astilbe would be scattered among painted and bleached oyster shells. Each one hand embellished with the couple's custom wedding monogram designed by a local artist.

But the showstopper would be above it all—an enormous oyster shell chandelier, designed and commissioned by the same artist. The one-of-a-kind installation would hang at the center of the tent and throw sparkles all over the dance floor.

Kayla turns and watches as a worker from the rental company lugs a white Adirondack chair towards the beach. Dozens of chairs were being brought to line the shore and scattered around the bonfire. Even the portable restrooms had been a hill Kayla managed not to die on. After extensive research, she'd found a type of luxury restroom trailer that had satisfied both Caroline and Sophia. The private restrooms with quartz counter tops and soft jazz piped in were coming from Jacksonville. She'd even managed bathroom attendants.

Tonight at the entrance, everyone would receive a swag bag complete with their own set of oyster shuckers. The couple's wedding monogram was—of course—etched into their wood handles. There were monogrammed flip-flops and beach towels. The debate over the towel's embroidered wedding hashtag another battle with Sophia. Social media turns every aspect of getting hitched into an opportunity to add to the giant e-scrapbook of life.

Everything seemed to be running smoothly, and Kayla exhales, fishing around in the "give me box." On the way there, a radio talk show host had been discussing some psychological condition called "decision fatigue," and Kayla had decided that *yes, she was definitely suffering from that among other things*. Decision fatigue or something much worse. With most of her weddings, it wasn't just helping the bride make her choices that was the challenge, it was the consequences that came with them. Once a reception hall was booked, they were stuck working around its aging décor, its broken outlets or leaky toilets. Only this time, Kayla had upped the ante. Once she'd decided to take on the Bancroft wedding, the consequences sometimes started to feel like drowning, like fighting an undertow constantly trying to pull her under.

This morning, when Ruth texted asking for more security, was the last straw. She'd had no choice but to go to her father, a fact that had both infuriated and deflated her. She didn't want to need him like this, to have him come to her rescue again. She could already hear his subtle, endless ribbing, and it felt like a breaking point. So she'd gone another way with her persuasion.

"Mom would be happy we are doing this as a team."

"The *mom* card? Really—you're going there?"

Even then, Kayla was glad that they could finally talk about her, speak about the missing piece in both their lives. The first year after her mother's death, Kayla had cried every day for eleven months, thinking she might never come up from her grief. Then one day, the ache lessened. Though it still caught up with her sometimes. On a regular Tuesday, answering an email or pumping gas, the pain would smack against her, taking her breath away.

After they'd come to an agreement about her father's terms, he'd given her a hug, the kind of outward affection he wasn't prone to showing. It'd been almost nine years, but in the moment, the loss was fresh again. He'd squeezed tighter as a sea of emotions bubbled to the surface, his thick chest the sudden comfort she wasn't sure she even deserved.

Kayla's hand brushes against what feels like a hard pebble in the bottom of the box. She extracts it—just some ephemera that must have made its way in amongst the swag bags accidentally—and tosses it onto the beach. Lying in the sand, the little white pill sits defiantly like a pale tourist. Kayla stares at it, unsure how it got in the box. The unassuming tablet could be Tylenol or something heavier. Anyone could have passed by and dropped it in. Sometimes being in charge of a wedding means keeping potential problems in your pocket. With all the activity on the beach, no one notices Kayla's two fingers pluck the pill from the fresh sand.

Chapter Fifteen

Ruth

～

Kayla and the wedding vendors look like they're ahead of schedule. The beach sand is raked into soft lines and a massive bonfire is already lit. Behind it, the giant sailcloth tent is fully assembled, servers in starched white uniforms go in and out with silver trays of marshmallows and rows of chocolates. Ruth closes her eyes as the mellow notes of the evening's band, *The Good Vibrations,* floats up to the porch.

Behind her, two women from the salon are setting up in the living room for hair and makeup. Ruth joins them as her mother calls from her bedroom, "Did someone make sure that planner had them check the beach again? I don't know where all this trash is coming from. I keep finding wrappers and things blowing into the garage. I don't want a hint of garbage anywhere out there. Not so much as a speck of seaweed."

Ruth shouts back that it's under control and takes a deep breath, wondering if tea might calm her nerves.

There's a knock at the door, and Mayor Bob is there, his arms loaded with flowers. He is dressed in a salmon-colored oxford and khaki pants, a selection which Ruth guesses by the cut of the trouser, the artful drape of expensive fabric, has involved her mother somehow.

"Two dozen red roses for this gorgeous lady and a mixed bouquet for the lovely bride." He lets himself in and hands Ruth and her mother their bouquets then bows, a princely move revealing a patch of bald Ruth wishes her sisters were there to see.

"That's so sweet, babe." Caroline looks at Ruth. "I don't see anyone else around here making such thoughtful gestures . . . Where is your father anyway? I hope he isn't late."

"My pleasure, ladies—two roses like yourselves should have fresh flowers every day." Mayor Bob leans in to plant a peck on Caroline's cheek. A second later, his cell buzzes at his waist, and before answering it, he bends down to brush a speck from a shiny Gucci loafer. "The work of a civil servant is never done–" He turns to the kitchen and covers the speaker with his hand before he whispers, "Always putting out fires . . ."

Ruth watches as he helps himself to a beer from the fridge. Finding the bottle opener before he ducks into the walk-in pantry to take the call, the ease with which he knows his way around their kitchen not lost on her.

Blessedly, the mayor hadn't been at the actual rehearsal that morning. The quick run through—designed to keep the amount of time Caroline and Thad were near each other to a minimum—had gone off without incident. Ruth had always imagined she would marry at St. John's Cathedral on Reid Street, but Blue Compass's only Catholic Church was yet another casualty of the storm. The unassuming cathedral with its white shiplap exterior and century old architecture had been no match for Kerry's 150-mile-an-hour-plus winds. Its A-line roof caved in, destroying the arched wood buttresses and stained-glass windows that had once felt magical to her. Only a small part of the rectory survived, and its priest, Father Ron, had practically been camping in it for the last year. It was one of the reasons they'd had such luck with the stark traditionalist. The stout priest who under normal circumstances would never agree to hold a full Catholic ceremony at the Beach Club, hadn't needed much finessing. That morning, he'd actually seemed buoyant, younger than his sixty-two years as he stroked his salt and pepper beard, repeating, "How joyful to simply perform the rites once again."

Father Ron's other poorly kept secret was that he enjoyed a good party, on occasion more than one celebratory drink. His attendance tonight—and infamous dance moves—was something she'd been promising Teo was well-worth the price of his seat at the dinner.

Of course, there'd been plenty of attention paid to wedding manners. Southern etiquette had dictated all out-of-town guests be included in the rehearsal dinner. The headcount tonight was basically the same as the wedding, a fact Ruth still found absurd.

"We are ready for you, ma'am." The taller of the two hair-dressers gestures to Ruth and she sits down in a kitchen chair facing the bay.

"We said loose waves, right?" The stylists name—Stevie—is embroidered on her shirt, and she holds up two fistfuls of Ruth's thick hair as Jo suddenly flies into the room. Her sister's bathrobe is draped open and a single giant curler pins back her bangs. "Have you seen Beau?"

The fuchsia-lined letters across Jo's back practically scream "Matron of the Bride x 2"—the "x 2" lined in cheap giant sequins. The robe had come with matching slippers too, the fuzzy toe of each embellished with a giant plastic diamond ring so tacky Jo had refused to even try them on. Ruth had her own lounge set as well. The shiny *"Bride"* stitched across her robe making her feel like a demented Pink Lady.

The bridal freebies are courtesy of Sophia and definitely not her usual high-end Instagram endorsement. The product's fabric is fire hazard cheap, and Sophia's skin hadn't touched that kind of polyester—well, ever. Ruth recalls the staged photos of the robes and slippers on her sister's feed, the black and white filter and Sophia's artful arrangement vastly improving their cheap aesthetic. The camera angle had obscured just enough of the persons wearing them so that someone might infer it was Ruth and her sisters, though it most definitely wasn't. Ruth knew she should have asked more about the endorsements, but she was afraid of the answer, fearful that knowing how much Sophia was making off of her wedding would put her over the edge. Ruth bit her lip, not thrilled about the realization that Sophia's financial situation clearly wasn't what she let on, that her sister's ulterior motives might be fueled by it. Until a year ago, Sophia had worked at a successful public relations firm, though Ruth never had the impression she *needed* to work. Sophia's social feeds were always filled with her and someone famous or beautiful doing something interesting or beautiful—generally both. It was a perk of the job that had launched Sophia's own internet celebrity, and Ruth imagined had later boosted the wedding's notoriety.

"Beau . . . Beau, baby where are you?" Jo steps into Caroline's bedroom, still searching for Beau when a gray blur in a seersucker short suit and a magician's cape leaps from the stairs and buzzes by. Beau is waving some kind of wand and lunges at Ruth. "Boo!" Behind her, Stevie yelps, knocking over a tray of bobby pins.

Ruth bends over to gather the metal pins as the child runs off again, but not before he whips around in a triple spin move that makes his cape flap. At the same moment, JD appears from the stairs. "Did you find him?"

Her brother-in-law's hair is damp, combed back so that the hint of recession is prominent with his furrowed brow. Jo joins him, and they amp up the sugary-sweet calls, their voices poorly masking their annoyance.

Ruth passes Stevie the handful of bobby pins and holds up a finger. "I'll be right back." She's gone only a second and when she returns, she calls to her nephew with an impish grin, "Beau—my little Beau Beau . . . Aunty Ruth has something for you."

She lurches, flinging open an empty cabinet. Next, she checks under the couch. She sings, "I've got a surprise . . . I know you like reptiles . . ." The turtle figurine her father has given her is in her hand, and she twists it, calling, "Guess I'll just keep this little turtle for myself." With that, a cabinet flies open. Beau is there, his knees squished to his chest, but JD gets to him first, grabbing furiously for whatever he has tucked behind his back.

"Aha, Magic Man." He grabs at the mysterious object then his eyes go wide.

Beau frees himself from the cabinet as Caroline charges over, snatching at the long purple cylinder in Sophia's hand while Beau leaps for it too.

"Gimmee. Gimmee. I want my waaaand."

Caroline's mouth drops open. With one hand, she holds the pregnancy test up to the light. The other hand is fanned out over her chest as she fingers a single strand of pearls at her neck. "Two lines."

Jo's body goes limp. "I woke up with that taste of metal in my mouth." Her voice tapers to a whisper. "I went to the store . . ."

Caroline's red lips scrunch. "Dear God—what is with this family and timing . . . You can't wait to get pregnant? Sophia can't wait to be divorced?"

Jo sits down and puts her head in her hands. A slow grin spreads across JD's face.

For a second, no one moves, then Jo finally looks up, coughing out an exasperated laugh—the sound maniacal, like something a Disney villain might offer up with an evil proclamation.

"Pregnant. Really?" she stammers, "That's just . . . wonderful—hysterical, *really*." She buries her head again in her hands. "Ruthie—I guess Teo gets to be an uncle again. Somebody hand me one of those diapers, I think I just peed my pants a little."

Chapter Sixteen

Marcus

⌐

Marcus' cruiser shudders as he cuts off the ignition at the curb of Summerhouse. Though he had always planned to show up for tonight, he hadn't told his daughter as much. Originally he was going to drop by the rehearsal dinner under the ruse of checking everything out.

This was much better.

From day one, he'd thought this wedding was more than Kayla could handle. These kinds of high dollar affairs were planned by big event companies. Businesses with resources and connections. Kayla's mother had started Two Be Wed selling prom dresses out of her trunk. Sure, Kayla had always had that same gift with a needle and thread—even more so than her mother, and the little place was doing well. But this whole thing was ambitious even for his daughter.

As he walked from the curb, it hit him again how parenting could split you, make you do things you never dreamed. That you became two things at once—even when they were polar opposites. It wasn't that he wasn't proud of where his wife, and then later Kayla, had taken their little shop, but they both knew that there were just too many ways this thing could go sideways.

It wasn't like she needed to work so hard either. While he'd made it a point not to spoil her—even when he could, he'd done his best to keep her humble, instill a work ethic. Part of him still felt guilty for how hard it had been for her growing up. Being biracial is never easy, and it hadn't been uncommon for her to come home sobbing. His own rage, white hot as she repeated the awful slurs she'd been called. He sometimes wondered if he hadn't spoiled her too much to make up for it, that his leniency at home was one of the reasons things went from bad to worse at that school in Atlanta.

Marcus had felt it right away—the same way he knew when a perp was lying to him: at the back of your mind, there's that itch you can't scratch. The way his middle schooler wouldn't quite meet his eyes anymore. It had all started way too early— the drinking and partying. You see a lot of things as a cop, and you think you're prepared, but when it's your own kid running with the wrong people, it's different.

Still sometimes, he wondered if they'd made it worse— forcing a move on a teenage girl already struggling. He and his wife had just been so desperate to get her away, to give her a fresh start. It hadn't occurred to them that she could find a worse brand of trouble right here in Blue Compass.

Damn it, there were lots of reasons why this was a bad idea. Whatever was or wasn't going on right now, he was exactly where he needed to be. He sure as hell wasn't about to let some second-rate, crackpot criminal ruin a year of his daughter's hard work. In the past few months, he'd hardly seen Kayla. When he did, she looked exhausted.

Marcus is still settling on a surveillance strategy as he heads to the beach side of Summerhouse. The Bancroft property was once flanked on both sides by thickets of greenery. The sparse groves of Palmetto trees and mangroves planted for privacy were now a sad hedge of naked sticks and dead bushes. There was an almost unobstructed view of the undeveloped acre between Summerhouse and the Beach Club. He wants the best view of it all, and he laps the perimeter again before settling on an out of the way spot on the porch.

"Excuse me, sir."

Marcus leans against the railing of the porch, stepping aside for a man in a starched white uniform, his shiny silver tray arranged poshly with marshmallows and what looked like rows of chocolates. Marcus looks around again, this time without the eyes of a cop. The smell of barbeque and firewood is tantalizing. Even the beach sand is somehow spotless. An unexpected surge of pride washes over him as the guests begin to arrive, many of them stopping to snap photos of Kayla's handiwork. Jade sticks out amongst them, ignoring the party as she makes a beeline for where Marcus is standing.

"You went with the blues too?" Jade tugs at the cuff of her polyester collar and Marcus nods, wondering if he even owned regular clothes anymore. "I had all my civvies packed for the trip—figured it couldn't hurt." A flash of hurt darts across Jade's face then disappears. "I'm supposed to be on a plane to Barbados right now . . . gonna have to *seriously* rethink some things after this weekend."

Marcus nods in commiseration, hoping he looks it. Jade keeps him in the loop regarding her long term, on-again, off-again relationship. She'd had plans to pop the question on their trip. Then this morning, she'd texted him that she'd been stood up at the airport. After that, it hadn't taken a lot of convincing to get Jade to work the party. Though Marcus hated to admit it, secretly he'd also been a little relieved. She was his best cop and a hell of a crime tech. That girl-friend of hers had been trying to get her to move out of Blue Compass for years. "Busy is good—and we all appreciate you stepping in."

"It's a bit much, isn't it?" Jade takes an appraising look around the beach, eyeing the trailers of Adirondack chairs backed into the sand, the generators and catering trucks encroaching on the newly sprouted sea oats still struggling to take root. "I'm just not sure how much I buy the whole *'look at how much money we have and aren't we saints cuz we're spending it on the town'* thing. It's . . . I dunno—yick."

"They're not calling it the 'Panhandle Wedding of the Year' for nothing." Marcus shrugs. "At least we are eating good. I heard there's a mini filet mignon station and that she-crab soup of Coastal Caterings." They both look out, spotting Tim, the retired Blue Compass beat cop originally hired to work the event. He is standing at the oyster table alone, a paper napkin stuffed into his uniform collar, shoving down oysters as fast as he can shuck them. "Seriously, what could be more fun than watching a bunch of white people drink too much and try to dance?"

Jade turns back from the bay with a wistful sigh. "Ignore me. I'm just in an awful mood. I dunno—maybe it's just the shit show that's my own life, but I've got this ominous feeling. It's a full moon tonight. I'm keeping my eyes peeled."

Chapter Seventeen

Ruth

It takes Nicholas exactly fourteen seconds after the band switches from background music to cover songs to shed his sport coat, find his straw cowboy hat, and drag Ruth out onto the dance floor. Sophia and Jo are dancing too, the twins in the arms of their parents. The band has just begun a shag arrangement, and Teo finds his mother. The two of them saunter across the parquet dance floor in a perfect Carolina two-step Ruth knows they've been practicing at home.

Amidst all the movement, Caroline catches Ruth's eye. She is at the bar, her burgundy sundress fluttering in the breeze. Ruth watches as guests drift to her, lipsticked lips full of smiles and air kisses before they rotate out of her orbit to make room for someone new.

Everyone from Caroline's circles is here. Not just the who's who of Savannah, but the ones Caroline preferred in Blue Compass as well. At some point, Ruth and Teo gave up on curtailing the guest list and began calling it what it really was, *The Real*

Housewives of Savannah and Blue Compass. Though she'd been watching them for years—an anthropological study of older middle-aged women with time and money—she still didn't understand her mother's people or their predilections. That first summer in Blue Compass, there had been a seismic shift. Caroline's social stratosphere suddenly skyrocketed, a moment she imagined her mother had been waiting for her whole life.

Ruth had just finished her first year at Morton Day, the social workings of her new elite prep school still strange. Too quiet and too awkward, she'd happily settled on the sidelines, her nose in a book as she secretly cataloged the middle school drama, studying it like an amoeba under a microscope—completely fascinated but never really wanting to get too close. On the last day of classes, Caroline had picked her up in a brand new BMW, (a *just because* from Blake), and they'd driven straight to Blue Compass. Her mother was new to the Nautilus Cove's Homeowners Association and had wanted time to prepare for her first meeting as their new president. Ruth had watched the meeting from the screened porch, could still remember the sound of her mother's gavel on the dining room table. It was then that the other members had begun deferring to Caroline. Not just on every board matter, but her every whim. The room literally swarmed Caroline, who—the very definition of queen bee—sat at the head of her own table, sipping tea.

It was there, among the expensive bags and dark tans, that Ruth saw it. There were no trust fund types here. No family names or legacy wealth. The people of Blue Compass were *new* money. American success stories. People who'd pulled themselves up by their bootstraps and would gladly go home and work the sixty hours a week it took to afford their shiny second homes. They were more impressed by the horsepower of your boat or the location of your stadium seats than by your pedigree. The nuances were subtle, but Ruth had seen them all too well. She'd watched the other type in her new school. Girls who clustered together—like attracting like—a glossy sheen that came from a lifetime of asking for things and knowing with complete certainty they'd be brought to you.

There was a small group of the well-heeled tonight, a few known Savannah family names who had made the trip. A coup mentioned by Caroline too many times to count. (*The Wellseys are here. Make sure you welcome them!*) Her mother's competitive streak was as famous as it was merciless. From checkers to her children's achievements, she only ever participated in games she could win. It was why she'd stayed in Blue Compass after Blake had passed. Her wealth ballooning with the size of her late husband's life insurance, all the while cataloging Blue Compasses' many faults. Her mother could have easily found another place to sit in the sand, but Ruth saw it that day: Not just any place—anyone—would wrap their arms around a former working class beauty queen. There was a kind of quiet assurance it took to maneuver in certain circles. But here in Blue Compass—the terrain was more hospitable. Her mother could hone herself, a practice she would later apply to the tighter spheres in Savannah. Ruth had seen it that night, and now again as she watched her mother at the bar. In this remote microcosm of white sand and southern drawl, it had taken time, but Caroline had not only learned to navigate, she'd found a way to reign.

Ruth watched as the town's prominent real estate agent and fellow self-made matron, Mandy Lowe, paused midconversation with Caroline to pluck a crab puff from a server's tray, and it hits

Ruth that she's starving. She steps away from the dance floor and turns to head to a catering station near the back. In the process, she tumbles on her wedges on the lip of the dance floor and runs headfirst into Colt Thistle. She apologizes, laughing at her clumsiness. "Gosh—sorry. Hey, what you got on that tray?"

Colt holds out a silver platter of bacon-wrapped stuffed shrimp, and she eagerly takes one. He looks around. "Everybody is talking about what a nice party this is—I hope you're having a good time?"

"How could I not? Though I don't love being the center of attention." Ruth takes another and pops it in her mouth. "But I'm glad you're here."

"I get it—I don't love attention either." Colt shuffles the tray from one hand to the other.

"It's all kinda surreal." She looks around at the flowers and candlelight, the chandelier rustling overhead, "But it's crazy beautiful in here, right?"

Colt is silent a second, and she feels him studying her. He opens his mouth to say something then stops.

Once upon a time, there had been a moment—a flash, really—where Ruth had considered a life in Blue Compass, had considered Colt as something more than just a friend. She'd just graduated from college and was interviewing to teach at high schools all over Georgia and Florida. There was a surprise call from the Blue Compass principal, a sophomore English position and an open avenue to make a life here even though she hadn't offered as much as a résumé. The position was hers if she'd wanted it.

Ruth hadn't been dating anyone at the time and had been looking forward to a quiet summer. Alone in Summerhouse for the first time that year, she decided to watch the sunset from the porch and think when she found Colt at the bottom on the porch stairs. He was hammering at something, a red tool box on the ground in front of him. Shirtless and sweaty, his long torso was already a deep summer bronze.

"Your mom asked me to take care of this step before everyone gets here." He stood, giving her the same one-armed hug he did at the beginning of every season. Ruth convinced him to join her for a drink in the rocking chairs. She grabbed two beers from the fridge, the kitchen already fully stocked courtesy of Colt's mother.

"Cheers to another summer and to your graduation—congrats." They clinked bottles.

Colt had been chattier than usual, and she was about to tell him about her job offer when he told her that he already knows. "You know the Blue Compass rumor mill has been chewing on that little morsel for days."

The wind picks up and blows back his hair, Colt's head looking strangely empty without a baseball cap. "Are you considering the job? You could be a beach bum year round—do a lot of good here."

Ruth remembered not being sure what to say. It was her first job offer, and she didn't yet know how she felt. "I'm definitely thinking about it." As they both took another sip, he'd done something she never would have predicted—he'd reached over and taken her hand. Without a word, threading it through his as they rocked in silence, the sun turning shades of yellow and orange as it set. As they finished their beers and kept talking—she remembered that there were lots of words that really didn't say anything. His hand still in hers, his fingers thick and rough with calluses. It hadn't felt wrong—exactly. But not right either.

Later, she'd realize that she just hadn't had enough of her own calluses, didn't know who she was outside her little liberal arts college and student teaching. The world was still fresh. She thought there was more left to do outside the safety Blue Compass could give her. The next day, her first choice in Savannah had called and offered her a two-year contract.

Caroline catches her eye now and winks from her post at the bar. Her mother would never have let her marry Colt, and maybe that was part of his appeal. A good guy but too much local flavor for Caroline's estimation. And maybe Ruth had bought into the idea that she was too good for this place too? She would never have admitted it back then, but now, in this tent with its gaudy, bespoke seashell chandelier, she wonders whether she's ever made a choice that was solely for herself.

Chapter Eighteen

Teo

〜

"Hey, pretty lady—whatcha thinking about?"

Teo sneaks up behind Ruth, who is deep in thought, and lets two fingers tiptoe up her spine. "Everyone having a good time? *Housewives* seem happy."

"I am too—*now*." She pulls into him, and Teo closes his eyes, enjoying the familiar way that they fit together. She smells like firewood and lavender. The band finishes up Beyonce's "Crazy Love," and they both watch as Caroline makes her way up to the front of the room.

"Time for the toast," he whispers. "Dun dun dunnn."

Ruth rolls her eyes as Caroline steps onto the skirted stage. He watches as the guy from Summerhouse the other day (*Colt something?*) parts the crowd and hands her a microphone and a glass of champagne, an uncomfortable glance before he disappears into the crowd. He knew it was unfounded but there was something about that guy that he didn't like. He squeezed Ruth again and turned his attention back to the stage.

"Thank you all for being here tonight." Caroline finds the center of the stage, adopting the rigid posture of someone comfortable in the limelight as she surveys the room. "We are so pleased all of you could be here, especially those of you who had to make a long trip. You know, having daughters has been the greatest blessing in my life." A spotlight is suddenly on her, and she tugs at the cord of the microphone, her voice without a trace of nerves.

"Over the years, Ruth has grown into such a special woman, and I've always tried to help her—to raise her and teach her— always knowing it was so important that she become the best version of *me*—I mean *herself* that she could be." There's a quick head tilt, a confident wink and just the right sprinkling of laughter to let her know the crowd gets her joke. The band belts out a few notes of Neil Diamond's "Sweet Caroline."

Bum Bum Bummm . . .

Next to him, Ruth lets out a sound. The sigh, part gasp, part resigned disbelief.

"Yes, I have tried to teach my daughter many things over the years." Caroline's voice grows warmer, and she tilts her head contemplatively. "But she has taught me, as well. My youngest is someone who really *cares* about people and will always go the extra mile, so it's no surprise she found Teo, who is so similar. I'm just so thrilled to have you—and your lovely mother, Maya—join our family." Caroline reaches out toward them at the back of the room. "Let us raise a toast to this beautiful couple and the amazing life ahead of them."

Applause and toasts break out as cameras flash. Teo sees people turn, feels eyes all over both of them. They respond, all teeth and clapping as Ruth blows her mother a fake air kiss that makes him feel queasy. The little devil on his shoulder thinking, *this is too much.*

A noise cuts across the room, a jumble of snorts and squawks loud enough that a few heads turn. It's coming from the corner table, the vicinity of the *family* table, and Ruth's face drops.

"Wait here. I'll check it out." Teo squeezes her hand, grateful for an opportunity to leave the spotlight Caroline's created on them. He whispers through a gritted smile. "Just keep smiling."

Ruth's sisters are at the table with JD and Nicholas, their backs to Teo in a sweaty, secretive football huddle. The table in front of them is littered with glasses and empty bottles, tiny plates and cell phones. Smoke from lit cigars billows. Nick wheels around slowly, rolling his eyes and shaking his head in a *you're not gonna believe this* manner.

"We were just at the bar over there with your old pal, Bob." He gestures toward Mayor Bob, who is deep in a conversation with one of his law partners across the room. Nick empties the rest of his beer then pulls back a chair. "You're gonna want a seat for this."

Then he leans into him and whispers the goods. Later, Teo would give the same information to Ruth, a flawless blow-by-blow and imitation of the events as they unfolded:

As Caroline stepped on stage, Mayor Bob was gushing ad nauseam about Ruth's mother. *Her gorgeous body, how young she looks, the way everyone loves her.* Which had prompted the other men to head to the bar for shots. At some point, between the licking, slamming, and salting of several rounds of top shelf tequila, the mayor let it slip he had a ring—a revelation that sent JD beelining for his wife.

"They barely know each other."

"Got it from the horse's mouth. It was like he wanted my blessing or something."

"He wouldn't—*couldn't*?"

"Mayor Bob is gonna pop the question to Mom?" Sophia stammered, "Like next week?" The rest of her wine disappears from her glass.

"As soon as Ruth and Teo take off for the honeymoon."

"She won't say yes . . . *will* she?" JD looks over to Jo.

Jo runs her hands through her hair. "Jesus, this is the night I get to stop drinking—really?" Jo sucks in her cheek bones, and finds Caroline's ramrod straight posture. Her hand on her chest, she reaches up to finger an imaginary necklace at her throat, nose in the air. "Jesus, what is it with this family and timing?" She smothers a laugh as she flicks a bent limp wrist around the reception tent in every direction, the impression of Caroline's mannerisms flawless. "*You* can't wait to be pregnant? *You* can't wait to be divorced. *You* can't wait to be engaged."

Pausing, she drops her hands to her hips, Jo's voice returning to her own dry tone. "Dear God, I think we've covered all the major life events, don't you—what's next? Someone gonna drop dead right here at this party?"

Chapter Nineteen

Kayla

The desserts were coming out on time and the toasts had gone off without a hitch—well, relatively speaking. After the mother-of-the-bride speech, there'd been an impromptu and unscheduled "boyfriend of the mother of the bride" speech that was not on the schedule and mostly a series of compliments for Caroline and her good taste. Caroline Bancroft and the mayor weren't exactly the most logical couple, but it wasn't like Kayla was about to jump on stage and pluck the microphone from his hand? Anyway, there was no time to worry about poor taste or the rumor mill. At the moment there were way more pressing issues—like the massive thunder cloud forming overhead.

The evening had been plugging along as planned, and she'd been feeling pretty good about herself. So she'd stopped to take it all in, to look around and admire her work. The last hints of a peach sunset were melting into a cloudless sky. After that, it had seemed reasonable to duck out, heading to her car for just a moment to kick off her shoes and rest her feet. Maybe even close her eyes.

But a previously menacing cloud has turned a disturbing gunmetal gray. Slack-jawed, she glares up at the monstrous haze as it stretches out from the horizon, hovering over Summerhouse like its location is personal.

Kayla makes her way to the tent's entrance and opens the weather app on her phone. Off in the distance, there is the rumble of thunder, followed by the flash of lightning. Around her, a soft wind blows at the table skirts. The flaps of the tent stir. Kayla's eyes dart around the party. Guests are still crowding the wooden oyster tables. The horseshoe pits and corn hole tournaments are still in full swing. The few children brought by their parents roast marshmallows over the bonfire. Under the tent, the band is taking a break, but the reassuring sounds of laughter, clinking dishes, and party chatter remain. If anyone is concerned by the quick turn in atmospheric pressure, they aren't showing it.

Kayla prays the rain will hold off as she tries the Weather Radar app again on her phone. The wi-fi symbol isn't spinning, and she wills it to move. She turns to keep an eye on the storm's approach and sees Justin Sellars, humming and strolling up the beach toward her in a soiled Coastal Catering apron. He is studying the sky too, his hands threaded over the paunch of his midsection like an expectant mother.

"Sure hope it's not gonna rain." He tosses back his head, the laugh long and strangely inappropriate.

"You guys good back there if it opens up?" Kayla adjusts her face. So far, the food has been spectacular and on time. In a few more steps, she hopes she won't catch the scent of alcohol on him.

"Oh, we'll manage." He's still humming an unrecognizable tune as he looks at her and then at the massive party in full swing behind her. "We've got a tent too, ya know—I'm not too worried. I've been doing this a long time . . . seen my share of disasters." A clap of thunder rumbles softly overhead, and he smiles, taking a peppermint from his pocket and popping it into his mouth. "Guess, I better get back at it. I got lots of things to watch out for—" Justin turns and saunters back toward the catering trailer, whistling the same tune, as if he had nowhere better to be.

There's no time to worry about what's going on with Justin Sellars because the first drop of rain hits the tent a second later. Kayla looks around as guests shift in their seats, pull out their phones. It is the kind of soft drizzle that sometimes goes away and probably would have gone unnoticed if not for the theatrics in the sky. But then another gust of wind blows through the tent, this one strong enough to extinguish candles and whip table skirts in the air. Kayla's heart lurches as the chandelier overhead whips back and forth.

Across the room, Sophia spins around, her scowl finding Kayla. Sweat forms at her temples and under her arms, and Kayla turns, hating that this girl has such an effect on her.

The rain picks up and suddenly a third strike of thunder makes the power flicker, the crack triggering a squawk from Summerhouse's alarm system as the beach disappears into darkness.

Around Kayla, the sound of rustling quickly transforms into a patchwork of fluorescent rectangles. Cell phones light up the tent like fireflies, while outside the bonfire smolders, red cracks of lava-like light illuminating the sand in an eerie glow. Even the full moon has disappeared behind a cloud.

Kayla's mind is already racing when somewhere behind her, Summerhouse's house generator flips on. There's another endless squawk as the lights inside return and cast a shadow down the still black beach.

Kayla takes off toward the house, cringing from the awful sound as her mind ticks off directives: More lights, turn off that damn alarm, get the band to play something upbeat to keep the guests in good spirits, figure out where the hell they're going to move the party if the storm doesn't pass quickly.

Her father is already in the main garage under the house. She finds him with the metal door of the giant Generac generator flung open, the heavy-duty beams of his flashlight assessing the power boxes and fuses. At the alarm pad, Kayla smashes buttons, not knowing the code and wondering who does. Impulsively, she presses 1234 and exhales as the system spits out a long beep and the sound stops.

"I think the generator will only power the house." Her father sends the flashlight beam around the triple car garage one more time looking for something of use. The room is empty. A wall sink, sandy cement floors, spare catering chairs.

For a few seconds, Kayla's mind goes south. She entertains the juicy thought of abandoning everything, of leaving these people to fend for themselves in the darkness and just walking into Summerhouse and pouring herself a glass of wine.

Her father shakes his head. "Shit—it usually comes right back on when this happens. . . ." Her father's thought is cut off by two muddled pops like fireworks in the distance. The fireworks weren't supposed to happen until nearly midnight. Kayla's heart jumps when a second later the alarm squawks for the third and final time and the lights return.

Chapter Twenty

Ruth

～

Five minutes earlier

Ruth is sitting in an Adirondack chair and enjoying a quiet moment when the first drops of rain land. The breeze has picked up, and the drizzle is so soft that she considers staying put, although the sky looks way too dark. She isn't ready to go back inside and deal with all the gossip, her mother and Mayor Bob rubbing up against each other on the dance floor.

There's another drop or two, a slow rumble as the cloud overhead seems to swell. Ruth jumps in her chair as thunder cracks overhead. The beach goes black as the screech of what she knows is Summerhouse's alarm rings out. Her guests—now shadowy figures—lunge closer to the tall fire. Around her, everyone is looking for their phones or their husbands and children, a palpable sense of uneasiness in those who aren't used to Blue Compass's fickle power grid. Ruth searches for her own phone, wondering where Kayla is. Her eyes are just starting to adjust when motion in another direction makes her turn.

In the mangled silhouette of the pier, there's a figure.

Its gait catches her attention, the steps deliberate like this person has somewhere to be. A second later, the form disappears into the darkness toward the clubhouse and an uneasiness rises in her chest. Kayla has ensured all the exterior lights around the Nautilus Cove pool were off for tonight's dinner. Caroline insisted on preserving the surprise and ambience for the wedding.

Ruth searches, straining to find whoever is lurking in the shadows again when a second alarm rings out. This time, the squawk brings with it the lights of Summerhouse. The sudden glow backlights the beach and as her vision adjusts, the beach is awash in contours. When her eyes adapt, she finds the man again. Down the beach to her left, he's at the entrance of the pier now, and he crouches down, a blur of movement before he steps onto the landing. Her stomach drops as she watches, thinking *it can't be*? Then her mind whispers *run*—the directive so strong she takes off without thinking, shedding her shoes as sand and rain pelt her skin.

Ten seconds pass.

Then thirty.

She's nearing the pier, her eyes fixed on the end. But it's still too dark, the black reaching into nothingness in front of her. The crack of a gunshot rings out, and her heart slams into her chest.

Once.

Then twice.

Behind her, the party, which had been paused by the power outage, lunges back into sound. A confused collective mass as everyone turns to watch what can't be seen off in the distance. Later, some would swear they heard three shots. Others, a splash.

There's thunder then more lightning. The power flickers again, another squeal from Summerhouse's alarm as light floods the beach. Ruth's eyes adapt, and she looks again.

The man is gone.

Chapter
Twenty One

Marcus

❧

The sound is unmistakable. Muffled and three hundred yards away, Marcus takes off toward the gunshots, making it to Nautilus Pier in seconds. He reaches for his gun, the beam of his flashlight leading him.

"Police—hands up!"

There is no answer, and he steps closer. Inching his way onto the landing, the light shoots through the darkness as a warped plank gives slightly underfoot. The figure is at the far end, frozen as the beam creeps upward, a split second of jagged wood, bare feet, two hands in surrender, finally the wild eyes of Ruth Bancroft.

"He was there—then he wasn't," she shrieks. "Someone's *in* the water."

Marcus trains his flashlight over the waves, the beam catching hints of white cap on the black water. Before he can stop her, Ruth darts to the other railing, leaning into a piece of bucking guardrail, adrenaline and shock making her reckless. Marcus shouts for her to step back and fights to steady himself before he lunges for her. The light from the party down the beach isn't enough and the pier is a minefield of holes and hazards. The rocks below are covered in barnacles as sharp as razors. If she goes over, chances are she'll strike her head or a vital organ. He tears her from the edge, her body trembling as he struggles with his free hand to find the radio at his shoulder.

"1013, 1013. Code 10–33, Nautilus Cove Pier. Send all units."

Ruth's fighting him for no reason. A tangle of fists and kicks as he tries to gain control. They are only a few feet to the exit walkway, and though she isn't heavy, he's forced to drag her, his feet searching for stable planks as he inches forward. They are near an open edge when she bucks then jerks against him, making his heart hammer with fear they'll both go over. At the entrance, he shoves her forward, the momentum sending them both tumbling to the safety of the sand.

On the ground, she's everywhere. Not wanting to but needing to, he straddles her and she pushes against him trying to free her wrists from his grasp. "Jesus, stop it—what are you doing?" Grabbing her by both shoulders and shaking her till he gets her attention. The terror on Ruth's face disappears as her head snaps back, and she's frozen, rigid with sudden recognition. He releases her, and shouts, "Go! Get help now!"

Ruth shoots up and scrambles backward, eyes wide in the beam of Marcus's flashlight. As she takes off down the beach, his mind wonders what the hell she was doing there.

When she's gone, Marcus trains his flashlight over the water again. There's a flash of something, what might be a hand or an arm, and his heart leaps, but when he looks again, it's gone. The waves close over it before he can be sure.

Marcus pulls out his cell from its holster, smashing in a number he'd long ago memorized. He'd learned the hard way to have the personal numbers for the Blue Compass Search and Rescue captain. Two summers ago, just down the beach—on a dare—a young girl leapt from another pier. The rescue captain hadn't been near his desk that afternoon, and it had taken too long to respond. That family was fortunate when her body washed up two weeks later. Sometimes they never did.

Another flashlight is bouncing toward him. Down the beach, Jade bolts past Ruth, gun drawn. When she's in earshot, Marcus yells, "I need eyes on the north beach. Gunshot— possible 10–32."

Jade reaches him, panting. She scans his face, the pitch black scene around him. "OK. North—got it. Tim's securing the tent."

She tears off toward the strip of beachfront houses past the pier, and Marcus's mind is already jumping ahead. The phone line trills for the third time, and Marcus finally gets through. The voice of the Captain assures him that all water units are on the way. He hangs up, trying not to think about how they still didn't have the kind of sonar technology they needed for this kind of rescue. That a bigger department would and that two years of budget cuts and a hurricane later, they were no better equipped than they'd ever been. More light is the next thing under his control. Even with the glow from Summerhouse and every exterior light the pool offered, it wasn't enough light to illuminate the scene fully.

As he dials, he wades knee deep in the bay. A flashlight search of the rocks around the pier's pilings yields nothing. Finally, he catches a glimpse of the first rescue boats slicing through the water at full throttle. Behind them, the department's two jet-skis bounce up and down in their wake. Headlights fill the clubhouse parking lot. The exterior lights switch on and flood the beach in milky illumination.

More units arrive and the flood of activity seems to progress as his shoulder buzzes with radio calls. Each time, the chorus of *negative, still looking* from the search captains shoot frustration through him as his mind finds more tasks that need immediate attention.

Jade appears, putting on plastic gloves. "Possible bullet hole on the pier. Weather's gonna make everything a mess."

Marcus inhales, steeling himself for the night to come. No one is going home. No one is sleeping. But first, he reaches for his personal cell. First, he will call his daughter—this time to make sure she's OK.

Chapter Twenty Two

Ruth

❧

Later, Ruth wouldn't remember Marcus running toward the pier, her reckless behavior, or her panic as she fled back. Not the murmur of party chatter under the tent nor their frenzied whispers, *What's happening? Who is it? Who would be crazy enough to go on that pier?*

But she would remember the center of the dance floor, the fear as her eyes darted in every direction. The panicked faces. Her own, ghost-white reflection in the drum kit's chrome side.

Finally a scream, her own voice pleading as she fell to her knees. "Dear God, where is Teo—I don't see Teo anywhere."

PART 2

PART 2

Chapter
Twenty Three

Ruth

The family watches in silence. From the screened porch, three police cruisers are parked on the beach, their headlights pointed at the pier. Someone has managed an industrial spotlight, and it's aimed at the rocks.

Around the pier, scuba divers emerge and disappear into the black water like fireflies. There are jet skis and boats, their individual lights catching the swells as the lettered abbreviations of different maritime agencies bob up and down. The Florida Department of Natural Resources boat had arrived first. Behind it, two Blue Compass Safety vessels and finally, a thirty-foot trawler from the Coast Guard. On land, Ruth counts at least twenty officers milling in and out of the party tent as yellow police tape flaps in the breeze. Every few minutes, the same garbled retort floats up from the activity below, the words landing like a fist. "Mariners in the vicinity of Blue Compass Bay, be on the lookout for a single man in the water . . ."

It wasn't what she thought, but it was another kind of nightmare.

Ruth reaches out, her icy hand around Teo's forearm. He is right there in that rocking chair, she tells herself again. She closes her eyes and tries to shake it away. In an alternate universe, it might have been funny. If it had been some bad sitcom, an awful laugh track in the background as she collapsed at her own rehearsal dinner, screaming for Teo who was found safe in those fancy bathrooms. It really might've been a punchline—if, at that moment—everything wasn't so completely, horrendously real. There's still one person unaccounted for, one person from the list of staff and guests that no one has heard or seen since the blackout. One body that had suddenly vanished.

Her father was the man on the pier.

She had to keep repeating this too. Though on the surface, it seemed to make sense. He and Teo were of a similar height and build. Even Nicholas had joked about the likeness between them. Ruth's stomach churns as she tries to accept it. Her father's state of "missingness" is anything but a false alarm.

The rain has stopped and white caps churn in the coal-colored waters in front of them. On the beach, the party tent's openings mirror the motion, white fabric whipping in the wind. Ruth can't make out the activity beneath the tent, the blur of sounds and moving shadows, but she didn't need to see inside to know what was going on.

"No one leaves until we process every last person." This from the same surly police officer who questioned her after the necklace was stolen. For no reason, Ruth was beginning to hate her, this woman called to the scenes of the worst moments of her life.

Guests, employees—the police quarantined everyone. Right now, huddled in the tent beneath them, the last of her guests were waiting their turn to be interviewed. She and Teo—bride and groom—had gone first. The same interrogation she imagined they'd all received: who, what, where, and did you see anything unusual?

One by one, she watches as the guests spill out, women wearing their husband's jackets and carrying their shoes. The rehearsal dinner staff, wide-eyed and harried, their white uniform tops stained and unbuttoned as they take the long way around the house to the driveway. Someone had thought to give Bart the Summerhouse golf cart, his Nautilus Cove uniform caked in sweat and sand as he shuttles anxious faces up and down the driveway to their cars.

So far, they haven't found him—this bit of hope is paralyzing. Part of her is afraid to even move, the irrational whisper at the back of her brain telling her that changing anything about her position on the rocking chair might trigger a discovery. Her father could have snuck out early, or he could be stranded on a sandbar somewhere, safe but unable to get to them. Of course, he wasn't answering his cell phone—it was probably drenched, or ruined, or lost. She rocked back and forth, her mind ticking off alternatives, desperate theories she clung to like a toddler's blanket.

Caroline is bringing in tea from the kitchen when Ruth hears someone at the beach screen door. Mandy Lowe is carrying her sandals, the old friend of Caroline's soaked, her teased red hair slicked against her forehead as she knocks on the screened door frame.

"You-hoo . . ."

Caroline sucks back a breath, sets down the tray and rearranges her face. She bequeaths a half smile on the unwanted guest as she opens the door.

"I just finished talking to them—well, down there. I wanted to check on y'all." The curvy real estate agent's drawl is thick and soupy, and she wraps Caroline in a hug that seems to Ruth to go on too long. Mandy is a Nautilus Cove neighbor and the only woman on Blue Compass's City Council. It's no secret that the outcome of the ordinance vote also stood to make her a mountain of money. Mandy might be Blue Compass born and bred, but it was her penchant for selling high rise condos to the surrounding beaches that had put her squarely in the "yes" column for Ordinance 23. As with all things in Blue Compass, there were other ways these two women were intertwined. Her mother had once told her that Mandy blatantly chased Blake before Caroline showed up on the scene.

Caroline releases herself, and Mandy sits down without invitation, a "How y'all holding up?" as she pours herself a cup of tea.

Ruth suddenly wants nothing more than to escape this woman, but she isn't about to abandon her station on the porch. Moving to the furthest rocking chair, she's a captive as Mandy adds sugar to her cup and grills Caroline on everything that is none of her business.

The small talk is flowery, cloaked in Southern manners as the two women circle each other, Mandy fishing for details while Caroline dodges them just as artfully. (Well, bless your heart. Aren't you a doll for asking! Of course, I won't speak to the press—not a peep. I just can't say for sure about anything else right now. No one knows what's going on . . .)

Finally, Caroline sees her out—a lie about Jo's kids needing their Gammy to read them a bedtime story—before she slams the back door, wiping her hands as if they're dirty. "Like I need her telling me what to do. I hate to say it, but there's gonna be a whole lot more where that came from—this town already had nothing else to talk about."

Ruth's stomach knots as she moves to the porch's bar cart. It is her second drink on an empty stomach and when she gets there, her eyes go wide as she sees the police chief, Marcus Jennings. He is standing in the kitchen, a second surprise interloper who has tracked a line of wet sand from the front door to his spot at the kitchen island. She charges in as Maya offers Marcus a hand towel, Nick and Mayor Bob exchange glances before they all fumble with excuses and retreat to other parts of the house. When they are gone, the chief puts the dish cloth down and dives in, confirming that the processed fingerprints belong to Thad.

"It was lucky we were able to process them so fast with the weather and conditions out there. The whorls were pretty degraded, but my tech lifted a single perfect print from the underside of the wood railing." He stops, his expression a perfect blank poker face. "All we know for sure is that Thad was on the pier. Unfortunately, the tide was going out, which makes things more . . ."—he clears his throat—"—complicated."

Ruth hears the chief, grasps the words leaving his mouth, but doesn't feel anything. The words roll over her and land, a cold opaque nothingness as she waits for him to go on. He takes out his phone, finding the recording app then sets it on the island. "I need to get back out there though I do have a couple quick questions. Usually, we like to start with those closest to him. Do we know if your father had a significant other or was close to his parents? Anyone we need to notify?"

They all look at each other, shrugging, until Ruth says, "I know he'd been doing the books—accounting for a restaurant in Atlanta called Alfred's. He never mentioned a girl—a friend or anything like that."

"It was just him. I think he had a place in Buckhead," Jo adds.

Marcus nods then turns to Ruth, his voice light. "I know a lot of people have already asked you this, including myself, but I have to ask again. You're absolutely sure what you heard and saw out there—and you'd only had one drink. One glass of red wine?"

"Yes—but like I said—it was dark and the power went out. The sound—" She swallows hard. "It was twice—this horrible pop, pop and when the lights came back—he was gone."

Everyone gets quiet and Marcus stares at Ruth as he waits, finally standing. "I'm sure I don't have to say it, but technically, according to police procedure, you're supposed to be my number one suspect. Last one to see him, last one at the scene . . ."

"What?" Ruth's voice cracks. "Why would you say that? Why would I—" She looks around the room as it tilts.

Teo steps toward the chief, and Marcus puts up a hand in mild defense of his statement. "I said technically—we aren't anywhere near all that—I just like to be upfront . . . treat everyone with respect. As long as we keep the lines of communication open, there's nothing to worry about." He exhales and pats Teo on the back, a move Ruth understands is meant to de-escalate the situation, although it makes Teo's jaw tighten. "There's a lot happening down there. We need to help each other—we need to remember this is an active crime scene."

He turns to open the door, everyone's mouth still open when Caroline blurts out, "Fine—you need information? My ex-husband's father died when he was a kid, and I heard his mother passed away about three years ago. He doesn't keep in touch with anyone because he's never anywhere long enough to set down roots. Unless you count strippers at The Cheetah Room."

Ruth's stomach catches on the words. She welcomed Thad back into their lives, assuming they would have more time together to rebuild a relationship. She believed him when he claimed to have learned how to be a better man during his absence. It dawns on her just how little she knows about her father's day-to-day life.

"We would tell you more if we knew anything—" Sophia's voice quivers. She still hasn't fully stepped into the kitchen, is hovering near the dining room table, and she raises her voice to make sure he hears her. "He wasn't the easiest guy to get to know."

Marcus nods, telling them he needs to get down to his team, thanking them again, he pulls up the hood of his rain slicker. In the doorway, he looks back at Ruth like he's calculating something.

As the door latches behind him, everyone is suddenly talking, their words swimming together. Teo and Jo are sounding off on police procedure. Their voices soothing, full of placations dressed up in their legal understanding of what was happening. Someone wonders if Ruth needs a lawyer as Ruth turns toward the porch, remembering the glass of wine Chief Marcus interrupted. She finds it and empties it, pouring another and draining it just as quickly. With the burn at her throat, the world begins to shift. A new and absolute understanding settling in that it would always be this way—her universe forever divided. A sudden slicing into "before" and "after."

Before her father went to the pier, after he disappeared.

The phone in her pocket buzzes, and she almost doesn't answer. The voice on the line is baritone, unfamiliar. "Hello, this is Trey Rosenthorp. I am calling from RDX News. We wondered if you'd like to give us a comment on the status of your missing father?"

Ruth checks the screen, the number is blocked. "Who is this? How did you get this number?"

"Listen, this is a big story—huge. Someone is going to tell this story. Just the way it is—like it or not. Everyone will be after you. I'm offering you a chance to be the one to set the narrative."

"Leave me alone."

"What are the police telling you about the chances of his survival in that water?"

Teo takes the phone from her and barks, "No comment. Don't call here again," before tossing the phone on the table. "What did they say to you?"

"He said like it or not—someone's gonna tell this story—that we better get ready because everyone's coming for us."

And the man is right.

Fifteen minutes later, the first news truck rolls up outside Summerhouse. The driveway is already blocked by police cruisers, and the Bancroft women gather around the kitchen window to watch as Bart stands at the passenger window, chatting nonchalantly with the Channel 9 news van as if it's the most normal thing in the world.

Chapter
Twenty Four

Marcus

~

Marcus has worked through the night under the tent and his adrenaline is waning. He'd just hung up from a call with Davis Ray from the Bay County precinct. That boss hog of a sheriff had called him at 5:00 AM, and it was clear he was already nosing around. As if calling at that time of morning wasn't message enough, he could practically feel the man wishing him to fail. They both knew it would be the final nail in the department's coffin.

Marcus kicks at a pile of sand and barks at someone to bring him coffee then goes back to the timeline he's creating, the problem of obtaining Thad's digital footprint. He needs credit cards and ATM usage, cell phone records. Since the victim had no wife, no responsible party who could sign away permission, he was stuck waiting on warrants. Stuck waiting on Bryant Kessler,

Blue Compass's less than enthusiastic city prosecutor. Marcus had to haul him back from a vacation in Austin, and they were already behind the eight ball.

He dives back into the file in front of him and is so enthralled that he barely notices the bustle inside the tent pausing. There is a noise behind him. He looks up, surprised to find Caroline Bancroft in the doorway. He watches as she takes it in, her lavish party in disarray. The tables, stripped of their coverings, are now only circles of marred wood. In the corner, the centerpieces and dishware have been stacked in plastic racks. The bar, once lined in bottles of top shelf liquor, is a row of precinct laptops and police gear. An officer with his back to them pecks and fumbles with Blue Compass's ancient radio system.

Arranging his face, Marcus hopes he can get rid of her quickly. From what he knew of Caroline Bancroft, she was a pragmatic woman. It hadn't taken long after Blake married her that he and his old friend had lost touch. Though he'd never know for sure if his slow elbowing out had been intentional or not, at the moment it was one of many things he was trying not to hold against her.

They shake hands, and Marcus leads Caroline to a table at the back of the tent.

"What can I do for you, Ms. Bancroft?" Her eyes are glassy and almost don't crinkle, the dark shadows highlighting her careful cosmetic assistance. "Unfortunately, there isn't anything new since we talked a few hours ago—"

"Please, call me Caroline." She sits down. "Actually—well, there's something I need to tell you—something I may have *left* out."

Marcus sits down, his back already killing him from the god-awful catering chairs. "Ok. I'm listening."

"It's just that Ruth was upset and what you said—and *all those people* before that." Her manicured finger traces a water stain on the table's top. "Well, when we knew it wasn't Teo and then—well, I realize now that it might be important . . ."

"I am gonna stop you and turn on the tape recorder if you don't mind. It's good to keep a record of as much as possible."

He takes out his cell phone, and Caroline waits for him to press record. She tells him that two days before the rehearsal dinner, she had been stopped at the hair salon one town over. A man approached her in the parking lot.

"He was looking for Thad. And right away, I was uncomfortable. He had obviously followed me, and there was something about him. Not just his size—I mean, he was big, and he had this thing on his neck—a tattoo of wings or something—but it wasn't that, exactly. I mean I spent enough years with that man to know that there can be more bite in a dog that's silent than one with a big bark." She pauses and looks away. "He couldn't keep a job or be a decent father, but find him someone with lots of money and awful morals, and you can bet Thad Hargrove would end up working for him or owing him—usually the latter." She clears her throat, wrestling with something. A second later, she spits out, "I know a strongman when I see one. I didn't tell that man anything."

Marcus raises an eyebrow. He's never taken Caroline Bancroft as someone who would know the slang term for a bookie's collector. "How can you be sure?"

"I know the *type*. The kind who comes looking—I've seen what happens when you're in a hole and you haven't paid—it's been a long time, but you don't forget that kind of thing."

"Can you tell me about Thad's history of gambling?" When he interviewed Sophia she had mentioned something about cards, although she'd quickly corrected herself. Thad's wilder days were supposed to be in the rearview, which was why he'd been on this beach at this rehearsal dinner at all.

Caroline spits out an incredulous laugh. "We got married in our teens, and when you're young that sort of life seems exciting." She leans into the table, hugging herself as she goes on. "Thad refused to hold a real job, to believe there was any better way to finance our life. He was always sure the next big break was around the corner. There were years of on-and-off harassment, middle of the night moves to different cities, always with babies in infant carriers. A beating once that dislocated his shoulder."

Caroline confessed to being equal parts terrified and relieved when one day, he packed up and left her and their three daughters. All of this is news to Marcus. Blake was always protective over Caroline's past, and he expected everyone in Blue Compass to treat her like she had always been part of the community, protected by his love for her and Blue Compass's love for him.

"We had no one and nothing." Her face is stoic as a breeze whips through the tent, her eyes shoot to the oyster chandelier overhead as it clatters.

"Did you happen to see what this guy was driving—maybe, get a plate?"

She shakes her head. "He was waiting at my car, and I just wanted to get out of there. He could've walked there for all I know." She swallows hard.

"Do you think you could ID him? I can probably get the sketch artist down here from Bay County today."

"I guess."

Marcus hesitates, choosing his words carefully. "Let me ask you—what was your relationship like with your ex-husband?"

She raises an eyebrow, and he can see her choosing her words. "For the last seventeen years, there hasn't been much of one. He would turn up from time to time—but I usually tried to stay out of that." She looks beyond the tent's plastic window to the water. "It never ended well for the girls either. Though my daughters never wanted to hear that from me . . ."

"Any chance—well, that necklace was worth a lot of money—the gambling, did he ever—"

Caroline cuts him off. "I never knew him to be a thief—even when his back was to the wall. But I supposed anything's possible." She mulls it over a second then huffs. "That would take too much forethought—something he has zero of. And we didn't exactly go around advertising its worth. Honestly, Thad Hargrove was the proudest man I ever knew. Believe it or not, I think he would see that kind of thing as beneath him."

Caroline drops her eyes to her lap and picks at an imaginary piece of lint from her pants. Her mouth sets into a hard line. "Chief, I am not a stupid woman. Let me be clear. I am here only for my daughters. Maybe this is wrong to say—given all this—" She gestures around the tent. "But as far as I see it, he did all of us a favor when he disappeared the first time, and I'm not shedding any tears that he's gone now."

Chapter Twenty Five

Kayla

~

Kayla is in her office at Two Be Wed, hiding from the world and telling herself she's finishing paperwork that can't wait regardless of the shit show that just went down. There are already two messages from news reporters on Two Be Wed's voicemail, and one of her brides has just called to cancel her services.

She looks around the newly finished sales room, and it hits her how bad this could be for her, too. Her mother had always said that their job was a privilege, that it was a gift to help people create their most important moments, but it was the challenge that drove her. She liked finding a way to cut a dress so that any woman—regardless of her shape or size—could feel good about herself. She liked the test of managing multiple egos and personalities, seeing what it took to get people to behave or do what she wanted. Even choosing the right mix of vendors and accessories for the shop felt like art to her. This wasn't just a paycheck, it was a creative outlet. Kayla was terrified it might all go away.

Behind her, there's a shuffling sound and Kayla twists to find her father in the doorway. He looks tired as he puts his own set of Two Be Wed keys back into his pocket. He is damp and needs a shave. "I just realized Halloween is next week. Hope you're not gonna be handing out the Halloween candy at the house by yourself this year."

Halloween was a big deal in Blue Compass, a weekend long trick-or-treat fest for the shoppers on Reid Street and what was left of the year's tourists. Of course, last year had been its own kind of terrifying—watching Kerry's aftermath from a motel room in Tallahassee, her numb shock as the hideous scene unfolded on an ancient RCA.

Kayla rakes her hands through her hair. "I'm not sure anything compares to the horror show last night. What are you doing here?"

"Got any decent coffee back there?" He steps into her office and heads to the coffee station on the credenza, a shift in his posture as he turns, offering her the back of his navy uniform as he fidgets with the machine. "Shop looks great by the way—who did you say did most of the work?"

"Colt Thistle did a lot of it—except the plumbing. Why?"

Her father clicks the button on the Mr. Coffee and picks up a rainbow Blue Compass Beach mug, wiping it out with a napkin. "How was he—you have any problems with him?"

"He's pretty quiet. Didn't talk much, but I was working from the house mostly—why?"

"He do all the locks too?"

Kayla sits up in her chair. Flashes from her teenage years, familial interrogations that could mean the difference between being grounded and freedom. But now she's not sure what she's supposed to be in trouble for. "That's a weird question—why?"

"It's probably nothing . . . unrelated, but after the Bancroft burglary, we got a list of all the people who worked on their renovation. Somebody's letting themselves into places around here—yours, the Bancrofts . . . now this mess on the beach." He puts down the cup. "Colt Thistle was the only handyman who worked there and here. He also has a record . . ."

The coffee starts to brew, the coffee maker choking and hissing in the background as Kayla's mind reels back to the day before the Bancroft dress fitting, sees herself finding Two Be Wed's alley door unlocked and open. She croaks, "You said that was nothing to worry about—that it was just the janitor?" Had that really only been six days ago? Something felt wrong, out of context. She tries to get her father to look at her. "Colt? No way. I know he's been with the Bancrofts for years. It makes sense he would help out there. What kind of record?"

"There was some kind of altercation when he went out West. A couple bad checks after that." Marcus gazes over her shoulder, studying the new pastel painting behind her desk. A piece she'd chosen for its calming effect, the canvas in shades of blue and green mimicking the sea. He blows out a sigh. "It could be a bit of a stretch, and this stays between us. Though I guess, on some level—there's no conflict—and you need to know."

"Need to know *what*?"

"That sister—Sophia—she's been getting some threats on her social media. We flagged one in particular. The guy seems pretty obsessed with her, with the wedding. It's not Colt's

Instagram handle but the boy has commented a few times—so we know he follows her too."

The room gets dizzy as he goes on. He tells her that he's working on a warrant for Instagram. That the particular follower they're interested in appears to be a fake profile. That the only accounts he follows are related to Blue Compass and the Bancrofts—including her shop.

"The guy's account photo is one of those cartoon clown avatars, and he's never posted a single thing. We can get his identity, but all this press coverage—" He scratches at the back of his head, "I'm told to expect Instagram's gonna fight us at first. That these companies like to give the impression they care about their users' privacy—we'll get what we want eventually—but it's the time frame that concerns me." He drains his coffee and puts down the cup. "We got some other leads we're looking into. In the meantime, I want you to change the locks."

"Is that really necessary? It's not exactly the simplest—or cheapest thing for me, right now." It was true enough. She had only received the initial deposit from the Bancrofts for her commission and everything else had gone to vendors. Two Be Wed had been operating on credit and fumes for a while now. But her real motive is to see her father's reaction. It was just too hard to believe anything like that about Colt Thistle or some mysterious fake user, but if he was really worried, if changing the locks was more than just a precaution—if this was *real*, then his next gear would be irritated. Probably angry.

"Hell yes, it's *necessary*." He scowls, "You think I would come all the way down here if it wasn't? I already got a guy. One of the boys at the precinct's brother can come by tomorrow and take care of everything."

Her father's phone buzzes at his waist. He looks down to see the caller—Mayor Bob, and his face goes from annoyed to genuinely pissed. He sends the call to voicemail.

"You and old Bob still quite the love affair, huh?"

Marcus rolls his eyes. "That guy's the last thing in the world I need right now."

A moment later, she's walking him to the back exit, still talking herself down from the panic pooling in her chest. Propping open the emergency exit door to the back alley, she reminds herself again who she lives with. Who would be stupid enough to mess with her?

Her dad opens the door to his police cruiser then stops, his face now serious. "You know, the other thing—there's a possibility we might have to deal with *that* too." His brow furrows. "With everything going on with the Bancroft family—well, things like that just don't stay buried forever."

Kayla's hands go cold, and she nods, knowing he's right. It washes over her suddenly: All the kinds of horror one life can hold, all the power your choices possess. Her hands tremble as she clicks the soon-to-be-changed lock into place behind him. She just hopes she's made the right ones.

Chapter Twenty Six

Ruth

❧

"Is something burning?" From her seat on the couch, Maya glares at Mayor Bob, who has returned clean-shaven and loaded with groceries. He's at the stove, stirring something in a pot, pretending to be some integral part of this family.

Nick is next to Maya on the couch and reaches out to put his arm around her shoulder as he rolls his eyes, "Come on, we can never have enough food—there's plenty of room in that kitchen."

There's plenty of room for all these people too, Ruth thinks, crossing her arms. Generally, she enjoyed Nick for the good time he was, but it felt like the house was shrinking. There were people everywhere. There's a loud clunk from the sink, and Ruth's eyes dart to her mother's bedroom door on the other side of the living room. Her mother has another headache and has been acting off since she came back from the beach yesterday. Her abrupt confession about a run-in with a stranger looking for Thad has shaken everyone.

Ruth keeps trying to picture Caroline's description of the stranger with a tattoo. For some reason, the sketch artist still hasn't called, and Ruth paces the length of the first floor impatiently as the sun streams in. The first hints of the sunset are spectacular, an amalgamation of orange and yellow that feels wrong with the police scattered in front of them, a few boats still on the water. The waiting is unbearable, and it is all she can think about. Where her father is, could be, why he went out on that pier in the first place. Her dread about what Search and Rescue might discover had a life of its own. It was like waiting to get back test results from the doctor. The prognosis of life or death. Either you had cancer or you didn't.

Only this time, the results never came.

And yet, somehow, the rest of the world was ticking forward. That morning, the trawlers in the bay had sculled by at the same time they always did, oblivious to the rescue boats in front of them, their nets heavy with fish. An excavator had maneuvered past the media vans to a damaged house down the way, the sight only the first of a thousand papercuts. All day, there'd been the familiar sounds of construction on a house down the street. The high-pitched squeal of a drill and the ratcheting of a jackhammer starting and stopping. Summerhouse's eight-thousand square feet was closing in, the effect like a fishbowl as everyone navigated around each other in clumsy disbelief.

From the kitchen, Ruth feels Mayor Bob's eyes on her. She turns away as he shoots her another look of sympathy, the same *I'm so sorry* face that everyone is walking around with. She'd heard it in the first of the phone calls before she'd stopped taking them, seen it pasted on Father Ron's face when he'd come by to check on them. She was almost getting used to it now—the downcast eyes, their faces arranged with just enough sadness. The same *"How you holding up?"* Only Mayor Bob's face had not quite mastered it. He kept gritting his teeth, an uncomfortable clench with that mouthful of cat-like teeth on full display. Her mother was dating the Cheshire Cat.

JD, Jo, and Teo are on the porch, and Ruth joins them on the row of rocking chairs. Beneath them, there's murmuring, a group of police officers talking. There's fewer of them than last night, and their voices are too muffled to discern the tone. She turns to Teo, and it smacks against her that she should be married right now, the reception in full swing. It was more hurt, more emotions she wouldn't, *couldn't* process right now.

"Anyone—out here?"

Sophia is in sweat pants and freshly showered. She takes the last rocker. Tucking her knees up under herself, she checks her text messages for the hundredth time.

"God—he's such a dickbag." She slams her phone down on the table between them.

Ruth reaches out and touches her arm. They'd been making coffee earlier, and Sophia had blurted out that right after Thad disappeared, she'd called Sam. Her husband had taken too long to pick up and hadn't seemed too concerned by her news. That after she filled him in on all the details, she'd fallen apart, and his reaction had been cold, distant. Ruth knew Sam had never been a huge fan of their family, had voiced a loud opposition to letting Thad come around, still it surprised her that since the rehearsal, he'd only sent Sophia a single lousy text message—one which hinted at "needing to take care of things when everything got cleared up down there." It seemed hard-hearted, even for him.

Beau enters the patio in yesterday's pajamas and carrying his iPad. He stretches out his stick arms toward the bay. "I left my bucket out there—we go get it."

Teo twists toward him in his rocker. "Buddy, we can't go to the beach right now." He reaches to pick him up and the boy flinches then pushes him away, his voice shifting into a full whine. "I neeeed my sand crab bucket."

JD goes over to him and kneels down to Beau eye to eye. "Listen son, I know you wanna see the policemen down there—that it looks like there's a lot going on and it might be cool, but we can't."

Beau stamps his foot. "I. Want. My. Bucket."

JD stoops to pick him up, and Beau recoils, his body limp a split second before he launches into a rebellion of bucks and kicks. He's strong for his age, a fighter, and his face turns red as he throws his weight against his father, sending JD backwards. "My bucket, damn it!"

JD regains his balance as Beau opens the porch door and makes a run for it.

"Beauregard Bancroft-Hunt!" Jo lurches to grab at him, missing as he bolts past her and down the landing stairs to the beach.

Everyone's eyes go wide as JD runs out the door. They all follow behind him, a barefoot chase down the sandy stairs.

Two steps from the bottom, Jo freezes. "Holy shit—get Beau." Her voice quivers with the scene in front of her. "There's something—it looks . . . there's *something* in the water?"

"What?" Ruth is behind her and rears around. A group of uniforms are huddled at the water's edge. Their backs are to Ruth, the circle tight enough to conceal the scene in front of them. A stout patrol officer in an ill-fitting uniform turns to stop Ruth when she approaches. "You can't come down here, ma'am—*miss*."

"Is it him?" Her stomach seizes then drops as the man doesn't answer.

The back of another uniform steps to one side and the wall of bodies open, shifting just enough for Ruth's eyes to snake between them. A million invisible sand gnats scurry all over her as her eyes dart up and down. A dark gray bloodied mass sways in the water. It's the size of an oil drum, and the creature is missing a flipper, a mangled hole chewed into what's left of its paddle tail. The bloated carcass rocks gently as the waves break, the wrinkled manatee so grotesque that for a moment Ruth forgets to be relieved.

"Looks like the propeller of a boat got him."

The brusque police officer is crouched over it, her voice familiar. "That's the third one this year." She shakes her head, snaps on a rubber glove. "They just can't hear the boats. Mother Nature didn't design 'em that way."

Ruth pushes past the patrol officer and finds herself on the edge of the crowd, suddenly fixated. She can't turn away from the manatee's creased face—its sunken empty eyes like black marbles, the leathery bristled snout frozen in a smile too human-like. Her stomach curls, and she chokes back a retch.

Then Teo is next to her. His arms guiding her toward Summerhouse. She's cut her foot on the way down the beach, and it's bleeding, a shell slicing through it at the bottom of the stairs.

She stops and stares down at her oozing red heel as it hits her too fast. She breaks free from Teo, sprints to the garage. A second later, she retches until she is empty, barely making it to the basin sink on the back wall. When she's finished, she wipes her mouth and turns, suddenly noticing the eerie sounds of the cold, cement space. The wind has picked up and is whistling through the wood louvered wall that shares the beachside. It echoes around her, the shrill howl and the shush of the ocean outside.

Chapter Twenty Seven

Marcus

᠆

Someone said the bride had gone to sunrise Mass in Panama City. Who could blame her? He was furious that his boys had let the family get down there, that no one had stopped them before they got to the water's edge. Someone from the Florida Fish and Wildlife Commission had just hauled away the manatee carcass, and his patience was waning. A few hours ago, he'd finally managed to sneak away for a nap and a shower. Now he was back, knowing that it was time for some difficult conversations, that it was important to get ahead of things. The water search was already winding down. The divers had found nothing, and most of the other agencies had already trickled off one by one. He'd settled on keeping one of his boats in the water a little longer. Mostly for the optics of it for the family. Still, it was getting harder to work in the elements. The sand and the water degraded things—evidence, security, his boys' concentration. Slowly, they'd been moving the investigation back to the precinct.

Marcus is leaving the tent when he spots her. The wisp of a girl, fighting her way to the front door, all elbows and arms as she shoves her way through a crowd of cameras and reporters at the top of the landing steps.

The mob is a new development. In a day, its size has grown from a handful to twelve. There's also a fresh mess of crackpots and gawkers, bored townspeople with their cell phones out spilling down the road. It looks like he will need to spare one of his boys just to work crowd control—a fact he deeply resents. As it stood, he only had two full-time, nontraffic patrol officers and one was already wasting time maintaining order with the protesters at city hall. He and Jade weren't exactly a robust investigative force and, though it was frowned upon, he'd assigned a few beat officers with tasks that couldn't wait. The clock was ticking and Bay County would likely be stepping in with "help" at any moment. The FBI had called this morning too. Everyone was coming. *Like black flies on a fresh carcass.* So, though he hadn't liked it and he'd been careful with his selection of officers, it was starting to feel like he may have made matters worse.

This morning, the cell phone records from Thad's phone had come in. Hundreds of calls confirmed his associations with a plethora of shady Atlanta characters. Though it had been what *wasn't* there that interested Marcus. For ten days in October, Thad's phone had gone dark—presumably turned off. This made it impossible to track his whereabouts during that time. It also begged the question whether he had done the same thing again now.

They'd also finished searching Thad's car and the rental property where Thad had been staying. Neither yielded anything too helpful. Now it was time to update the family and make a graceful exit. He already knew he hadn't made any friends when he'd made it clear Ruth was a suspect, but her reaction had been more important than currying favor. It was definitely a reach, but he'd learned long ago that you never really knew anyone. Everyone had secrets.

The reporters are closing in on Ruth as Marcus makes it to the landing stairs. Cameras flash, the mob of microphones and boom mics surrounding her as she fumbles with her keys.

"Ruth. Ruth—who would want to kill your father? Do you think they'll find his body?"

"Ruth, do you still plan to get married?"

"Ruth, do you blame the wedding planner? Care to comment?"

"Ruth, Ruth—why won't you speak to the press? What are you hiding?"

Marcus is about to intervene when she ekes her way inside the house, slamming the door. As he crests the stairs landing, he snaps, "Off the property, now—last warning before I start throwing people in jail."

The reporters scatter, and he watches them hustle back to the street before he reaches up to rap his knuckle on the Bancrofts' oversized door. Ruth opens it, her face red and blotchy. "Give me a second" as she waves him inside. Grabbing a bottle of water, she takes a greedy chug. "God. That camera was six inches from my face."

Marcus shakes his head. "Unfortunately, until that gate gets fixed, there's not much we can do, as long as they stay on the street and off your property. The minute they set foot on those front stairs again—call me. I can have somebody run 'em off."

She nods. "Mom and the HOA are working on it. Once the gate's back then they can't just come in the neighborhood anymore? Right—it's trespassing?" She puts down the water bottle, and Marcus imagines how arbitrary it must feel. It was ridiculous that the presence of the metal arm at the front of the neighborhood's entrance made the street private. That every time a teenager plowed through it or if the actual barrier was missing, a technicality in the ordinance changed the enforceability of the law. It didn't matter that the little brick gate house was there, that the rest of the entrance's infrastructure was fine. Right now, he was stuck.

Marcus stays near the door, not wanting to invade more of her personal space. He has just begun filling the girl in, carefully choosing the right words, the right details when the fiancé comes into the room, looking like he's just rolled out of bed.

"All dad's stuff was still at the rental house—just like you thought." Ruth tells him with a grimace, and Marcus notices the lines around the girl's eyes. They belong to someone much older. Again, he thinks how young she is, so close in age to Kayla. It was almost impossible to grow up these days—with the internet and 24/7 media. God, it was a rigged system.

Marcus nods, "Your father's keys were still on the dresser. Car in the driveway. No wallet, but a suitcase full of clothes."

"There was a bullet too—in the pier—though that's all they will tell us about that." Ruth turns to look at Marcus, a depleting frankness in her tone.

"Teo, you're free to go over there now and get the rest of your stuff from the rental. We appreciate your patience."

Marcus clears his throat. "As far as the investigation, we are doing everything we can. There are plenty of leads we're still looking into—you will probably notice that we are moving things back to the precinct now. There are just a lot more resources there and—"

"And it means you're going to be functioning on the assumption of recovery—" The fiancé turns and gets a glass of water, fidgets with the kitchen faucet before he finishes. "Not rescue?"

"I don't like to get bogged down in the terms. This just opens up some other avenues for us—investigationwise. What matters is we keep looking." He has the urge to reach out and pat the girl's hand and fights it.

Marcus heads back to the beach, reiterating how important it is that no one in the family talk to the media. As he scales the stairs back to the tent, he replays the whole conversation in his head, hoping he hadn't sounded too patronizing. It was a lot of tragedy for a young girl. Again, he thinks of Kayla. Both were too trusting—it was just one of the many reasons they all had to be worried.

* * *

An hour later, Marcus is the last person left under the tent. The rental company had finally come by and taken away the last of the reception furnishings. Without the wood parquet dance floor, the stacks of linens and glassware, the space had an eerie emptiness to it. The chandelier above him was all that was left, marooned as a breeze sends it pitching and swaying.

Marcus grabs his laptop from a chair, searching for the report on the Summerhouse robbery. He had been reading it earlier and something is still nagging at the back of his brain.

Before he can get to it, an email pops up, and he is relieved to read that the social media warrants are finally done.

Marcus pulls up the Summerhouse robbery file. Glad to see the investigation has already been input into the system, he reads for a while, scrolling through the details. Then he stops abruptly, cursing as he slams the lid shut and stomps out the tent.

Five minutes and one lap around Summerhouse later, Marcus returns with sandy feet. He pounds out the number to the precinct on his cell. The officer answers on the first ring, and he growls, "Detective Richter, how many exterior doors does the Bancroft house have?"

"What—the *who*?" There is the sound of paper rustling. He stammers, "Umm, the Bancroft house. It looks like we fingerprinted seven doors, sir."

"Seven? You're sure?"

"Yes sir. I got the results right here."

"That's interesting because I just took a walk around the property and there are *eight* doors. The little arched one in the thicket—it opens into the garage. It's nowhere in your report."

In front of him, the sky goes gray as Marcus stands to stretch, realizing how badly he needs another nap. He hangs up with the first hints of a fresh headache as a hard wind shoots through the tent, rattling the chandelier. For the past two days, his officers had worked beneath it, the gentle sound of polished shells bustling against each other as it teetered in the open air. Like everything else, the noise suddenly irritates him. A second later, a new gust of wind blows through—this one, stronger.

There is a creak and Marcus looks up. Then a groan. A split second of realization before the massive thing gives way. He dives to the ground. His heart in his throat as the multitiered shells break apart on the ground, crashing inches from where he was just standing.

When he opens his eyes again, his ears are ringing. He looks around. The beach is quiet, not a single person around to witness the near miss. *Good*, Marcus thinks to himself, *no one needed to see that. It's not a bad premonition. Definitely not another ominous reminder no one needs that they were all running out of time.*

Chapter
Twenty Eight
Teo

❧

Teo stares out the bedroom window, wishing for earplugs—or headphones—anything to drown out the noise beneath him. One floor down, Mayor Bob and Caroline are fighting—a knock-down-drag-out. Their angry voices carry up with too much clarity. It's the first time he's heard anything outside absolute bliss between the two of them and from what he can glean, it had all started with a phone call. This morning, someone was on the phone with the mayor, and Caroline had clearly heard something she didn't like—something about the city council vote and which way the mayor was leaning.

They were the same questions he hadn't worked the nerve up to ask himself. In the short time that he'd spent with Mayor Bob, the man had been ever the politician, artfully dodging any direct conversation, skirting the subject. Sometimes completely disappearing from a room when someone brought it up. It was one of those things that had seemed so important until their own personal tragedy had eclipsed everything else.

Something slams beneath him, and Teo hears, "Damn it, Caroline—I'm doing this for us—*all* of us. I'm trying to save this place."

Teo doesn't envy the mayor. The town is a pressure cooker. Since the first time he'd come here with Ruth, he'd imagined bringing their own kids to the handful of shabby restaurants, buying them slushies from the one grossly overpriced gas station. The charm of Blue Compass was its size, its come-as-you-are vibe. Everyone knew the name of the street vendor where you bought bait, the old lady who sold boiled peanuts off the main pier. Now you could almost feel the town unfurling, the seams being ripped apart by the uncertainty of what the future would look like.

Teo picks up his phone, searching for a song to play loud enough to drown out their voices when Caroline screeches, "Damn *you*, Bob—that's not just a metaphorical mob outside your office—it's a *real* one."

"You need to trust me Caroline—let me take care of things . . . I want to be the one to get you the things you want . . ."

She spits out an incredulous laugh, her voice up two octaves and even clearer. "I have been taking care of myself my whole life—you need to take care of this town. I don't need you—or anyone else—swooping in to save me—Jesus, shut the door!"

A door slams and Teo's even more uncomfortable, wondering if he's the only one hearing this fight. He rummages deeper through his suitcase as his phone pings. For a second, he thinks it's a media alert. Like everyone in the family, he'd promised to stay away from all the media coverage of Thad's disappearance, but *Google Alerts* had become his guilty little secret. He had to keep up on some things for his pro bono work, though with everything happening, the coverage was all mixed together. It wasn't exactly easy to avoid the press even if you wanted to.

He opens his messages and sees that it's actually a group text from Ruth.

Mom done with sketch artist. Photo totally creeps me out. They release it later today

Teo takes a deep breath and clicks on the attachment. He enlarges it and as the picture slides into focus the room closes in on him. The man's thin lips, those dark eyes. The sketch of his tattoo is pretty close. The wings weren't quite that anime, but they peek out of his collar just as Teo remembers.

It's the night of the bachelor party, and Teo bursts into the men's room—in his current dizzy state—and Thad is already in there leaning against the grimy sink. His reformed soon-to-be father-in-law is chugging from a silver flask, his eyes shut in concentration. Seeing Teo, Thad slips the flash of metal into his sportscoat, the movement so smooth, it's as if the flask was never there at all. He offers a small smile, squeezing past in the tight quarters. Mumbling something, his breath unmistakable. It's Teo's own drink of choice, Jim Beam.

The brawl came a minute later, he realized. Thad must have headed straight to the bar. From Teo's vantage point, there'd been only a partial view. The back of a rumpled fishing polo, wide aggressive posture. A hard shove and a punch that didn't land. The light of the front door opening as someone fell backward into a table, bottles flying. A group of bikers leaped to their feet then chaos broke out. Someone grabbed Teo and a second later, he took a blow to the face, a kick to his shin. He remembers lunging, swinging, and missing. Then they were all on the concrete, a tangle of fist and limbs, sweat and adrenaline.

Goosebumps form as the picture fills out for him. There was only one person who had not joined in, one person in the whole bar with no interest in the free-for-all: *The man in the leather jacket*. A chair had landed at his feet, and he'd actually stepped out of the way. At some point, Thad had broken free and made a beeline for the exit, the stranger ten steps behind him as they escaped out the front door.

So, it was what he'd suspected all along—but hadn't wanted to voice. Thad Hargrove had never quit drinking. It was part of the role he'd played for his daughter, for the rich people at the wedding. A story he'd concocted, the contrite father making amends just in time to walk his only daughter willing to forgive and forget down the aisle.

And this man had followed him there. Stalked Caroline days before. Might have been watching all of them. Might be watching them even now. Teo sits down on the bed, his mind spinning. Beneath him, Caroline screams something, the sound muffled, now an afterthought to the tangle of his own dilemmas. Did he have to tell Ruth? Would the truth matter now anyway?

They were all just waiting for Thad's body to wash up somewhere, to give the family closure and provide some kind of memorial. Teo's head began to throb. He hated Thad Hargrove, hated him for what he had done to Ruth as a child, hated him for ruining their wedding and putting him in this position. His own father had believed that lying was the worst of all sins. And if Thad was willing to lie about his drinking, omit the details of a stranger he'd seemed frightened enough to run away from, what other dangers had he brought with him?

Chapter Twenty Nine

Kayla

~

Across town, Kayla hangs up with her father and exhales. She's on the back porch of their cinder block lanai, the sky full of stars. The air suddenly has the tiniest bite to it, the kind that always felt long overdue by late October, and she leans forward, tucking her hands beneath her thighs, letting her body weight pin them to the patio chair. *God, she wanted a Marlboro Light.* The last cigarette of the day had always been her favorite, and she'd never wanted one as badly as she had this week. She closes her eyes, settling for a deep gulp of air, the first breath of deep relief she'd taken in weeks.

Colt Thistle had a solid alibi.

Her father's voice had said it all—even over the phone, the change in tone was palpable. Jade had finally tracked down several wedding guests who after their initial interviews had made hasty exits back to Savannah. Each of them were sure they'd seen Colt Thistle smoking a cigarette by the Summerhouse stairs when the lights went out.

Her father hadn't offered more, but Kayla knew there were other theories about the crime now. A sketch artist's rendering had been left briefly out on their kitchen table. There'd been rumblings about Caroline Bancroft, Sophia, and even Ruth. Hefty insurance money for the stolen necklace. The Instagram account with the threats of the creepy clown avatar still kept her up at night. But her father had clammed up even more than usual. She, like everyone else, was stuck getting her information from the usual sources: her phone, the internet, and television.

It was alarming how the "The Blue Compass Bride" had blown up. *Lord, did the media love a pretty white blonde.* Since the rehearsal, there'd been a few stories in the press, but it seemed even the minor minutiae of the Bancroft girls' lives was now leading the twenty four-hour news cycle.

She'd come outside to escape one particular story she couldn't seem to shake. Her face, plastered across her dad's favorite cable news show. The awful shot from her high school yearbook, her eyes heavily lined in purple liner, her hair a messy pile of ropey braids. The television caption beneath the grainy black and white photo read: Blue Compass Drop-Out Drops Back Into the Center of Crime Scene.

She turned the TV off immediately. She didn't need to watch anything to know what was happening. Somehow, the whole thing had become her fault. Her father was her alibi and this was a worst-case scenario. Now, her voicemail was full of messages she wasn't checking. She was either the media's new favorite punching bag or star witness depending on who they were interviewing. Not that it mattered, the insinuation was always the same—she wasn't talking so she must have something to do with it.

On her way outside, she'd noticed that the red light on their home answering machine was blinking. She pressed it, a sense of foreboding as she placed the voice on the line.

Hey Kayla—It's Colt. Hope you don't mind that I called you at home. I've been calling your cell and it's full. Believe it or not, I still had your number written down somewhere. Anyhow, I wanted to let you know that I've been getting some calls about the rehearsal dinner—reporters and stuff. I'm guessing we all are. Anyhow, I don't want you to worry. I am not gonna talk to anyone—I don't care what they offer . . . Also, there's something else. Something I wanted to talk about from the other night. Give me a call. OK? I texted my cell.

Her finger had pressed delete instinctively. This morning the last of her winter brides had canceled their services, and the idea of losing not only her safety, but also Two Be Wed had hollowed her out, made her want to bury her head and pretend none of this was happening. The whole thing had been a terrible idea—she saw that now. Though she still wasn't ready to admit it out loud. It was one thing to suspect something in the deep corners of your mind, another to finally speak it.

The first time Ruth Bancroft had walked into her shop, it'd been years since she'd seen a Bancroft sister. At the time, she'd been in a funk. Her business stalled because of the storm, she'd felt stuck on the sidelines as the wedding industry descended into an artificial hellscape of bleary-eyed zombie brides. Insta-everything was taking over, the entire planning process suddenly consumed with an unobtainable social media perfection that demanded the impossible from its vendors.

So Ruth had felt like a breath of fresh air. That day, she'd asked all the right questions, been genuinely concerned with the substance of the day, the sincerity of the ceremony, and the experience of her guests. There'd been something about the look on Ruth's face, the innocence of her *"simple but maybe romantic beach wedding?"* that had made Kayla genuinely want the job. Even after Sophia and their mother stepped in and things began to spiral, she'd honestly believed she could pull it off.

Who was she kidding?

Kayla stood up, double checking the lock on the patio door before she turned to go inside. Her father had been right all along. They were coming for her. It was only a matter of time.

Chapter Thirty

Ruth

Ruth had taken to camping out on the porch. It was a good place to gather herself. There was no quiet in the house. No place to be alone. The television was always blaring, the twins' toys and tablets were an endless assault of high-pitched animal noises, blinking lasers, and overstimulation. Under normal circumstances, the introvert in her would have had trouble functioning, on the porch the shush of the ocean was endless. The roll and crash to drown out her thoughts. It was steady, reliable.

She wills herself to get up and reenter the house when she hears Caroline in the living room. Her mother's eyes are circled in shadows, her Botoxed forehead betraying an actual line. Caroline is handing out sleeping pills, everyone taking them like Tic Tacs. The old bottle resurrected from her medicine cabinet.

"These work well. Just don't take them with more than one drink . . ."

Ruth takes two, thinking it won't help, but pocketing them anyways. At night, the house had another persona. Even with everyone around, there was something unsettling, a feeling she couldn't place, a creak in the wood floors as she paced them in darkness. Sometimes, it felt like Teo was acting strange too. Jesus, maybe she was losing it.

In the kitchen, Jo is alone at the counter, surrounded by a giant tray of cookies and petit fours. The remains of the rehearsal dinner's dessert table flanked by bottles of wine from yet another provision run courtesy of Mayor Bob.

"There's still a ton of these." Jo dips a knife into a jar of Nutella then spreads it thickly onto an oatmeal raisin cookie. "This is just too awful to be real." Ruth takes a seat as Jo's phone pings on the counter. Her sister looks down at it—tracing her finger over the calorie tracking app that has just popped up, the screen reminding her to log a meal.

"God, you ever just get so sick of it?"

"Sick of what?"

"The cycles of things—of *life*." Jo takes a healthy bite of cookie and chews as she talks, a smudge of chocolate goo clinging to the corner of her mouth. "You know what I would normally be doing right now? What I *should* be doing—running. Every morning, running my ass off to lose the baby weight leftover from the twins. I mean, God forbid something jiggles on a Bancroft, right?" She takes another bite. "But then all that exercise just leaves me starving, so I'd end up right here—eating again. Which—*of course*—would make me feel terrible, so then I want to go for a run again since that's the only thing that makes me feel better. But then I'd just be hungry again . . ." She blows out an exasperated breath. "*Nothing* ever changes."

Ruth dips a finger into the jar of Nutella and lets her go on. This was her sister's way, the world her courtroom. Everything talked out and litigated to a silent jury of her self-selected peers. Sometimes people just needed to rant.

"And I know this is all selfish—but I'm pregnant again so now dieting is out . . . God, I'm *pregnant.*" Jo stuffs the remainder of the cookie in her mouth. "JD and I are barely hanging on as it is . . . And I can't even have a proper pity party because Dad is gone—really gone." She sets her head on the counter. "And isn't that just what he does? Isn't that *his* cycle? He disappears and comes back—only this time, we're all living in an episode of *Murder She Wrote,* and it's real." Jo lifts her head before she buries it in her hands. Her voice cracks. "Once again, Dad has sucked up all the air in the room—out of our lives." Ruth reaches out for her sister's hand. "God. I am awful—but I'm going to say it—just say what everyone else is thinking. I mean how long are we supposed to do this? How long are we supposed to hold court and 'pretend grieve' this stranger, our 'father' who showed up six weeks ago?"

Ruth is frozen, a hundred layers of sad, some part of her repulsed, some part of her glad for the voice echoing her inner thoughts. Jo sits up and takes another cookie. "God. I'm climbing the walls—I wish we could *do* something."

Ruth scoots back her chair. "Me too—sometimes, it feels like the walls are closing in. I'm just not ready yet—I feel like if we wait a little longer, then maybe it will be obvious what comes next."

Chapter
Thirty One

Marcus

≈

It's past 10:00 AM on Wednesday when Marcus pulls his cruiser onto Highway 98, seething as he heads toward the Looksee Lounge. There'd been another press leak this morning. An anonymous source had gotten hold of pictures of the rehearsal tent after Thad went missing, full police interviews from some of the guests had been leaked. It's more mud on him and his department, and he quickly switches off the local news, wanting to avoid further reminders of how badly this investigation is going.

A minute later, he pulls into the LookSee's gravel lot as Patsy Cline finishes her second refrain of "Crazy."

This morning, he'd decided he needed to go at things in a new way, needed some fresh perspective, and he knew Sally Banks, The LookSee's bartender, was the girl for the job. Sally had been tending bar in Blue Compass since most of her patrons were in diapers. Marcus guessed she was in her late sixties now, but her mind was a steel trap—especially when it came to her customers. She'd been helpful to him before, and he hoped today would be no exception.

The front door of the LookSee Lounge was already open, a stream of daylight beaming into the windowless rectangle of a restaurant like a headlight. Sally was wiping down the bar. A pair of cut-offs and a LookSee T-shirt, she is fit for a woman half her age, her arms and legs tanned to the color of cognac. *Tanning Bettys*—was that what Kayla called them? Her nickname for naturally pale white women—usually of a certain age—who believed looking your best meant keeping your body an unnatural leather color year-round. Marcus didn't find it funny, but it sometimes amused Kayla, the older she got, the more those kind of Panhandle ladies cornered her, admiring her medium brown skin, asking asinine questions like what type of cream she preferred in the tanning bed.

Sally greets Marcus with a smile, aqua eyes buried in deep wrinkles. "How's it going, big guy—what can I get you this early?"

"I'll take a sweet tea and a grouper basket to go."

She pulls a pen from her apron and writes his order on a scratch pad, ripping off the top sheet before slamming a bell on the stainless-steel window ledge. "Go order."

Marcus waits, taking in the packed bar, unusual for this early in the day. "Pretty crowded, huh? How the reporters tipping these days?"

Sally rolls her eyes. "Better than the regulars." She turns to face him. "It has been quite a year—first Kerry, then the ordinance mess, now this . . ."

"I was hoping we could chat about the night of the bachelor party—I've been told the men were here?"

She nods, handing him his drink in a Styrofoam cup.

"Anything stick out?"

She laughs, the raspy voice of a lifetime smoker. "Honey, everything sticks out right now. We got so many strangers around here—strange roofers, strange electricians, construction workers from God knows where." She leans over the bar toward Marcus. "But I remember that night. That groom's pretty *unforgettable*. It was a pretty normal night except for the little tussle there at the end. Only thing I reckon is that Asian fella everyone's talking about."

Marcus raises an eyebrow, "So you heard about him too?"

"Heard about him? He was *here*. Sat right there at the end of the bar, didn't say two words."

Marcus pulls a file from the stack in his hand, finding the sketch artist's rendering, he holds it up. "This the guy?" She reaches for it, and he lets her have it. "We're just getting ready to release this to the media—you're the first to see it."

She studies the sketch for a minute. "That's pretty close. Maybe his nose is a little different."

"Did you see him and Thaddeus Hargrove interact?"

"I don't remember him talking to anyone. Which stuck out like a sore thumb around here, just sitting there all alone— usually them vacation boys wanna karaoke or hit on anything that moves . . ." She thinks for a minute. "Then again, it gets pretty loud in here on karaoke night. And we were busy."

"Any idea what started that fight?"

She laughs, "Honey, I seen worse ones than that after Sunday brunch. Seems like it was over before it started."

She turns to ring him up.

"Anything else?"

"Well, let's see. There was George Ricken who wouldn't shut up about his boat getting stolen. Walker Hoover moaning about his tiny insurance settlement. Justin Sellars was at the end of the bar, pretty loaded—nothing new there. Oh yeah, there was a table of them DC boys too."

"What about the father? Was Thad Hargrove talking to anyone? Anyone that wasn't with the wedding party?"

"Order up." A grizzly looking chef with a ZZ Top-length beard hands Sally a grease stained white paper bag through the window.

"He was at the bar for a bit, but unless I'm taking drink orders, my back's to everybody. I did notice one thing: That guy was carrying—the one with the tattoo—though that ain't much different than anyone else around here. I'm surprised it hasn't already bit us in the ass." Her eyes shoot to a sign above the cash register that reads "No firearms. We don't care about your permit."

"You sure—you saw?"

She nods, "He leaned over, and I saw one tucked into his shirt. Some kind of small handgun."

"Any idea what kind?"

"Nope just saw the bulge—that's it."

The word "bulge" seems to amuse her and Marcus reaches for the bag. "Thank you, Sally—this smells great." He hands her a twenty-dollar bill. "Keep it—and let's keep this chat between us."

On the way to his car, Marcus eats a french fry and checks his messages. When he'd left the precinct that morning, the place was buzzing. The sketch artist's rendering was an adrenaline shot to the investigation. Everyone was suddenly laser-focused on finding the tattooed man. Even Blue Compass's laziest beat cop was offering to canvas on his time off. Still, Marcus wasn't convinced.

It was interesting that this man had been there that night, but it was a little too tidy. Marcus wasn't keen on starting a targeted campaign against a tourist, a tourist of color no less. No one else had seen this mysterious man on the pier or at the rehearsal dinner—including himself. And from the look of the sketch, he would have stood out. And how did the necklace play into it? Bookies and their muscle liked to threaten people with their fists; they generally shied away from any payment that wasn't green and especially from any kind of harassment that left a digital trail.

The sketch was already making its way through the precincts in Atlanta. Maybe someone could ID him there. They needed a better idea of who this guy was. Forensics had finally come back and identified the bullet as coming from a Glock 19 semiautomatic. It was a bit of information he'd held back from everyone but Jade. A matching gun would go a long way.

He'd been avoiding the FEDS and holding back the sketch as long as he could. He still wasn't sure if releasing it might do more damage than good. Marcus had always known that at some point, the race card was going to enter into things—and he didn't like it. Blue Compass didn't exactly have a bustling ethnic population. It was a community still catching up with the rest of the world in a lot of ways. Though, he liked to think that things had improved some. Less than two months ago, he'd been reelected for the second term in a landslide victory. It was a feat that once would have been unthinkable for a Black man in this kind of town, especially on this stretch of the Panhandle. Excluding the occasional perp walk where a less than original racial slur was slung at him as he ducked a criminal into his cruiser, race wasn't the kind of thing he gave as much thought to as he had early on in his career. He'd always been able to count on his own boys to take care of it when it did happen. For the most part, they were good men. Some of them, he owed more than he liked to think about.

Still, he was a Black man who'd grown up in the South and that hadn't come without scars. When he and his wife, Cecilia, had gotten together in their late teens, his future father-in-law had threatened him with a baseball bat. Thirty-five years later, he could still hear Ceceila's father, his throaty rage that their relationship was "against nature."

Most days, he still couldn't believe his wife was gone. What a bad cliché—she'd just run out for milk. A semitruck on a three-day haul had crossed over the double yellow line on Highway 98 right in front of Toucan's Beach and Grill.

He and Kayla had fallen into each other in the aftermath. There hadn't been much choice. Though, at first, she had been touch and go. After the funeral, she'd spent two solid weeks in bed. Then finally, one morning, he'd found her at the kitchen counter, making pancakes. The next day, she cut ties with whoever her awful boyfriend was at the time. She started cleaning up her life, her appearance. Slowly, his daughter reappeared. Later that year, she got her GED and decided to reopen Two Be Wed. Life had forced her to grow up too soon. It was probably why Kayla had handled Hurricane Kerry better than most people. The tragedy had focused her. He knew how lucky he was—that she tended to hold on to things. His job came with resources, he'd use them to protect her and her business in a heartbeat.

Marcus pulls his cruiser back onto Highway 98, taking in the sparkling blue water on his right, struck again by the beauty and misery one road could possess. He's late for a meeting at the precinct and his phone pings. Jade's two-word text making his stomach drop.

Feds here

The Honda in front of him slows down, and he decides to pass it, his heart skipping another beat as he pulls left, his cruiser in a blind spot for only a second. Then he speeds up—running toward the eye of the storm, just like he always did.

Chapter
Thirty Two

Teo

～

Ruth is parked out on the porch again, the same rocking chair, legs crossed. A rote concentration on the empty beach, blue sky, and water, her mouth agape. So Teo challenges the twins to another game of Chutes and Ladders. It's obvious she needs space and he's trying to give it to her. He'd felt it this morning in her flinch when he brought her coffee and tried to land a kiss on her cheek. The way she'd bristled when he asked her if she'd thought anymore about checking her email, made a joke about going down to the courthouse to elope.

His mother had warned him to have no expectations, not to put pressure on her. He was trying not to take it personally, but he and the twins had just finished a cartoon marathon on Nickelodeon, and he was running out of patience. To make matters worse, he still wasn't sure whether to bring up the LookSee, to tell her what the sketch artist's rendering had brought back. He'd been just about to broach the subject yesterday when she'd wanted to have a talk of her own.

"I don't think we should sleep in the same bed anymore while all this is happening."

Teo had tried not to show his frustration. "Are you serious?"

"This morning, Rhea and Beau came into our room and got in bed with us—it was awkward—not right. Teo, we aren't married. It's confusing for them."

"Ruth, they are four years old. I—"

"I need to do something—*feel* right about something," she'd snapped. "Can't you just give me that? This house is making me crazy."

"Ruth, they are leaving tonight anyway—what good is that now?"

Her face falls. "They are?" She pauses, "Oh God, that's right—" She wrings her hands. "I feel like I'm starting to lose it. I've gotta get some sleep."

He hadn't said more. He was forgetting things, too—his own fitful sleep was full of nightmares, faceless creatures stalking the house and drowning in the bay outside. Summerhouse was like a vortex, the insomnia like a perpetual state of jet lag— your brain didn't function like it should.

A few minutes later, Teo checks the clock, knowing it's time for the twins' nap. He peels Rhea from the window she's staring out and throws her over his shoulder as they head upstairs. When he tucks them into their bunk beds and goes to shut the blackout curtains, Beau bolts up. He pleads, "No. Too scary."

Rhea shakes her head in agreement, her eyes suddenly glassy. "Dis house. Dose noises. Dey went away and came back."

Teo pushes back the heavy fabric again as wide as he can before he returns to their bedside. He's halfway through a second reading of *The Cat in the Hat* when their eyes grow heavy. He whispers, "I'm gonna miss you two—your daddy's taking you home later."

Beau rolls over, relief washing over his face. "I need a go home. I don't like it here."

Teo looks around and tugs up the soft summer quilt. "Yah bud, lately, I know what you mean."

A minute later, Teo creeps out of their room, tiptoeing till he gets down the hall to the room where Nick is staying. The door is open, and his friend is packing to leave, his suitcase spread out on an unmade bed. Thad had only booked the rental through the wedding night, and Nick was supposed to be on the first flight out the next morning. He'd said he felt strange leaving when the investigation was just getting started, so he had stayed on with no other option but to move into Summerhouse. Teo adjusts his expression as he hovers in the frame watching Nick prepare to go. It was another thing he'd been trying not to think aboutall day. He knew it was selfish, but he was still dreading his departure. His friend had already stayed way longer than he'd planned, had let his original plane ticket lapse without booking a new one. Last night, he'd caught him up way too late, studying a thick Gross Anatomy textbook by lamplight—even after the two of them had slung back way more alcohol than they should.

So this morning, Teo had spent the early hours in a frustrated search for return flights. Though he'd expected the cost of a last-minute ticket to California to be expensive, he hadn't expected every airport near them to be sold out. When he stumbled upon a bargain ticket leaving out of the Savannah airport, he and Nick had conspired, turning the extra travel into the solution to another problem.

Other people's lives need to go on.

Not just Nick's, but his mother's too. Maya's patients needed her, and she'd already canceled days of clients. Thankfully, the two of then had somehow talked her into going back to Savannah with Nick. His best man was like a second child to her, and had given an "Oscar-worthy performance" falling to his knees in front of Maya, pleading, *"Puleeze,* I need you—I've got issues—narcolepsy, test anxiety, fear of abandonment, multiple personality disorder. I absolutely cannot survive the six-hour drive unless you keep me awake the whole way."

It was a pathetic farce but the display had worked. His mother's bags were packed at the door with a promise to return if and when anything changed.

Nick looks up at Teo. "You ever notice how much nicer rich people's towels are?" He shoves a shirt into his open duffel bag. "Seriously, it's like drying your bottom with angels. I am *really* gonna miss taking a shower here."

"Take all you want," Teo sighs, "I don't know how I'm ever going to thank—"

"Please." Nick swats the words away and looks up. "Did you decide what to do about Ruth and her dad's—" He mimes someone chugging from a bottle.

"No—I'm so pissed I can't think straight. Between worrying about Ruth, wondering if she's some kind of suspect—and that." He blows out hard. "I feel so useless."

"Why don't you have someone look into Thad? Seems like the police are the useless ones around here—there's gotta be some private investigator firm somewhere?"

Teo's eyebrow arches. "That's actually not a bad idea—" He considers the idea a moment, and in the silence that falls between them they can hear the noisy mob of news vans outside. "Why didn't I think of that? But first let's get you out of here—I just hope you can get through those fools outside without running someone over."

"Wouldn't be the worst thing that's ever happened." Nick laughs.

"It's getting . . . bad." As the words leave Teo's mouth, he feels something behind him. He turns to see Ruth drift down the hall. Her face is gaunt, eyes hollow, a ghostlike gait as she heads toward the bedroom. She looks up at him for only a second, and he nods, not realizing he is holding his breath.

The exhale only comes a moment later when he sticks his head into her room and finds she's finally trying to sleep. He hovers in the doorway, watching her back rise and fall before he peels himself away to head downstairs.

In the dining room, Sophia and Maya are at the table, two uneaten plates of leftover salad and two untouched bowls of chicken soup in front of them.

"Nick's almost ready, and Ruth is trying to sleep—I think."

"Good. Let's keep it quiet." Maya takes a spoonful of soup, looks at it, then sets it down.

"She's in there in the weirdest way—and it's so hot." Teo scrunches up his shoulders in an *I don't know* posture. "She's got all these blankets—like she's in a cocoon or something."

Sophia's mouth draws into a tight line. "She all balled up, put 'em over her head?"

Teo nods.

"That's a throwback from when we were kids." She twists in her seat like she's checking the room before her voice lowers. "It was like our little—I don't know—kinda hide-from-dad thing? When Thad would come home all hot mess again, we always ran to my room, got under the covers, piled on the blankets and pillows. Got to the point where Caroline would even bring me Ruth—as soon as he walked in the door—she was just a baby."

Teo sets down the glass of tea he's poured. How had he never heard this about her before? She'd always been upfront about the trauma of her childhood, but maybe it was worse than he realized.

"Me and Jo—we always just waited." Sophia closes her eyes, presses her lips together, and it's obvious she's reliving it. "Sometimes we pretended it was a game. We'd sing little songs to her but God—that was Casa Hargrove . . . you do anything long enough, and it almost starts to feel *normal*."

Teo waits for his mother to say something, imagining psyche terms like trauma response or repression syndrome, but she just stands up and says, "I'm very sorry you had to go through that."

It's silent for a moment, and Sophia scans the bay, her eyes stretching to the pier. "Yeah—and I guess, karma is a bit of a bitch, too—huh?"

Maya reaches over and grabs both their plates. "That is a lot for a kid—a *family*—to go through. Any of you ever see anyone—talk to anyone about it?"

"I don't know if that ever occurred to Caroline. She met Blake and things just got so much better. I guess it was easier to not think about it anymore." She exhales. "I really don't even remember whole chunks of it—but I still sleep like that sometimes too. We all like a lot of blankets."

Maya is at the sink, scraping plates. "It would be perfectly natural for all this to be bringing up old emotions for everyone.

Sometimes this kind of stuff lands later . . . you think you're going along fine, and then suddenly you're not." She pauses, "I can—umm, after all this, we could probably *all* use some support. I'd be happy to refer you to a colleague—Teo, you too—I know a few good therapists who—"

Sophia's laugh cuts her off. She puffs out her chest, and Teo can't tell if she's embarrassed or indignant at the suggestion. "Maya, that's very—*nice*—but not really my kind of thing. Obviously, I wasn't close to Thad—and this whole thing is just—I don't know—*confusing*." She drums her fingers on the table. "But hey, if you know a good divorce attorney . . . now that—I'll take." Sophia stands up and the back of the chair presses into the pile of mailed boxes and packages lined up in the corner of the dining area. A cardboard box falls from the top, and Teo winces. UPS and FedEx have been working overtime, the steady stream of wedding presents, obviously mailed before the last few days, continually arriving. Until now, he'd been avoiding even looking at them, the physical manifestation of all the things he and Ruth had yet to talk about.

Sophia disappears upstairs, and Teo and his mother have barely finished restacking the boxes when Ruth appears from the stairwell. She looks at the boxes, then at the suitcases waiting in the doorway. "Hey—you weren't gonna leave without saying goodbye?"

"We were hoping you would get some quiet—but of course not." Maya comes over to her, encircling Ruth with both arms, a long hug before the three of them head to the garage. Everyone is quiet as Nicholas slides out of the garage's side door to pull the rental convertible into the open space beneath the house. As the garage door clicks shut, the sounds of reporters shouting from the road disappear.

Teo packs the bags into the car, and Maya is about to get in the front seat when she stops, "You're sure you don't want me to stay?"

Ruth shakes her head. "You have done more than enough—JD and the twins are going home tonight too. At this point, this is no place for—" She looks around and her voice breaks "—anybody."

"Oh my poor girl," Maya reaches out and tucks a stray hair behind Ruth's ear. "I remember when Teo's father passed, I was sure that the colors of life would never return." She pulls Ruth into her. "Eventually, you will find that we are all vessels built for the storm. No matter what happens, just know that there are no right ways now. It's enough to get up. Brush your teeth. Put on your shoes." She pauses then hugs Ruth again. "Teo loves you. I love you. You will survive this—we all will."

Teo shuts the trunk. He adds himself to their hug, reminding himself again that the safest place for his mother is *away*. It would be one less worry to have her back in Savannah. All that was keeping him sane was the idea of his family—intact. He kept telling himself that they were getting closer to putting this nightmare behind them with each person who returned to their real life. Teo kisses Maya on the cheek before buckling her into her car seat, nodding to Nicholas. "Drive safe. Five bucks for every journalist you mow down on the way."

Chapter
Thirty Three

Kayla

~

Kayla runs her hand over the rack of dresses in front of her, enjoying the comforting squeak of the plastic bag. She'd swung into Two Be Wed telling herself she needed to catch up on invoices.

But the groom called when she was pulling into her parking space, blathering nonstop: *Could they borrow Two Be Wed, or just her office? . . . he'd hired a private investigator and for obvious reasons, they couldn't meet with him at the house . . . they would be quick . . . in and out . . . he wouldn't be there, but Ruth didn't trust anyone she couldn't meet . . . of course, they would bring her check too . . .*

Kayla wonders what kind of PI doesn't have an office. Trust the wealthy to not think these kinds of hires through. But it wasn't her business, and she really needed that check. For whatever reason, Jo Bancroft had flaked on her promise to bring one over before the rehearsal dinner and with everything that had happened after, invoicing the Bancrofts hadn't exactly seemed like the thing to do.

A moment later, she lets Ruth and Sophia in the back door, and she can hardly believe her eyes. Sophia and Ruth are similar versions of haggard. Messy hair piled into haphazard ponytails, pasty skin, and dark circles under their eyes. She's never seen Sophia anything but perfectly made up. They head to the sales floor, slumped shoulders, heads down. When they get there, Ruth opens her laptop and an alert dings, Sophia's phone pinging at the same moment. The sound makes them both freeze until Sophia reads it and nods it away.

We are all just waiting for more news.

It was another reason Kayla agreed to let them use Two Be Wed for this meeting: the reporters follow them everywhere now. They couldn't exactly meander over to the coffee shop for a sit down with a PI—not that they ever would have.

The front bell chimes and the lobby door flies open to the sounds of shouts and flashbulbs. Jo pushes into the room, big sunglasses and arms covering her face. She wipes herself off and says, "So, I'm guessing you haven't seen it then?"

"Seen what?" Sophia looks up from her phone. "PI should be here in a sec."

Jo whips out a tablet from a giant sac purse. "It's that girl again—that dumpster fire of a blogger. What's her name–'Tania T'?" She taps on the screen then looks away as if she's ashamed of what's there. "I guess some of the media—the actual media—are reporting this crap too."

Ruth's eyes go wide and her fingers are already pecking away. Kayla's stomach pitches as the site loads, the blasts of hot pink and neon yellow searing.

*IS SHADY WEDDING PLANNER'S SECRET GRUDGE
KEY TO DADDY'S DISAPPEARANCE?*

Hey all you out there,

Tania T has got an exclusive storm cloud line item in the ever-evolving Blue Compass Bride Superstorm. And trust me, the plot thickens. This blogger has it from reliable sources that Kayla Jennings, wedding planner of ill-fated bride Ruth Bancroft, has not only a criminal past but also a Category 4 grudge against the whole Bancroft family! That's right—it seems the outcome of poor Ruthie's fancy soiree might've been sealed from the start! Ms. Kayla wasn't just quite the party girl in her day, but it seems some pretty ugly resentment has been simmering all these years! And we can't forget, Kayla was in charge of security the night big daddy disappeared—sooooo, a girl's gotta wonder: Is Kayla Jennings a menace to society or just plain bad at her job? Was she out to sabotage the soiree—or worse? Don't hate the messenger—I'm just asking the questions we're all thinking . . .

Kayla clears her throat, panic pooling in her chest. "I think that's enough—you obviously get the idea." What the hell were these girls really doing here anyway?

Jo shakes her head. "It's what passes for journalism these days. The firm had a case like this once. Someone with a blog and a big following makes up a story, then other outlets report their 'report.'" She makes air quotes. "As long as the show paints itself as *entertainment*, they can pretty much say whatever they want. They're just 'asking questions,' but the damage is done. Most people miss the *'no proof'* part. They are supposed to be news and talking heads with opinions. They got confused a long time ago . . ."

No one speaks and then Jo turns toward Kayla, her voice going hard. "Unless of course, there is proof—Kayla, is there—*proof*?"

"I always knew you looked familiar." Sophia's mouth falls open. "Did you go by something different in high school?"

Kayla closes her eyes, pinches the bridge of her nose, not wanting to relive it, but almost relieved the moment is here. "People called me Kiki back then." She sighs and walks over to lock the front entrance. "I think I was going through my white blonde pixie phase."

"So you guys did know each other?" Ruth asks.

There's a chilling silence. The sisters sit in a line on the couch, all waiting expectantly for her to explain how they know her. It seems cruel that not one of them remembers that night, a memory she's been forced to carry alone for all these years.

She'd just gotten her driver's license. It was the end-of-summer bonfire to celebrate the departure of all the tourists and the first time her father had let her drive alone. The timing was convenient since Jax's car was broken down again. There was that tingle of excitement as she pulled into her boyfriend's driveway, the smell of cigarettes on his Pink Floyd shirt as he reached behind her seat to set down his cooler and jacket.

Jax had the best fake ID in Bay County and was always willing to share. His generosity with booze often paid for by his cash from dealing weed to the locals and tourists. As they pulled onto Highway 98, Jax popped open two cans of Natural Light.

"The good stuff for tonight."

Kayla had wondered if he meant the beer or what was usually hidden in the pocket of the green army jacket.

The Blue Compass bonfire was a senior tradition held before the start of school. She was new to Blue Compass and nervous. As they parked, they found the remote stretch of beach already crowded. A crescent of lawn chairs and coolers surround a tall bonfire. Boys in backwards caps and girls in short shorts, red Solo cups littering the ground.

Jax flipped open his phone. "Be right back," before he disappeared into the crowd. Kayla grabbed another beer, fidgeting with the can's metal tab.

"I loooove your hair."

Kayla lit a cigarette from her purse, and realized the girls were talking to *her*. Low cut tank tops and frayed shorts, Kayla knew the two brunettes as senior cheerleaders. She didn't know their names, but was sure the third girl was Sophia Bancroft. Sophia might only be a summer resident, but she was treated as the exception to the locals-only rule, practically famous along the beach. Kayla touched the nape of her neck where her hair ended bluntly, taking a drag of her cigarette. "It's something I'm trying."

"This party sucks. All the hot guys are already at college." Sophia ran the toe of a Tori Burch sandal through the sand.

The taller of the two girls asked, "Is that Jax guy your boyfriend?"

Kayla shrugged, unsure how to answer. They'd been hanging out all summer, but he wasn't the kind of guy to define those things.

The three girls spread out a blanket and to Kayla's surprise scooted over to make room for her. Within an hour, they'd emptied Jax's cooler, and Kayla had learned the brunettes' names were Megan and Riley. That none of them were virgins, although the shorter brunette preferred "oral any day of the week."

"You're such a slut, Megan." Sophia rolled her eyes then stood up as the radio changed to a techno version of Alan Thicke's "Blurred Lines."

"Dance with me, Kiki. This is my jam." Sophia closed her eyes, piling her long hair on her head suggestively as she swayed to the pulsing rhythm.

The beer's going to her head, and Kayla let Sophia pull her up. Dancing wasn't exactly her thing, and she tossed her empty can in the fire before doing her best to imitate the other girls.

A couple of songs later, Sophia blew the bangs from her forehead, saying, "Hey—why don't you call your boyfriend and see what he's got that might pick things up?"

Kayla had promised her father she would be home early that night, but there was the first day of school to consider—the idea of walking in alone, diving headfirst into the wannabe waters of a new school. Then the prospect of having girls like Riley and Megan in her corner. She called Jax.

The line trilled twice before he sent her to voicemail.

"Maybe you know where he keeps—?" Sophia makes a gesture like toking a joint.

Kayla knew where he kept his key and his stash. No one was ever home at that house. Maybe he would be happy she made a sale? "Can you drive?"

"We walked down the beach, silly." Sophia smacked Kayla's hand, her glossy lips in a pout. "Didn't you drive?"

"I'm kinda lightheaded."

"Shut up. You're fine. I'll help. I got you." Sophia stood and dusted herself off, turning her back to Kayla. "I mean if you don't wanna hang out—we will just go home."

"No—wait." She hadn't meant to grab Sophia's arm. "I am good. I guess it's not that late anyways."

When the four girls got to the car, Kayla realized she hasn't unloaded her Dodge Dart from her afternoon at the beach. She saw her ride with new eyes: the foam peeking out from the ripped back seats, the secondhand beach gear piled to its drooping ceiling. "Shit." She kicked the tire, silently cursing her father. Her grandparents had offered to buy her a brand new SUV, but Marcus had made her use her own money on this POS instead. There isn't enough room for all four of them to fit.

"Just us two will go," Sophia commanded. "You two stay here."

Kayla still wasn't sure this is a good idea, but the prospect of not endearing herself to this girl is much worse. She put on her seatbelt, head heavy. As Kayla eases the car onto 98, Sophia talks at a breakneck pace. Kayla had mostly practiced driving on the back roads of Blue Compass and always in the quiet. She avoided Highway 98's busy two-lane until right before her driver's test. As it came into view, the sensation was like a tunnel, black and endless, and she dug her fingernails into the wheel.

"Let's hurry. I have a curfew tonight—can you believe it? My mom is so disgustingly head over heels for her new husband, and all she wants to do is play house with us. It's so gross." Wind whipped through the car as Sophia rolled down a window. The air made Kayla dizzy as her headlights stretched out like two smoky eyes in the darkness.

"Jesus, my grandma drives faster than you." Sophia shoved her shoulder with her hand and Kayla jumped, turning her focus back to the road, trying to breathe. It was only a mile down the road to Blue Compass and the first hints of town would offer enough light to let her relax.

A minute later, Sophia slammed her phone down, snapping, "Geez! Come on!" before she leans over, pressing Kayla's right knee hard into the gas pedal.

The car jerked with the surprise, swerving toward the double yellow lines. Kayla overcorrected, jamming the break, and there's a jolt before they skid in the other direction. There was only time for one more maneuver before they are off the road when, miraculously, Kayla rights them, her stomach in her throat.

Sophia spit out a laugh like it's funny, not terrifying, and they both look up. A split second of recognition of a brown blur in front of them, an animal large enough to fill the windshield. Kayla slammed on the brakes. But it's too late, the car swerved harder, trees spinning around them. There's the awful sound of metal on metal as the back side of the car skims a tree then skids ten yards into the "Welcome to Blue Compass" city sign. When Kayla came to, she found herself alone. The front hood wrapped around a steel piling.

*　*　*

"Black bears in Blue Compass used to be a bigger deal" Kayla mutters darkly as she steps in front of the sisters. "Two more feet and the engine would've gone through the dashboard and killed us both. But you've always been so lucky, Sophia. No one even asked me why two airbags went off instead of one."

Sophia is silent, her eyes glued to her lap.

"I still don't know. Did you just take off or call a cab?" Kayla spits out an exacerbated laugh. She'd foolishly thought she could avoid this moment. Since she took the Bancroft wedding, she'd somehow managed to delude herself that being this close to Sophia wasn't dangerous, wouldn't come back to bite her in the ass. "You know, we didn't even need to go anywhere that night? Those three ounces of Jax's pot were right there in the backseat the whole time."

The room is silent, everyone staring at Sophia. Kayla steps in front of her, willing her to look up.

Ruth snaps her laptop closed. "I don't understand any of this. Why is this girl—this *blogger*—coming after us . . . you—any of us?"

Jo shakes her head. "It's nothing personal. We're just content. It's whatever sensational thing people like her can dig up and throw against a wall——right now, that just happens to be us—or Kayla." She turns to look at her.

"It's personal for me," Kayla says. There's silence again, and Kayla wants to say something that will cut deep, make Sophia feel even an ounce of what she felt all those years ago when her father showed up on the scene, his jaw going slack when he saw her in the back of the EMT's van. "You should've stayed, Sophia. Your whole life you've been skirting consequences. And I was so stupid back then and never told a soul what really went down." She turns her back to them, both seething and terrified. They had no idea what her father had done to keep her out of jail, the jeopardy it had put his own career in. It hung over them every day—the fact that the department had swept it all under the rug for him. Technically, the accident had never happened. She didn't even have a mugshot. Now, her own decisions had made it so much worse. People were scrutinizing the department, the wedding, her life. If anyone found out Kayla had been traveling with a small pharmacy in her backseat, his career not just as Chief of Police, but as a cop would be over—for good.

"I'm not out to get you, Sophia—but is there some way—something you can do? Work your social media magic? This has to go away."

Sophia finally looks up at Kayla. "I don't remember much. I was pretty wasted, and I think I've blocked it out—I do that sometimes—when things are bad. I mean, I know I ran away—I made sure you were breathing. I was gonna call the cops but the sirens were already coming . . . I never heard anything else about it so I thought you were fine. I guess I was afraid to ask . . ." She shakes her head.

Ruth puts a hand on Sophia's, a gesture of solidarity that makes Kayla's body go cold. She guesses she should've expected that. The Bancroft women look after each other, and she has no place among them. Unless it was to act as scapegoat. How easy it would be for them to point the finger at Kayla, who was supposed to have security under control, who had seen the Bancroft necklace, actually clasped the delicate hook on Ruth's neck during final fitting.

Kayla feels Jo's eyes on her, the middle sister's pensive sidelong glance making it more difficult for her to keep calm. "This is ridiculous—I didn't sabotage the wedding—do anything. Do you know the hours I've spent—the crap I—" She takes a deep breath, "Jesus, do you have any idea how hard it is for a shop like mine to get an Alexander McQueen dress—the hoops I had to jump through? This is my livelihood—my *life*."

Kayla rubs the sides of her head, suddenly seeing it: What she hadn't wanted to admit, what was always there. Maybe in some sick way she *had* wanted to be close to the Bancrofts, to move in their circles. That from the beginning, she'd wanted to see how it all worked, to be the one pulling the levers and be in control.

And it was her father who might pay the price.

Sophia stands up suddenly, pushing off hard against the plush settee, she takes Kayla in an awkward one-armed hug. "I am gonna take care of this—I promise."

Sophia is still talking, rambling on about protecting Kayla from the jackals outside, a look of resignation on her face. Kayla sees it in the set of her eyes, there's an understanding of what needs to be done, what this new story means for both of them going forward.

They were in this together now.

"This isn't that hard." She meets Kayla's gaze. "We just need to change the subject. The press has been begging us to comment. I think now's the perfect time—don't you?"

It is always a perfect time in the Bancroft world, Kayla thinks, suddenly uneasy. She's about to pipe in, but Sophia nods definitely. "This is perfect . . . Mom's man has gotta be good for something. The ordinance vote is going to be the same day, so we're gonna need to be first." She nods again, assuring herself. "Let me and the mayor make a few calls—let's see what we can do about shutting this down."

Chapter Thirty Four

Ruth

∽

Later that evening, Ruth is skulking around Summerhouse, knee deep in her own pity party when she catches the faint sound of crying. She opens the door to find Sophia in pink pajamas, staring at a blank laptop.

"I can't do it." Her finger hovers over the keyboard. "I can do press—that's nothing. I can throw together a *national* press conference—one day, no problem—but this—*this*, I can't do."

Ruth looks at the blank screen, black with a bouncing white cursor. Sophia taps a key to wake it up and her Instagram account appears. "Do you know that since the rehearsal dinner I've gone dark on @sophiasez and gained one hundred and forty thousand followers?" She spits out an exasperated laugh. "I'm almost at a million . . . but it's gross, isn't it?"

Ruth shrugs. Nothing surprises her anymore.

Sophia goes on to tell her that right after the rehearsal, she'd posted a very generic, very off-brand "Thank you for thoughts and prayers. Please respect my family's privacy" statement. Since then, she'd been ignoring all the messages and texts that came in. This morning, she'd received a not-so-subtle DM from one of her sponsors about fulfilling contract obligations. And that each time, she tried to come up with something appropriate to say, the nightmare had shifted.

"It's so ironic—isn't it? If the social media that is around now, and allows me to chronicle my life, had been around when I was younger, I would probably have gone to jail." She runs her hands through her dirty ponytail. "I don't know how these kids do it. Teenagers do awful stuff—*obviously*—and like, now you have to think about how someone is gonna catch you with their smartphone or out you Twitter."

Sophia blows her nose with a wad of toilet paper. "Can't you just see my face with a big red line drawn through it? The word CANCELED in all caps? My brand is easy, sweet, flawless perfection." She tosses the tissue at the trash can and misses. "No one wants lifestyle tips from a former *mean* girl." She twists and grabs the pillow behind her back and fluffs it too hard, punching it before bringing it to her lap, and punching it again.

Ruth watches, thinking that maybe this was progress that her sister knew she was once a mean girl. Maybe some part of her should feel sorry for Sophia, for her marriage imploding, but anger wells up instead. At Two Be Wed she'd grabbed Sophia's hand, squeezing it hard to try to wake her sister up so she would apologize to Kayla and everything she'd put that girl through. And her sister's answer had been a press conference featuring herself.

The Good Bride

The day had been such a waste.

That investigator hadn't even bothered to call or cancel. Her whole life was starting to feel unsalvageable—and at the moment, she hated her sister for it, hated how she'd helped her create this giant wedding, convinced her to perform for strangers on the internet.

Sophia was right—she didn't have any business telling anyone anything. Whatever happened to humility, anyway? To quiet success? When did this look-at-me, peeping Tom, humble brag form of communication become not just socially acceptable, but the goal? She wanted to hit something.

Ruth feels Sophia studying her face. "Ruthie, I know you already have enough going on . . ." Sophia's voice is cloying, suddenly a sugary sweet baby talk like a mouse trying to sound cute. "Sissy is sorry. I'm all good now—*really*. I got this. Get some sleep—love you."

Ruth stands to leave, her jaw clenched. Their time to hash it out was coming—but not tonight. She's almost to her own room when she hears Sophia again. The same muffled cry, the same thump of her fist hitting a pillow. She pauses in the hallway, rage washing over her again. *Have at it, sister,* she thinks. *Over and over until something in this house feels as bad as you should.*

Chapter
Thirty Five

Kayla

It isn't even noon and every chair in the station's waiting room is taken. Kayla looks around, still surprised the whole thing has come together so quickly. Sophia Bancroft might be a piece of work but she'd managed to pull together a *real* press conference. The girl had even talked her father into letting them hold it at the precinct, a coup that had spared Kayla and her business more association with this never-ending nightmare. As skeptical as she was, most of her was desperate for this to work.

A deputy invites everyone waiting to follow him into a sparse conference room where rows of folding chairs are lined up. Sophia is already there in a folding chair, clicking away on her phone. The room has the fetid smell of a space with windows that don't open. The air is thick with the scent of chemicals, air freshener, freshly laid carpet, and new paint. The conference table has been pushed to one side and a makeshift stage is at the center.

At the podium, the city's part-time communications coordinator, Benita Adams, is fiddling with an ancient sound system. Both are relics from another era: the heavy electric box and the stout brunette. Benita is dressed in a wool suit, panty hose, and school marm block heels. Her reading glasses slide from a bulbous nose as she steps down from the stage and gives Kayla a quick hug. "So good to see you, little girl—we still miss you around here."

Kayla smiles. Years ago, she'd briefly worked in Blue Compass's administration building, her father's name likely helping her high school dropout résumé.

Benita pulls out a list. "I still can't believe what a good response we got for today—expecting it to be packed . . ."

Kayla looks down and yanks on her dress. She can hardly wait for this thing to be over. The mauve ruffled shift dress Sophia had picked out for her via Facetime is uncomfortably short, and her feet are shoved into her only pair of heels.

Sophia takes the list of the press outlets from Benita, and Kayla has a flashback of her time there. Benita at the city's enormous dot matrix printer, faxing tourism paper press releases to the major outlets outside of Blue Compass. The town barely had a website, still churned out weekly newsletter on a beast of a copy machine. The printer's miraculous survival from Hurricane Kerry was still a thing of town legend.

Sophia presses a finger to her lip. "Wow. This is *good*." She takes out a compact to check her makeup then angles it for a fuller reflection of her outfit. In a navy sheath dress and pearls, a pair of nude heels that Kayla had seen in last month's Vogue,

Sophia is channeling a blonde Jackie-O. She snaps shut the compact. "We made sure that awful girl isn't here, right? If that batshit blogger Tania T comes anywhere near this place, I want her arrested for trespassing."

Kayla squelches an eye roll as she looks around. Leave it to Sophia Bancroft to assume dominion over a public building like the police station. The room is already filling up, and Kayla has to tell herself not to gawk as familiar faces from a dozen media outlets stream in. There are a few local newspapers and crews, reporters from the big three networks and even some of the major cable news channels. They cluster in circles. Each crew around its anchor, the proportion of silicone and collagen separating the local broadcasters from the clearly more famous ones. The press conference is about to start when one last crew streams in. A burly camera man blocking her view before Kayla's mouth drops open and the crowd literally parts for Sela Mason, the reporter's star power silencing the room.

"That woman has two Pulitzers and an Emmy," Sophia whispers as the stick thin woman in a tailored white suit and the world's shiniest black bob struts past them. "OMG. I never get star struck, but Sela Mason has the number one show in the country—and five million followers." Sophia runs a hand over her own shiny blowout. "I love everything about her—God, her *style*—even that crazy gray streak in her hair is amazing . . . She's—like my hero." She watches Sela take a seat that one of her crew saved for her near the front of the room. Suddenly, the stakes have just gone up for Sophia, and Kayla is grateful it might work in her favor.

They are ready to start, and Kayla follows Sophia up onto the stage. At the last minute, Jo, Mayor Bob, and Caroline stream in. The couple is holding hands, their mouths set in grim lines. Jo takes the place closest to Kayla, linking her arm through in a sign that will read solidarity. Sophia steps up to the podium and suddenly there are flashes from the raised cameras. Kayla isn't sure where to look.

Sophia covers the microphone with her hand and winks. "Just like we talked about. A little razzle, dazzle. Kayla *who*?" Sophia seems to click more into herself. Her head high, chest out, she takes out a folded piece of paper from her pocket and sets it on the podium.

"Thank you for being here. My family—and I are devastated by the disappearance of our father, Thaddeus Jay Hargrove." She hesitates, glancing down to read from the paper though Kayla is very sure the speech is memorized.

"My sister, Ruth, and her fiancé, Teo Vargas, thank you for being here also. They chose not to attend themselves in order to keep the focus on our father. Our concern is getting information that will help find him or discover the person or persons who are responsible for this terrible act—" Sophia stops again and scans the audience. "We also want to set the record straight regarding the many *false claims* and fake news stories that have begun circulating." There is an over-enunciation on the *f* sound in *false* and *fake*. "We want to be *clear*. Our family believes that the perpetrator of this heinous crime is someone *outside* our direct circle. Everyone on this stage today has our full and unwavering support."

Sophia turns over her shoulder to glance at Kayla then whips around, wrapping her in a surprise hug. The length is prolonged, and knowing she needs to sell it too, Kayla tries to look touched as the cameras snap away.

When Sophia finally releases her, she smooths her dress then returns to the microphone. "Everyone on this stage has been victimized by the vicious attacks in one form or another from the media. There have been so many 'fake stories' promoted while legitimate leads like the threats made against my family have gone uninvestigated. That's right, ladies and gentlemen, there have been vicious, *credible* threats made against my family on my Instagram account, @sophiasez. Though I—my family— have fully cooperated and submitted their usernames to the authorities, the department can't investigate," she pauses. "*Why?* Because small police departments like Blue Compass can't get cooperation from the spineless media conglomerates that shelter these users' identities."

Sophia adjusts the microphone, and her voice booms. "Why is Instagram stonewalling the Blue Compass police department? What do they have to hide and more importantly, why do the current laws surrounding media companies shield their users when they make threats against *innocent* people?"

Sophia's voice breaks, and she pounds her fist on the podium. Kayla feels her face going red with embarrassment as the sister cries out, "My family needs *justice!*"

Sophia is just getting started, regaling the evils of big tech and droning on about fake media in general as every camera is dialed in, locked on Sophia's perfect features. For a moment, Kayla looks around, a surreal disbelief that everyone is furiously taking notes, bobbing their heads up and down in agreement. When Sophia finally seems to be wrapping up, she raises her voice in a finality that is way too Legally Blonde for Kayla's comfort. "I submit to you that *Big Tech* is the real villain here. Hasn't this beloved town been through enough? Let us shine a light and bring those to justice that harass, sow fear and discord. Help us Instagram—I *implore* you."

Kayla's jaw drops as a few people begin to clap, and she's suddenly aware she's being watched, so she joins them. Sophia grins then leans into the podium. "Thank you. We won't be taking questions."

The conference has run long and crews begin to pack up for the city council meeting. Sophia glides over to Kayla and Jo. Her face is flushed. "I think people really *got* it. That guy over there just told me how brave I am for going against my own platform." She gestures to a good looking man in an expensive suit. "I'm doing a couple quick side interviews with the more prominent outlets—is my hair OK?" Jo nods and smooths an errant hair behind her ear before Sela Mason taps Sophia's shoulder, and she's off to mug for a camera.

As the crowd disperses, Kayla sees Justin Sellars in the back of the room. She puts her hand up to wave—thinking it's nice of someone else who was part of the wedding team to show up—but the caterer ignores her, charging over to the crowd where Sela Mason is standing, a protective circle of her crew and security around her. Justin's face wears a giant pasted-on smile as he tries to make his way through and for a second, she almost feels sorry for him. Dropping her wave, she thinks *good luck with that*.

Jo reaches out to touch Kayla's shoulder, distracting her from eavesdropping on Justin's attempt at a new fifteen minutes of fame, "Listen, I'm so sorry about all this. I've been meaning to thank you for all your hard work with the wedding. I know— well, I know my family—that we aren't the easiest people to deal with sometimes. Some more than others . . ." Her eyes shoot to

Sophia, who has a hand gently cupping Sela's elbow, the closeness making it seem like these two women are old friends. "Anyways, we're leaving tonight—JD needs me and I gotta get back to my kids—Sophia's got some stuff she has to deal with too—we are planning to come back, but in the meantime if there's anything we can do for you—"

Kayla shakes her head, saying it's fine—though really it isn't. The check she'd finally cashed from the Bancrofts had included a 15 percent bump—in the notes section called "bonus" and though she'd appreciated the gesture, it wasn't enough to keep Two Be Wed open if no one wanted to work with her again.

"I gotta admit," Kayla says. "I thought this thing was an awful idea but—" She gestures toward Sophia who is laughing broadly at something Sela just said, her gel manicured hand over her heart as if she's pledging allegiance to her newfound best friend, "—just look at em." She shakes her head. "The power of a pretty face."

Jo nods, "She leaves everybody that way. Imagine being related to her."

Chapter
Thirty Six

Teo

~

Teo and Ruth are strolling down Summerhouse's driveway toward the street when she loops an arm through his and says, "I think we made the right decision skipping that press conference—don't you?"

He nods. "We'd just be a distraction—though I still don't get what they're hoping to accomplish? But if it puts the focus on helping your dad, then I'm all for it."

They stop at the end of the empty road, and he turns, elated to find the whole street quiet. As promised, Nautilus Cove's security gate was finally being repaired and though it isn't clear whether the timing had been fortuitous or planned, just as the reporters were peeling off for the press conference this morning, a security company from Panama City was setting up shop at the gatehouse.

Teo knew the hiatus would likely be short lived. Marcus had warned them it wouldn't take long for the media to find legal and not so legal work-arounds to the trespassing issue. Still, as he'd sipped his coffee this morning, he'd imagined with glee the sight of the reporters trying to return. All of them scratching their heads and asses about what to do now that the gate's new, red, metal arm blocked their free access to the street—and the Bancrofts' life. Even the investigator problem had found a solution. After the first PI had been a no-show—claiming he was easing toward retirement and not looking to work a case with this much media attention—Teo got busy finding a new one. They were meeting with a new one next week—a former cop with better references.

So today, he'd been feeling—dare he say it—hopeful? And when Ruth had suggested they take a quick walk, *"Just a lap around the neighborhood's one mile loop."* There'd been no reason not to agree.

Now, it was late afternoon and the sky was cloudless. As they turned right toward the Beach Clubhouse, he wondered if other things might be turning a corner too? He was starting to get some sleep, and it was allowing him to think straight, to feel human again.

"I love that some people still decorated for Halloween." Ruth gestures toward a Dutch Colonial house. Its front porch is dripping with pumpkins and gourds, a curated selection of orange, yellow, and white artfully arranged on haystacks. Nautilus Cove's layout was simple, one giant loop with two intersecting streets cutting across the large lots. The waterfront homes had long thin driveways designed to maximize the bay property that opened to wide water views.

"It sucks they canceled trick-or-treat . . . but seriously, how could they possibly have those kids running around with an ongoing investigation under foot?"

"Leave it to *my* family to ruin a whole holiday." Ruth kicks at a stone on the road. "God, this town must hate us."

On the left is another home in full Halloween mode, the yard strewn with realistic looking gravestones and cobwebs. On the porch, a masked-clad dummy dressed as Michael Meyers sits in a lawn chair, a real chainsaw perched convincingly in his flannel lap. Before Kerry, the neighborhood had once housed twenty-five homes, the architecture of each a different version of contemporary coastal. Once upon a time, they'd all been perfectly landscaped, perfectly maintained. Every flower box teaming, gas lantern blazing. Teo had seen it on holiday trips to Summerhouse for Thanksgiving and Fourth of July. All of it was a bit too perfect for his taste, but it was less so now. While most of the Nautilus Cove homeowners were in different stages of rebuilding, a few had pulled up anchor, taking the insurance settlements and disappearing. To all the other homeowners' chagrin, they'd left their gutted eyesores, roofless skeletons full of mold and garbage. Though the HOA had done initial cleanups, there were still years of legal battles ahead of them to deal with what now felt like a handful of haunted houses dragging down the property values.

They turn a corner and the Nautilus Cove gate comes into view. The metal security arm is already in place. A man in neon yellow coveralls is in front of a power box to its right, a drill in his hand.

"Don't you almost want to hide in the bushes and take pictures when the news vans try to come back?"

"Teo, let's just enjoy this while we can." Ruth turns toward Summerhouse then stops and looks at him. "I dunno—did we do the right thing? Should we be there right now at the police station—Sophia was pretty annoyed, and I feel guilty . . . maybe we didn't—" She looks at her feet. "What do you think?"

A pang of frustration shoots through him. He hated how Ruth twisted herself into knots for her sisters. The longer he's with her, the harder it is to watch. He takes her face in his hands. "Ruth, don't do that—you always do that—ask everyone else what they think." His eyes soften. "When are you going to start asking yourself? What do *you* think?"

For a second, she looks hurt, and she looks away. "I think it's all my fault that this happened and people would pay too much attention to us if we were there—"

He's about to disagree when his phone goes off, and he pulls it out to check it, the vibration setting was reserved only for work emails. There's a message from someone named Chuck Mathews. At first, he can't place it, but as he skims the content it comes to him. Chuck Mathews was fighting People First Insurance Company. The old charter captain was a fifth generation Blue Compass resident, and his first-row beach bungalow had been washed away by Kerry. Because of the advanced age of the house, the low income of the family, the insurance company had been grossly lowballing his settlement. Teo thought he remembered firing off a threatening letter to them several months ago, and he pushes down guilt as he tallies how long it's been since he's checked on the situation. It looked like the company had finally submitted a new offer. One with an expiration date of tomorrow.

"This is one of the guys I was helping pro bono." Teo turns back toward Summerhouse. "I shoulda dealt with this a while ago—and it looks like there's a deadline. I need to go back and deal, but let's revisit this conversation later tonight?"

When Teo gets to the kitchen, he finds his laptop and quickly reads through the new settlement offer attached to the email. He dials the number included. A second later, he's surprised when Chuck picks up. Like most of the people in Blue Compass, the old man cut right to the chase. It was one of many things Teo appreciated about the people who lived here. "I know it's last minute—and I'm the one who should have reached out sooner, but I just came across the same email, and I can talk for a minute right now if you have a moment?"

He tells Chuck that he's read through everything and that while the insurance company's new offer was by no means generous, it was at least now in the ballpark of reasonable. They chat about the specifics for a while, and Teo does his best to explain the legal aspects of signing off and accepting the offer. The two finally settle on Teo attempting one more call to the insurance company to see if they could nudge the number any further. Either way, he advises Chuck to accept and begin moving on with his life.

Teo's about to hang up when Chuck clears his throat, "I'm real sorry about all that—everything with your fiancée's father. Any word?"

Teo thanks him and is contemplating how to make a graceful goodbye when Chuck adds, "It's probably nothing. But I saw him a few nights before he disappeared—down at the park."

Teo raises an eyebrow. "Thad—before the rehearsal dinner? Are you sure?"

"He tall like you? Grayish brown hair, right? He was acting a little off. It's probably nothing."

"Off? How do you mean?"

"Listen, I ain't tryna speak ill of the—well, you know—the *gone*—but see, I was coming out of the backwoods—there's a pond out there with good bait and next thing I know, I hear gunshots. I come around and look, and there's that Thad fellow shooting at a tree?" He laughs, a throaty uncomfortable guffaw that echoes through the phone. "Maybe he was target practicing? I dunno—seemed pretty stupid to me? Anyhow, I wave and the guy takes off like he doesn't see me. I didn't know if he was in a hurry or something—but shooting at a tree ain't the smartest thing in the world to do . . ."

"Thad Hargrove had a *gun*? You sure?" Teo tries to hide his surprise. In the same moment, he reels back to a conversation he and Ruth had with Thad before the wedding. At a dinner in Savannah, Ruth had mentioned she didn't care for guns, and Thad had rattled on and on about how much he agreed with her, how they never made sense to him, only made situations worse. He'd even gone as far as to say he would never own one.

"Looked like a Glock to me—got one myself so I know 'em well enough."

Teo's mouth goes dry. The bullet in the pier was from a Glock. That bit of information hadn't come from the precinct. It had only been reported in the news from an anonymous source, that blogger Tania T, and it seemed unlikely Chuck was reading her posts.

As Teo hangs up, it washes over him—that thing that had always been there in the twist of his gut. Nothing about this man was what it seemed. Had Thad been shot with his own gun on the pier or was there something else going on? Maybe, the investigator could find out who Ruth's father really was. He needed something in this hellish week to fall into place.

Chapter Thirty Seven

Marcus

❧

Marcus can't stop thinking about the scene earlier—and at his own precinct, no less. The sister hadn't been halfway through that sham of a press conference when he'd stormed out. He should've known better than to let the mayor talk him into using their building, but he'd been playing the long game. There was already too much to do, and he didn't have time for another pissing contest. Before this mess, he'd planned to finish the afternoon with more important tasks ahead of the ordinance vote. Now, he was stuck at his desk, the department's priorities once again rearranged by the Bancroft family.

He was a big enough man to admit that some of what that sister said was true. Instagram was fighting the city's warrants. From what he knew, Bryant Kessler was still working through the latest round of paperwork. But so far, the city's reaction had been flat-footed. It was a David and Goliath fight, and up till now, he'd been the only person interested in picking up a rock.

The problem was that there were still too many other credible leads, avenues that needed deeper dives. Now that sister had thrown a spotlight on one he was reasonably sure was dead, the phone was going to be ringing off the hook with the press wanting updates and comments. *Jesus, Benita definitely wasn't up for the task.* This was going to be a delicate dance and a major waste of time.

Marcus leans forward on his desk, pressing a finger and thumb to his eyelids before picking up the phone to dial Bryant's line. It was time to light a fire under his ass. The phone hasn't yet connected when he catches motion in his peripheral vision. Someone is outside his door. It takes a second to place the wiry figure. Colt Thistle is slouched against the wall, looking lost.

He nods toward the reception area. "There was nobody upfront."

"Janice—at the desk—likes to take a lot of bathroom breaks." Colt looks confused and Marcus gestures, putting a hand up to his mouth and miming like he's smoking a cigarette. "*Bathroom* breaks."

He smiles, "Oh—gotcha."

Marcus has no idea what the boy could be doing there and is suddenly curious as he gestures for him to take a seat. "How can I help you?"

"I was thinking about the rehearsal dinner—about something I remembered, something I overheard . . ." He sits down and takes off his hat. "After you guys came to my house, after you questioned me that second time—well, I started thinking—" He stops, shifting in his chair. "At first I guess I was so shocked—then after you left I remembered, and it's something somebody should know."

"You never know what might help." Marcus takes out his recorder and sets it on the desk as the boy explains again that he's the head waiter at Coastal Catering. That he'd been at the rehearsal supervising and had helped set up the party.

"Anyway, so it's early—before cocktail hour, and I was heading back to the catering trailer when I hear two guys going at it, somebody yelling pretty good . . ." He pauses and fidgets with his hat some more. "Not that I was tryna listen. I just had to walk through there, and I didn't want to interrupt—so I waited."

"Turns out it was Mayor Bob and Justin Sellars—and damn, Justin was pissed about something. The guy's all sweaty and shaking—it's something about the mayor and Caroline Bancroft—" Colt eyes the tarpon mounted over the window. "I don't know if you heard, but the mayor was running all around that party—pretty much all over town—bragging how he's gonna pop the question. Justin seemed real worried about 'somebody getting confused' or *their* relationship changing cause of Ms. Bancroft or something? Dude's pissed enough to slam Mayor Bob up against the trailer."

Marcus is tapping his pen on the desk and stops. He didn't know Justin well—he was already in production on his show when Marcus started working in Blue Compass—but he'd always taken him to be a mellow guy, a drinker but somebody who life had kicked one too many times to think he was interested in fighting back.

"I dunno. Maybe it's not even related to all the stuff happening around here, but they got something going, Chief." He twists at the bill of his hat then looks up. "And I don't think Justin is doing so well. I know he hasn't been happy since he got back—that he's bitter and feels like Hollywood gave him a raw deal—but my last check bounced and then when he wouldn't let anyone in the catering building yesterday—it got me thinking . . ."

"Justin wouldn't let his employees into the Coastal Catering building?"

Colt nods. "We were trying to clean up from a job, and he refused to let us in. He said something about needing to meditate. That he needed to be alone before some meeting with some big shot. It was definitely weird cause he's usually so uptight about clean up—we had to leave a bunch of dirty catering pans in the alley."

Marcus scoots the tape recorder closer to Colt. "Can you recall any specifics about the altercation you heard at the rehearsal dinner? Any actual statements Justin or Mayor Bob made?

"Not that I can think of. The band was warming up in the background—so I couldn't hear everything. It was more of a *sense* of what they were fighting about." He shakes his head. "I've been meaning to get over here sooner, but I got tied up with my mom. It's been a bad week—she's not doing great either . . . but it's just—well," His shoulders go back. "Listen, I ain't accusing nobody of nothing, and I got all these reporters calling me, asking me questions . . . well, I just thought somebody should know."

"You aren't wrong. I appreciate you bringing me in on this."

As Colt stands to leave, Marcus wonders what Colt knows about their investigation. Somebody at the precinct was already talking, and the media leaks were bad enough.

He gets up to shut the door. His gut was on the fence. The boy seemed to be telling the truth, but the whole thing could also be a ruse to send them in the wrong direction.

Justin Sellars was an odd duck too. A bit of a partier, but a lot of bad habits around here were escalating. The waitlist for the hospital's rehab program was two years long. Mayor Bob didn't exactly have a lot of fans either these days. Like everyone that grew up in this town, those two had a history that went back years.

Marcus is still weighing his thoughts when his phone pings. "Bart Brinson is on the phone and he says it's urgent." Janice's voice has the slightest tremor to it. He can see her through the interior window that looks out on the main desk. She's cradling her cell phone with one shoulder, the curls of a tight perm tumbling over the hand that holds the precinct's cordless landline in the other. "He says it's *important*."

"Tell him I gotta get to the council meeting right now." Marcus stands up and tucks in his shirt.

"That's just it, Chief. Bart says to interrupt you no matter what—it's about the case. He says to stop what you're doing right now—" She reaches out her cell phone to him as he leaves his office and saunters toward where she's trembling behind the big intake desk. "They found something that changes everything, sir . . . now, please, darn it—you shut up and take this call."

Chapter
Thirty Eight

Kayla

~

The sun is overhead, and Kayla wipes away a bead of sweat from her forehead as she walks the few blocks from Two Be Wed to Blue Compass's school complex. She was in a hurry after the press conference but had stopped to change at her office, throwing on jean shorts and a baseball cap. At the last minute, she'd added some oversized sunglasses and though she's rushing the few blocks to the gymnasium, her now sneaker-clad feet thank her.

Blue Compass's school compound is a small plot of land six streets back from the beach. The tiny cinderblock elementary school building is situated next to its doppelganger, a modestly larger upper school. Both are newly painted the same soft beige, and share a red metal-roofed gymnasium. Though the buildings were open for school, the asphalt between them was one giant eyesore, a crater surrounded by three construction dumpsters overflowed with broken playground scraps, garbage, and building materials. The gym was the only municipal property large enough to house the large crowd expected so, like many other things the city did, they had simply roped off the danger and looked the other way.

It's still humid for late afternoon and the crowd of reporters, picketers, and townspeople seems to swell as Kayla approaches. An uneasy intensity billowing in the air with the heat as Kayla takes in their tense faces. Their signs punctuate the different emotions:

Blue Compass Belongs to Us.

Hell No—We Won't Grow.

Yes We Will.

Grow or Die.

There are a collection of strangers, faces both familiar and foreign, a handful of creepy-looking interlopers mixed into the crowd. A few are dressed in Halloween costumes. As Kayla crosses the street, a tall man in a Scream ghost face makes her look twice.

She steps between two news vans, and a few feet away a reporter launches into a live broadcast. "Today is the day this tiny coastal town has been waiting for. With millions of dollars at stake, and many feel the soul of this community, Blue Compass Beach is a beloved relic of the Forgotten Coast that some hope will stay that way. This area has never allowed buildings higher than four stories—though a single vote may change that today . . ." The camera pans the crowd in front of the gym's entrance.

"It all hinges on Building Ordinance 23—will Blue Compass embrace growth and vote to amend their building codes thus allowing high rise condos and obvious expansion? We will be right here as the vote goes down."

The journalist pauses as Kayla stops to tie her shoe, and she can hardly believe her ears when the reporter adds, "And coming up tonight at ten—Big Tech, social media and their role in criminal investigations, our panel explores . . ."

* * *

The gym is loud and full, the smell of a freshly lacquered floor as Kayla enters through the main doors. At the front, she's surprised by a security guard she doesn't know. He glares at her and checks her bag, a curt "no cell phones" as he rummages through her purse.

The gym is lined in rows of chairs and the room reads like a Who's Who of Blue Compass. Uniformed and plain clothed police are everywhere. Some standing, eyes erect in an obvious security capacity. Others, like the Bay County Sheriff, mill about. Kayla spots the owners of all the large construction companies, the presidents of several local banks. In the corner, she sees the Panama City Port's Authority CEO, the owner of the large development company, Beaman Corporation and another slimy developer, Jenson Inc. There are a decent number of businessmen and realtors, the familiar faces of Reid Street business owners. The crowd of murmuring voices carry below the gym's high ceilings.

Mayor Bob is in a mass of people near the front, and Kayla watches as he works the room, careful to give each VIP attention. He shakes hands and slaps shoulders. Caroline is next to him still in her pastel power suit from the press conference, and she imagines both their cheeks must hurt from smiling so much.

At the front, a podium has been set up and two long tables flank it on each side. The area is roped off and behind it, three members of the city council chat, their eyes down. Mandy Lowe is deep in conversation, arms crossed in a tailored navy suit. Cyrus Lacroix is next to her, his gangly posture exasperated as he glances around nervously like he's expecting a bomb to go off. Behind them is Austin Johnson, whom she hardly recognizes without his hardware coveralls. The store owner yanks at his tie, shifting side to side, clearly self-conscious of the crowd studying them. The three members are like cuts of meat in a butcher's display, everyone appraising and dissecting their body language for any hint of what will be served to the community in today's decision.

A staticky announcement gurgles over the speakers for everyone to please take their seats, and as Kayla does, she sees that on the far wall, the stadium bleachers are packed too. She waves to a few familiar faces, surprised to see Colt Thistle is sitting among a group of protesters. All of them are packed tight along the wood rows, their faces pinched. That morning, the news had run a story about some rumors of vandalism from the DC activist group. Though no one was sure what had been done and to whom. The group was rumored to be blaming an opposing pro business group that had recently surfaced in Blue Compass. Both groups are there, Kayla realizes, the tension between the two palpable.

A few minutes pass, and the crowd is getting restless. The clock above the basketball hoop clicks to 4:22. Someone behind Kayla reads her mind and wonders out loud where Justin Sellars is. His seat behind the council member's table is the only vacant chair.

The side exit door flies open and daylight suddenly floods the room as Kayla's father rushes in. He beelines to Mayor Bob and shuffles him off to the side of the stage, his face the dead poker expression that gives away nothing. The pair's voices start to change, and Kayla can see from the way their bodies shift away from one another that whatever this is, it's serious. Their sentences are clipped, brows furrowed. A second later, the mayor heads over to the other council members, whispering something before he makes his way to the podium.

At the microphone, Mayor Bob clears his throat and puts on his reading glasses. "My apologies that we're running behind. Let's get started."

He welcomes the crowd and launches into a patriotic and canned statement. Five full minutes later, he begins to call the council roster. His voice is slow and methodical as he checks off each name in the roll book in front of him.

—Mandy Lowe, *Present.*

—Cyrus LaCroix, *present.*

—Austin Johnson, *present.*

When they get to what Kayla knows as the last name— Justin Sellars—the mayor stops to adjust the microphone. He fidgets with his coat button. As he adjusts the microphone a second time, it kicks back a high-pitched squeal. From the back of the room, there is a commotion, the crowd turns as bright light fills the gym, and Justin Sellars bursts through the double doors.

"I'm here. I'm here. We can start!" He barrels down the center aisle, breathless, his rotund stomach lumbering toward the front as he fumbles to tuck in his shirt. "They had me. I mean— the media out there . . . my apologies. *Let's go.*"

Even from Kayla's vantage point, it's obvious something is off. The caterer's eyes are wild, his hands jittery.

"Bob, Council. I'm ready. Let's—"

"Thank you for joining us, Councilman Sellars. I was just, umm—calling the roll. It seems, though that we are going to declare a postponement—" Mayor Bob's jaw clenches. "There are some allegations—err, problems that we will need to work out before we can proceed . . ."

Justin skids to a halt in front of the podium. He looks as if he's been punched in the stomach. He snaps, "Problems? What sort of *problems?*"

"We can't get into all that right now. I will set a new date—to be determined." The mayor lifts his gavel high in the air to adjourn the meeting as Justin leaps onto the platform, lunging at his wrist. Justin's hand stops the strike midair.

"*You* don't have the authority." Justin turns to the crowd, his face purpled in desperation. "He's not God. He works for us. We were all elected together—the vote is now."

"I absolutely have the authority." An involuntary muscle spasms in the mayor's jaw, and Kayla watches as he makes a mental calculation. "Pursuant to code 1294, which states that city council members must be in clear and good legal standing with no *pending allegations* to participate in city business, I have no choice."

He smashes the gavel, and it echoes woodenly into the gym's elevated ceiling.

Justin lunges at the mayor, exploding over the podium. "You bastard—you're supposed to be on my side!"

The mayor's glasses fly off as Justin wraps his hands around the mayor's neck. The podium overturns as they both tumble backward. Justin is swinging wildly as the other council members scatter, chairs flying. A second later, the police are on top of them, but not before Justin lands several blows to Bob's face. It takes three officers to peel him off, and Justin bucks as they're pulled apart. A second later, the cops have Justin on his feet, still restraining him as Mayor Bob stands up, dusting himself off. Blood gushes from the mayor's nose down his suit and tie. "Jesus, Justin, what is wrong with you?" He throws his head back as he pinches the bridge of his nose.

The room has gone silent, and the mayor looks around, suddenly aware of his massive audience. He puts his hands up. "It's alright y'all, it's alright—just a little rough and tumble with an old classmate." He signals to the officers to release Justin then forces an awkward handshake with Justin, who is still panting and wild eyed.

Mayor Bob turns to the crowd, his face arranged with a nothing-to-see-here expression. "Let us boys handle this over a beer . . . and don't worry. We'll get everyone notified when a new meeting date is set." He looks again at the police who are already ushering Justin toward a side exit.

A second later, the door slams shut and the whole thing's over as fast as it began. The room murmurs, a collection of shock and whispers as Kayla's phone vibrates in her hand and everyone starts to shuffle single file into the aisle.

Outside, Kayla is still processing the scene around her when she checks the message. She's annoyed to find it's another media alert for Tania T. *God, that girl never quits.*

She's almost to Two Be Wed when the TikTok video loads, and Tania T is on the screen, a close up of her in the same red glasses, her hair parted down the middle into two space buns.

She's wearing a pair of oversized headphones and the background behind her is a nondescript studio of some kind with white walls and a large fig leaf plant.

"Hey all you out there,

Tania-T, here—just popping on for a second to give you a little tease about my upcoming exclusive story. And yup—it's about our favorite corner of the universe—Blue Compass! This 'T' is so big I am gonna be live streaming my podcast with a special cohost. The award winning Ms. Sela Mason will be joining me. So buckle up, bitches—the countdown is on and your mind is about to be blown."

A superimposed clock ticker is in the right corner of the screen and starts to tick down. It is set for twenty-four hours. Kayla stops and rewinds the video to watch it again. She can hardly imagine what more this girl could possibly know. Especially how she could get someone as famous as Sela Mason on her low-level podcast. Justin's little meltdown had just happened and was hardly earth shattering. There was no way she could already know and have done a podcast on that.

Kayla suddenly hates this girl even more. If today's press conference wasn't enough to deter her, what more could she do? Clearly Tania T wasn't scared of Sophia Bancroft or her money. Kayla's stomach churns as she closes the app and dials her phone. It was time for the last line of defense. It was time to call her father.

Chapter
Thirty Nine

Teo

~

Justin Sellar's scene at Blue Compass's city council meeting is leading the evening news. Ruth and Teo are getting ready for bed when the report comes on. It takes a second for the story to land as Teo listens, the news another layer of surreal: Sela Mason was accusing Justin of assault and harassment. Somehow the country's most famous journalist was alleging that their caterer had followed her and there'd been some sort of altercation?

Teo fumbles to find the remote and turn it up. The reporter on the television is one of those young, rail thin hipster types that usually covers the Hollywood beat, and Teo leans in as she says, "Sela Mason once hosted and produced a well-rated 'Where Are They Now' piece on reality stars—one with a less than flattering portrayal of the now infamous Coastal Catering owner and his failed Atlanta restaurant. Many are speculating on whether the show's reemergence on cable television could have contributed to the incident. Sources are also telling us that Justin has agreed to turn himself in to the Blue Compass Police station tomorrow morning—though it's not clear if the charges he's facing are related to Sela Mason or a confrontation he had today with the mayor of Blue Compass at the long awaited council meeting."

Ruth is in the bathroom, brushing her teeth, and Teo rolls over and watches her barefoot at the sink. With Jo and Sophia gone, Caroline and Mayor Bob locked in their rooms as usual, Summerhouse feels even quieter than normal. It hits him that *they should be in their own bathroom right now*, and he kicks back a blanket as the television replays an old scene of Justin cutting a red ribbon in front of his Atlanta restaurant.

Ruth comes out of the bathroom in a Hamilton T-shirt and polka dot pajama bottoms, tendrils of her thick hair falling loose from the bun on her head. She puts down the glass of water she's carrying and picks up the remote control on the nightstand. She presses the button to pause the scene and a close up of a younger Justin Sellars in a chef's apron freezes. "Well, Sophia will be happy with all the mentions of the press conference—but God, I dunno—maybe, there is something more going on with that guy than being just some kind of crazy food genius?"

Teo pulls himself up in the bed. "Justin brushed me off at the rehearsal dinner—even though I was trying to thank him— it was kinda weird. Before Sophia left, she told me she saw him at the press conference—that he didn't look like a guy about to go and accost anybody."

Ruth shrugs and peels back the sheets, then turns to her bedside table, fishing around in the nightstand until she unearths two blue sleeping pills. She picks up one and breaks it in half. "I may regret this—but not sleeping is part of my problem. I've got to start functioning better." She takes half the pill and tosses it back with water then leans over to kiss him.

It's too late to stop her and for a second, Teo's memory flashes on her father at the LookSee Lounge, his face slack and sweating, Thad's eyes are closed in concentration as he chugs from a silver flask. Then it's a picture he has to create himself, the kickback as Thad's hand fires from a gun that his mind conjures up. He needs to break the news to her that her father isn't who she hoped he was, who he claimed to be. That might be the key to breaking her out of this waiting game: an assurance that the man they probably wouldn't find wasn't worth waiting for.

"Hey—listen, in the morning, we should talk about leaving—some more long term stuff?"

She rolls over and mumbles, "That's fine—morning is good. I just need to sleep . . . I am so sick of being tired."

I am too, he thinks, a hopefulness rising in his chest. He reaches across her and grabs the leftover pills on the nightstand, feeling bold as he pops them into his mouth before he turns out the light.

Chapter Forty

Ruth

Something is screaming, squealing. The room is dark, and Ruth's eyes flutter open. She's been sleeping, dreaming. The vision is fleeting, unsettling. The dark figure with its back to her is there, then gone. She shoots up in a startled fog, left only with the feeling from it, a well of uneasiness in her chest.

The sound seems to be growing louder, and her heart thuds as she tries to get her bearings. It hits her that the squeal is only the house alarm downstairs. It yelps again, and she looks to her left to find Teo there, his back moving up and down with his sleeping breath.

She lies there a few seconds longer, clenching and unclenching her fist as the alarm screeches. *How does no one else hear it?* Then she peels back the covers and pads into the dark hallway. The oak floor is cold on her bare feet and the wood groans beneath her steps as she feels for the landing's arm rail.

In the kitchen, the undercabinet lights, which are always on, are switched off. The room is lit only by the eerie green glow of the appliance lights. The digital clock on the Viking stove reads 5:41. Across the bay, gray clouds have erased the stars and the red glow of the sea turtle lights blur into the inky darkness as she feels for the alarm pad.

The little screen lights up as she touches it, and she can see that her hands are shaking. She draws in a breath as she mashes in the last code she remembers, the alarm rejecting each attempt before finally she remembers that no one's changed the code from 1234. As the squeal ceases, there's a creak, and she freezes, the shush of the ocean suddenly in her ears. She forces a ragged breath, the crimson glow of the porch pushing in on her as she twists, steps toward it. The porch doors are open. The beam of a flashlight blinds her before the scene slides into focus.

She is staring down the barrel of a gun.

"Welcome to the party."

The dark tip of the handgun quivers, and Ruth follows it to the face of Justin Sellars. "But I guess you must be used to those by now."

Her caterer is six feet away, just inside the patio doorway. The flashlight is tucked under his arm, the firearm between his hands, an imitation of a cop in a TV show. His stance is wide like he's shooting at a target.

Only the target is *her*.

He jabs the gun toward her, and her heart slams into her chest as he inches closer to the tall table, quickly propping the flashlight there with one hand. As the beam of light shoots skyward, her eyes adjust and the full picture emerges, the world suddenly teetering on a knife's edge. Over Justin's shoulder, Caroline and Mayor Bob are lined up against the shared wall between the porch and living room. It looks like their wrists and ankles are bound, their mouths muffled by something.

Ruth puts her hands up in a sign of surrender, swallows hard. "Justin, please—what's all this?"

He doesn't move, doesn't speak, but she can see his mind is working. Then suddenly he's pacing back and forth in the shadow of the flashlight before he stops, turns to her, and jams the gun in her direction.

"We're gonna fix this—that's what this is—all of us are in this together now." A bead of sweat slides from his brow.

For a second, Ruth tells herself to stay calm, that there is some explanation, or that Justin means them no real harm. But even as she's thinking it, she's calculating the scene around her. This man has broken into their house, brought a gun. This man who looks like someone coming down with the flu. Still, the porch is the worst possible choice. Someone—anyone from the neighborhood—could meander down the beach. The sun's just starting to inch over the horizon and the view into the screened patio will be full and unobstructed.

Her voice breaks, "Whatever is happening, Justin. Please, don't do this—Teo's a lawyer—and Jo—or if it's money you want—"

"I don't need *your* money." Justin's nostrils flare and instantly she sees her error. In her mind, she filters through a lifetime of interactions with him. There are years of casual summer run-ins then later a handful of catering meetings before the wedding. All of them had one thing in common. Justin Sellars was nothing if not prideful. He was used to being the center of attention, used to giving autographs and being adored.

"Whatever it is—it's OK, Justin. Help me understand." Ruth scans the room as she pleads, cataloging its contents for weapons, objects sharp enough or heavy enough to give her a fighting chance. She needs to puncture skin or gouge eyes. Maybe cause a concussion. Besides the porch furniture, the room is useless. The bar cart is clear across the room. She squints to make out a broom in the corner, a flimsy decorative lantern on the pub table next to them. A sole ceramic coffee cup with an inch of old coffee inside.

Justin turns away from Ruth, checking his hostages before he whips back around, his eyes wild brown discs.

"The only thing you need to understand is that I'm not going to let them get away with it—that I'm nobody's patsy."

Ruth swallows hard, her hands still up, a useless shield against the barrel of a gun. "Let's talk about this. Help me understand."

Justin shakes his head in disgust. "Jesus, this *family*—everybody's always falling all over themselves to be liked—" He steps closer. His face softening as he gets within inches of Ruth's. The handle of his gun strokes her cheek. "You barely stood a chance, did you? And yet somehow—somehow, you resisted, somehow you managed not to let your insides rot away like the rest of them—I know you hated all that attention."

Ruth swallows a sob, fights the urge to recoil as he pushes back a stray hair with the steel end of the gun. His eyes are locked on hers, an intimate black gaze she's too frightened to break. He's frozen for a moment, suddenly zoned out until behind him, Caroline whimpers. The sound snapping him to attention.

"See, all that attention—I know what that's like. It makes you vulnerable. It lets people take advantage of you. That's why I was always there, always . . . always protecting you—like no one ever did for me." His eyes flicker, ticks of mania and rage spinning like a wheel as his words reassure him. "The dangers were everywhere. Your mother. Me. It was only a matter of time 'til you were next—I warned you that you were *next*."

It takes Ruth a second to piece it together. "*You* sent those messages?"

"Messages?" He laughs, the sound guttural and unhinged. "I don't know if that's what I would call them? I mean—I know my methods aren't perfect, but I was helping you, Love— warning you. My God, that house, that father of yours—Ping. Pop. Ping. Pop." He rakes a hand through his hair.

Ruth tries to adjust her face, to digest what he's saying.

"That father of yours . . . I'm not saying he didn't deserve it—nobody shakes me down. And sure, I thought about it. I saw him on the pier—but I didn't kill him." Justin spins around and points the gun at Caroline. "The real criminal here belongs to you."

Caroline's eyes bulge as a single tear slides down her cheek.

"OK, Thad—my father, tell me about that." Ruth turns away from her mother, hoping he will follow her motion, that she reflects a calmness he can mirror. It's a technique she's used with her high school students. *Project a quiet confidence.* But at the moment, her heart is pounding so hard, she's sure he can hear it. "My dad—shook you down? Why?"

But Justin doesn't answer her. He's fishing around in another pocket as he turns to the bay, another spaced-out silence as he stares out at the breaking waves, the dark streaks of sky turning to hints of orange. After what feels like an eternity, he says, "You know, my mom died on this same beach. Not far from here. Storm surge took her—everything. One swoop. House was in my family for eighty-seven years, and Kerry swept them both clear past Highway 98 . . ."

A vein throbs in his forehead. "She taught me to cook in that house—everything I know. I wasn't gonna just let them take the land. *Fucking taxes.* Government commies . . ." He turns to Ruth. "See, when you're famous, everybody wants a piece of you, wants to take what you have. I wasn't just going to let that happen. So when your mom's man comes to me, and he's looking for one more vote . . ."

There's another misplaced laugh, and he starts to hum a tune she doesn't recognize. Halfway through the second stanza, it hits her: "Pennies From Heaven."

When he's finished, he steps closer to Ruth. "My mom liked you—'Only Bancroft worth her salt' she used to say—but this isn't just about you anymore." He lips curl into a sneer as he whips around to Mayor Bob, jamming the gun at him. "You think I didn't know what you were trying to do—that I wouldn't find it right away?" He laughs, the sound maniacal and unhinged "—I bet you and that construction prick thought you were going to cut me out? Didn't think I would figure it out?" He rips something from his shirt pocket, and Ruth can hardly believe her eyes when it glints in the emerging light. Justin is holding her mother's diamond necklace.

He steps in front of Mayor Bob, an inch from his glassy eyes as Justin shakes the thick choker in front of him, his other hand still pointing the gun. "You stupid fuck, you can't frame me—you're going to take it back." He wipes sweat from his forehead with the back of the hand, and beads of wetness inch from his fat fingers onto the sparkling filigree. "You are going to fix it all, damn it—the vote, my money—I need my money."

At the same moment, Ruth spots something out of the corner of her eye, a tiny flicker of hope rising in her chest. It's propped in a corner where two lower screens meet the porch door. The pink gift bag that her father had given her. Wilted from the weather, it's been there since the morning of the rehearsal dinner. Next to it, the bottle of champagne sits unopened. Ruth had wanted to avoid questions, and so she had set it in the dark alcove where no one would notice, completely forgetting about it until this moment.

"I'm glad you wouldn't sell your land, Justin—you're so much smarter than that." Ruth steps toward the bottle, hoping her voice will draw him from Caroline. "It's definitely crazy what they say the land's worth around here. We all know it's worth more." She inches forward again, in her mind formulating a plan. She needs to keep him talking, buy time. She imagines striking him on the head or using the bottle to knock the gun from his hand. Either way, it is a suicide mission.

And probably her only choice.

"It's the money that always gets your interest—*huh*—" Justin shakes his head in disgust, and starts to pace again. Then something on the floor grabs his attention. He stops, frozen as he stares at his feet. A few seconds later, he reels around to Caroline. "You got more money than you could ever spend, and you're too busy looking down your nose at the rest of us. I don't know what Bob was so worried about anyway . . . maybe you should have tried being a better mother—worrying about your daughter instead of letting your girls, letting those babies stay in that house—that . . . that haunted house." He laughs and shuts his eyes. When he opens them again, in his place is a man barely tethered to reality. "Jesus, that slanted room, those sounds . . . Ping. Ping. Pop! Sometimes I thought it was me going crazy . . ."

Ruth's hands are still up, and she takes another miniscule step backwards. "It's OK, Justin. You're a good man. Please don't do anything you'll regret—"

Then a voice comes from below them, "Yoo-hoo—what's going on up there?" They both turn to see Mandy Lowe at the top of the porch stairs, the redhead's poodle panting quietly at her ankles.

Justin's eyes go wide, and his finger trembles on the trigger. It's now or never, and Ruth lunges for the bottle. When it's in her hand, she spins and launches herself at Justin. She's on top of him, and the world is flying backwards, a white-hot rage where her fear should be. His eyes are wide, and in her mind is every person who ever took advantage of her, used her goodness against her and took too much. As Justin's head makes impact with the floor, there's no time to think, no one to save her. So she rears back and saves herself, the awful sound of the bottle landing at his skull meeting the gunshot that reigns out through the porch.

The room is spinning, and somehow she's still straddling him. The gun is on the floor, a few inches away from his limp hand. She raises the bottle overhead and waits. Ready to strike. A breath from his bloodied face, and she knows she will attack again.

A dog is barking. Someone has her arm. Caroline's voice is behind her, free of her bonds, she's shrieking about 911. Mayor Bob is at Ruth's elbow as she tries to stand. He eases the gun from her shaking hand.

"Am I shot?" Ruth looks down, feeling her body for holes or wounds. She's dizzy, outside herself. "Alright, Caroline. Alright. You win. Champagne *is* good for something after all . . ."

Chapter Forty One

Marcus

❧

The thing about small towns is when the shit hits the fan, people get there quick, Marcus thinks as he stares at the little open door.

This wasn't your run of the mill shit—your usual "perp is spiraling out on meth" kind of stuff. This was *unbelievable* shit, the kind of Netflix is going to make this into a documentary bad shit that ends careers.

And it had just leveled up.

It's barely 6:00 AM and he's standing in the Bancrofts' garage, with rubber gloves and a flashlight, an evidence bag in his hand as he stares at a teal green sleeping bag—one that Caroline Bancroft swears she's never seen before.

The bag is on the ground, unzipped, splayed open enough to see there's sand inside it. The only other thing in the little arched closet is a crushed up water bottle, a few clear cellophane wrappers that might belong to some kind of candy. After he'd gotten through the preliminary interview with Ruth, she'd needed a break, so he'd gone to look around. Justin was looking at some serious jail time, and her account of what had happened, of what he'd said, was pretty unhinged. Marcus was still deciding who to interview next when he'd noticed the curved door beneath the stairs. It was open just a sliver.

With a gloved thumb and finger, Marcus picks up a plastic wrapper and shouts into the radio on his shoulder, "Somebody get Jade down here now."

She's there in seconds, her footsteps coming from the garage stairs above him. "The feds are with the daughter now." He nods, not happy about it as he hands her the evidence bag. "We need to print this and that bag ASAP."

Jade stoops to look into the slanted room, her eyes darting to the sleeping bag on the cement floor, a single light bulb suspended from the ceiling over it. "I'm gonna guess that Caroline Bancroft doesn't camp?"

Marcus stands up. "Ruth says Justin told them he was *watching* them—that the house made sounds." His chest tightens. "Christ— the press is gonna crucify us for not arresting this guy yesterday."

Jade's eyes go wide. "And that scene when we were cuffing him?" She blinks. "Are we gonna be able to make something— any of this stick?"

Justin Sellars had been rambling on the whole time they were reading him his rights. As they'd ducked him into the back of the police car, he'd hysterically blamed the mayor for everything from throwing the ordinance vote to global warming. Mayor Bob had been front and center for the whole scene along with half his police force.

"I dunno—we are looking at some pretty unbelievable—" He scratches at the days-old scruff he'd been planning to shave that morning. "Let's see what we find at his office."

Jade's phone dings, and she takes it out, skimming the screen. "Looks like the warrant's done—fastest one we ever pushed through." She turns to head out the open garage door. "I'm heading there now—"

"Text me whatever you find."

* * *

Thirty minutes later, Marcus's phone lights up with a series of messages. Jade was still picking through Coastal Catering's dank windowless office, one which she had described as a wasteland of garbage and pizza boxes, dirty laundry and beer bottles, vodka bottles and wine bottles. From the photos, it looked like when he wasn't lurking around the Bancroft's house, he was living there. The torn leather sofa had a bedsheet and pillow balled up in one corner, his desk piled high with late notices and unpaid bills.

The small catering kitchen was an even stranger find. The adjoining space was compulsively clean. Its gleaming pots and pans hung with stark precision, the giant metal ovens and prep spaces all spotless. The last photo to come in was a close up of a rusty razor and a toothbrush on the lip of the deep metal apron sink. Next to it were rows of empty pill bottles. The labels lined up like soldiers, the dosage of Adderall enough to medicate a small elephant.

Though it looked like the pills might only be the beginning.

Out in the open, right next to the medicine bottles, Jade had found two Nokia cell phones. Neither password protected. The black burner phones had dozens of calls to the bride's number, presumably hang-ups; their photo galleries an even bigger treasure trove. It appeared Justin Sellars had been tailing the family on and off for months. There were photos of the sides of their faces and shoes, the back of Ruth's car. Shots at the nail salon, on the beach in front of the house, inside their garage, a strange close-up of a rug he would have to confirm belonged in the living room. But it was the last photo that had raised the hair on his arms. The off-center shot of a modern gold and glass desk, a stack of file folders piled next to it. In the corner was a white ceramic coffee mug, the angle offering just enough rainbow colored letters for Marcus to be sure who it belonged to. He imagined Justin leaning back in Kayla's desk as he took it—

"The mayor wants you upstairs."

A woman in a black jacket with the gold words "Federal Agent" on it interrupts his thought, and he covers the screen of his phone as he stands to follow her.

He was ready to talk to the mayor too. He'd had his suspicions about Mayor Bob for a while now. There were years of cut corners, the mayor always flashing some new toy when he should be broke. Like a lot of the boys around here, he owned a thirty two-foot boat he couldn't afford, spent all his free time deep sea fishing, the kind of hobby where the gas alone should eat up a meager civil servant's salary. When he'd come around, showing off a giant engagement ring for Caroline Bancroft, it had sealed Marcus's suspicions.

And now Marcus's own end game is in jeopardy. There is a lot more than intuition that the mayor wasn't privy to—and it needs to stay that way a little while longer.

Marcus enters the kitchen and Summerhouse's main floor is a collection of faceless officers in the same black jacket and a few of his own boys, everyone stumbling over each other. The fiancé is in a corner, pacing behind the marble island.

The mayor and Caroline are on the couch, his arm around her shoulder protectively. "Someone get me and Mayor Bob some coffee." He turns to Caroline, who's biting her lip. "Excuse us, Ms. Bancroft—we need to have a little chat. Why don't you go see that guy over there—procedure dictates we file your necklace into evidence, and we'll need some signatures . . ."

Marcus takes a seat at the long dining table and puts back his shoulders as he waits for Mayor Bob to join him. He was good at interrogations, good at getting suspects to trust him. Sometimes the urge to confess can be overwhelming. It feels good to get things off your chest, to talk yourself clean. That was exactly what the mayor needed to do. There were still a lot of pieces that didn't fit together and though Marcus wasn't quite ready to put all the cards on the table, he knew enough to know he wasn't going to go down with the ship. The mayor was elbow deep in it—he was sure of that much—it was time to muck through this filthy mess.

Chapter Forty Two

~

Hey all you out there,
   Tania T here!
   Now I know your ears have been ringing with the latest report about Blue Compass and that crazy caterer, but trust me—Justin Sellars and his attempted kidnapping has nothing on this scoop! As promised—my "T" is bigger—much bigger.
   In the immortal words of the queen herself (a little vintage Taylor Swift aka her 2017 Reputation tour): Are You Ready For it?

   THAD HARGROVE IS ALIVE.

Chapter Forty Three

Ruth

~

"Why is it so cold in Savannah?" Ruth rubs her arms up and down, turning to look out into her sister's Ardsley Park courtyard.

It's been almost two weeks since they left Blue Compass, and she's with her sisters in Jo's sunroom, the evening strangely cold for autumn in Georgia.

"I still can't believe it was one of my followers that spotted him." Sophia's porcelain skin flushes with importance. "I mean—I know he'd dyed his hair and grew some crazy beard . . . but they obviously recognized him." Sophia hugs herself as she takes a seat in an oversized outdoor lounger. "It still pisses me off how that awful blogger knew before we did."

Ruth rolls her eyes. "The guy was a policeman, Sophia. It's kinda his job to *notice* people—"

"The whole thing would be almost sad—if it wasn't so disgusting—" Jo enters from the kitchen to the patio where her sisters are waiting, her arms full of snacks and a bottle of wine.

She carefully releases the goods onto her glass coffee table and begins to fight with the jar top on a container of salsa. "If they really found him weaving all over the place in a stolen car then I don't feel sorry for him. He *deserves* jail." The lid pops, and she sets it down, sighing before she falls into a chair. "He and Justin can rot away together for all I care."

Sophia is scrolling her phone and puts it down to reach for a wine glass and the bottle. "Maybe I should reach out to that cop? He's a hero—we could meet up."

Ruth looks over at her, her irritation with her oldest sister jumping three notches. "Sophie, please tell me you're not thinking of using this situation for a photo-op? Some policeman follower of yours pulling over our dad and foiling his fake death doesn't exactly call for a 'meet-cute.'"

After Tania T had broken the story, a grainy telephoto picture of a frail looking Thad took the internet by storm, the hashtag #ThadDadLives trending for days. That first week, Ruth had stayed mostly at Jo's house. It was like old times, all of them staying up late into the night rehashing how their father had failed them—the three of them consumed in long, bitter rage fests at Jo's kitchen table. Ruth wasn't sure if those loud, wine-soaked family dissections had woken something inside her or simply fueled an already growing flame, but she wanted to hold on to that feeling, to cultivate it. She sensed that this united front wouldn't last. Sophia's suddenly waning anger seemed to confirm her suspicions.

Jo leans back in her seat, the slightest hint of baby bump at her waist as she takes an outdoor pillow from behind her back and moves it to her lap. "God, I'm so sick of talking about that man . . . of hearing about that man. There's got to be something else in the world we can talk about?" Her eyes widen as an alternative strikes her. "You're not gonna believe the phone call I had with Caroline this morning."

"Mom?" Ruth sits up. "About what?"

"You know how all she's talked about since we got back to Savannah is listing Summerhouse? Well evidently, she's found some therapist Maya recommended and has tabled the idea." She laughs, "She wants to . . . and I quote—'work through her overly trusting nature of men'—before she decides."

"Hmmm . . ." Sophia taps her chin with her pointer finger. "I wonder if some sort of therapy and trauma feature on @sophiasez might be good? There's a ton of natural tie-ins that—"

Jo's snort cuts her off. "Nice to see you back to your old self." She pops a chip in her mouth. "How many times have you posted something cryptic about our family drama today?"

Sophia sticks out her lower lip. "Yes—I am *working* again, but only under the parameters we agreed to. Do you know how many interviews I've turned down?"

"We *all* agreed not to talk about Dad . . . or to Dad—that the juice isn't worth the squeeze—and it's not." Jo turns to Ruth. "Alright, Ruth—out with it. What do you want?"

"Who says I want something?"

"Ruth, you never ask us for happy hour." Jo crosses her arms. "Teo says all you do is run since we got back—what's going on?"

Jo's presumption galls her and she almost changes her mind. She didn't need their permission. Ruth turns to face them both, looks Jo square in the eyes. "I'm going to see Dad."

"No, you're not—" Jo starts to snicker and then stops, the quick appraisal of Ruth's rigid posture, her resolute expression making her mouth fall open. "Jesus, what is with everyone today? Mom's talking sane? You're talking nuts?"

"No way" Sophia's eyes bug out. "We said ice everyone out— 'Don't feed the beast'—that's what *you* said." She slams down her wine glass. "Christ, I gave up an interview with Nancy Grace!"

Jo drops her head and blows out her cheeks. "I get it, Ruth— you want answers. I do too, but you're not going to get what you want—he's not capable of that."

"It's not that—" Ruth feels her emotions ping-ponging. Her sister wasn't wrong. She did want answers. Those first few weeks, it had been hard to shake off the sense of something eerie that seemed to follow her wherever she went, the sounds of Summerhouse, the eyes of strangers. The world had more layers now. It wasn't the safe place it once was. She saw now that being good couldn't protect you. People still stole, lied, broke your heart regardless of how good you were to them. Maybe they did it because you were good to them.

Ruth turns to Sophia. "Don't worry sis, I'm not gonna tell anyone what he says to me—we all know that this—our little agreement—benefits *you* the most. The less everyone knows, the more interest it creates for you and @sophiasez—right?"

Sophia's head whips around. "That's not fair."

Jo dips a chip in the salsa, exhaling in frustration. "Ruth, you have nothing to prove to that man. Just wait on the investigator. We *will* get answers—eventually."

"I'm allowed to think differently than you." The words feel good and Ruth says them again. "I am allowed to think differently than both of you. It's *OK*." She watches as a bird lands on a wooden feeder outside the window, avoiding her sisters' faces as their mouths harden into straight lines. "I am so tired of you guys reducing me. My whole life . . . it's like the older I got, the less you heard me. The less you *wanted* to hear me. You can dress it up in sweetness and sarcasm, but it feels the same." She crosses her arms. "What I think matters . . ."

Sophia's face goes beet red. She stomps her foot. "Oh hell no, Ruth. We kept our end of the agreement—that's not fair. I forbid it."

Ruth takes a sip of wine to steady herself before spitting out, "I am twenty-seven years old—you can't *forbid* me to do anything. It's already set up."

Sophia doesn't stop. It's unfair for her to not get the first crack at Thad when her platform is the reason they found him in the first place. Jo can't let go of this being a fool's errand, a waste of time and a slap in the face to the Bancroft women who were trying to go on with their lives. Both of them are blathering on as Ruth stands to leave. She knows those faces. She might be rethinking some things lately, but one thing never changed: There was no stopping a Bancroft sister who'd made up her mind.

Chapter
Forty Four

Marcus

～

Marcus is standing in the parking lot of the Panama City Correctional Facility, the hot sun reverberating off the black pavement as he waits for Ruth Bancroft. She's already on her way there when it hits him that he should probably warn her. Thad Hargrove isn't in the medical unit, but he looks like he should be. Her father is on week two of a pretty brutal detox.

It had taken more than a week to extradite him back from Alabama and in the time he's been in their custody, he's lost even more weight. His skin has a yellow pallor to it. His right eye is swollen shut, still a marbling mess of purple and black from some sort of drunken brawl he must have had before they pulled him over.

The good news is that he's eating again and was agreeing to see Ruth. The last thing any of them needed is that girl driving down here just to have him refuse the visit. Marcus could still hardly believe the feds were being so hands-off. That they'd been able to keep the news of Thad's reappearance under wraps for as long as they had. Somehow, his big talk about his connection to the wedding and the town, to Kayla and the family, had been persuasive enough to let him go at it alone—for the moment.

He'd been waiting for that chance since the morning of the city council meeting, since the moment Janice had given him that call. So today—when he'd finally gotten it—it'd been difficult but necessary to go at him with kid gloves. Of course, Thad had been full of the predictable double talk and denials, and had lawyered up pretty quickly. Still Marcus had gotten enough to start tracking his whereabouts after the pier. He could already place him in a bar in Fort Walton three days after his disappearance. From there, it was pretty clear he'd gone on some sort of bender, that it wasn't the work of a clear-thinking individual that had sent him sailing through a four-way traffic light in a stolen car, his identity confirmed right away with fingerprints despite the flurry of his obscenity laced denials.

Marcus is at the front desk double-checking preparations when Ruth pulls up. He's surprised to see she's made the drive alone. In the last couple of days, the fiancé had called him several times, clearly not happy about Ruth's plans to drive down and reconnect with ol' Thad—though it wasn't as if he was gonna be the one to talk her out of any of this. It was Marcus who had called her and asked her to come here today. She steps out of her car in wide leg pants and pointy flats, her shoulders back. She's carrying a light jacket and relief washes over him that she looks more pulled together than the last few times he's seen her.

"You find it OK—any problems at the gate?"

She takes off a pair of big sunglasses and squints. "No problems." She looks around, her expression unchanging as she eyes the cinderblock building, the tall fence of barbed wire and chain link metal that outlines the ground's perimeter.

"Low-security facilities aren't generally as tough to get things scheduled—though they are only giving you an hour."

They walk through the main doors, and he flashes a badge to the prison officer. Ruth stops, covers her nose, and gulps back a breath—her face has the familiar look of recoil everyone got with that first kick of stagnant air and acrid metal. It was something you never got used to.

There's a second set of interlocking doors, and Marcus gives her a quick run-down of the visiting rooms rules and logistics before they check in. As she fills out the paperwork and finds her license, Marcus strikes up a conversation with the overweight officer waiting in the metal cage, their small talk providing the tiniest distraction he can offer as her trembling hand passes back the stack of papers.

"You're sure you want to do this? No one would blame you . . . you don't have to do anything—"

For a second, she's frozen, and he regrets his choice of words, tries not to think about how much is at stake. The investigation was at a standstill. With Mayor Bob full of denials and no evidence to prove a connection to Justin or the stolen necklace, he was running out of options.

She exhales, yanking at the bottom of her white oxford shirt. "No, I'm ready. If I haven't talked myself out of it at this point, then nobody's going to." She turns briskly and pushes through the metal detector alone.

Chapter Forty Five

Ruth

~

The visitor's room is the same assault on Ruth's senses as the rest of the penitentiary. There's a grime that hangs in the air. The hard click of interlocking doors, the collection of old body odor and metal, cinder block and humidity. As she steps inside, she's surprised to find the space more school cafeteria than the creepy institutionalized dungeon she'd imagined. The drab room is almost empty. Behind the rows of gray hexagon picnic tables is a single vending machine. A lone prison officer stands erect in the corner.

Her father is sitting at the centermost table. His body is hunched over the metal grate top, arms crossed, head buried. He lifts his head to acknowledge her then drops it back in the same position as if the exertion is too much for him. The two-second glimpse is enough to see that he does look like hell—his face is gaunt, eyes sunken, flaccid skin stretches over newly hollowed cheekbones. One eye is hamburger.

"I haven't had anyone to talk to in weeks." Thad looks up again and mumbles, "I should've known it would be you to visit first." He offers a weak smile, the wrinkles around his eyes creasing over the purple and red marbled skin before he buries his head again.

"The whole way here, I've been trying to decide what I would say to you when I saw you." Ruth sits down. She tries to keep her tone measured, the same sweetness he would have grown used to during the weeks leading up to the wedding. "I thought it would just come to me, what a daughter should say in a situation like this, but it still hasn't."

After a second, her father lifts his head again, looking her up and down. "Ain't life a kick in the pants when it doesn't do exactly what you want?" His eyes dart around the room. "Looks like they cleared the place out for you—lemme guess some kind of VIP visitor crap?" He puts his head back between the sleeves of his orange jumpsuit.

She wants to snap at him, to bark that he's not worthy of VIP status, but she reminds herself why she's there. She still remembers his moods. She puts her elbows on the table and leans on them. She can wait. A minute clicks by on the round clock above the vending machine. Then out of nowhere, Thad slams his fist on the table. "Oh hell, Ruth—I ain't well—and rather than lying in my bed convincing the powers that be I should be in the hospital wing, I'm here—with you." He huffs, "What are you doing here?"

His words break something inside her, and it takes everything she has not to fly across the table at him. "What am I doing here—what are *you* doing here? What is this?" She jams a finger at his sunken chest and then around the drab room. "What the hell is *all* this—"

"There she is—" His laugh cuts her off as he claps his hands together "—there's my girl." He leans back, seeming to draw energy from her outburst. "You know, you were always my favorite—you were such a trip when you were a baby—that temper! Your sisters would mess with you, take your shit or whatever—but that fire—your face would go red, and you'd fight back like hell." He scratches at the back of his neck. "It was fantastic—"

He reaches across the table toward her hands, and she flinches. "Don't touch me."

Thad shoots back, his hands up in surrender. "OK. OK—geez, sorry. Yours is the first friendly face I seen in a while—I much rather of died than what I been through these last couple weeks—just thought my daughter . . . but whatever—"

She looks at him, closing her eyes and making a calculation before she says, "What's happening, Dad? What are they saying—your lawyers? This thing is serious—the amount of money and resources, the ancillary crimes attached to searching for you—right now, everybody wants your head—"

"I can't afford a decent lawyer—and the public defender's been here once." He crosses his arms. "Come on, Ruth—you here to do something about that? What do you want?" He pushes up his sleeves and scratches at his arms and neck.

She can't look at him so she stares at a stain on the linoleum floor. "I don't know—I just thought—I thought maybe you could tell me, and I could decide . . . I thought maybe some sort of explanation? That there's some sort of regret?" She exhales, "It wasn't just my wedding. It's my life. I blame myself for letting you back into it."

He scowls, "Damn it, Ruth. Life is hard—you don't know that because your mother got to you. She made all you girls soft, but shit catches up with everyone." His face is dark. "Regrets? Hell—everybody's got regrets—but there's two types of people in this world: Those that do what needs to be done and those that don't have to—" He leans back.

Ruth tries to remember what Marcus said on the phone to her, that the only thing Thad said to the police after they picked him up, while he was still detoxing in the drunk tank, was how sorry he was for ruining his little girl's big day. "The least you can do is explain all this. It would help me if I knew why—if I understood . . ." She looks away "—something?"

He stares at her for a while, and she can see he's making his own calculations before finally he says, "You're a big girl—old enough to know that things don't always go according to plan— but I had one—a good one."

He scratches again at his arms and neck, raking his fingernails back and forth as Ruth tries not to look at the ragged lines of angry red skin. "See, it was just that last run of bad luck snuck up on me. I couldn't get a game, and I owed people—the kinda people who don't take kindly to not getting paid, the kind who don't just bust kneecaps or take a finger." He clears his throat. "So I did what I needed to do—I got out. I had always planned to come to your wedding anyways—I figured why not go early. Let things cool off?"

"I'm guessing it doesn't hurt that half the homes in Blue Compass are either vacant or half-finished? Not a lot of functioning security cameras?"

"That's my girl—" He gives her a proud nod. "So anyways, I had made myself at home, had plenty of time to look around—maybe, find a game. Do your due diligence—I always say."

"And Justin Sellars? He has a lot to say—seems to think—" Thad's laugh cuts her off.

"That sweaty, fat fuck. All I wanted was a little finder's fee—you're *my* daughter after all. I bet your mother was dropping what—five? six figures on the food to impress all her snooty friends?" His brow creases. "At first, he laughed in my face. So, that's when I played my pocket ace—told him what I knew, and he shut up real quick." He scratches at his neck again.

"See, this is one of those things I never got to teach you. Over the years, I've found that if you're real quiet you can pick things up—*useful* things. Like when you find a game a couple towns over, and some sloppy fish is losing his ass at the poker table and won't shut up about all the condos he's gonna build, the piles of money he's gonna make off some poor little hurricane town. The idiot drops five Gs in one hand and doesn't bat an eye cause money means nothing to him—because Beaman Development Corp got a couple councilmen *real* friendly to his 'cause' if you know what I mean."

Ruth fights the urge to look surprised. Beaman Corp sounded familiar, but there were several developers who'd set up shop around Blue Compass, a few faceless entities that blended together.

"So everything's all fine till the bachelor party." He finds her gaze. "I kept myself pretty straight for you—always knowing this was gonna be it—see, the plan was always to disappear a few days *after* your wedding—God, that woulda been so much simpler. But then Angel walks into the Looksee, and I knew plans had to be accelerated, and damned if Justin Sellars doesn't show up and corner me at that bar at that exact moment." He huffs and rolls his eyes. "The guy's all poking at my chest and slurring his words. I couldn't exactly have him talking in front of a bar full of people, so I gave him a right hook and got out of there—created *a little diversion . . .*" His smile disappears as he says, "But then Angel chases me down anyways, and that's when I remembered how close Summerhouse was to the LookSee—like I said, I do my due diligence." He shrugs. "I still don't know how Angel found me in Blue Compass—the whole time I was in Atlanta I never told people about my business, who my daughter was—but that damn house is built up so high. All those garages and storage places. It was as good a place as any to wait Angel out and—"

"That was the same night Caroline's necklace was stolen, wasn't it?"

Thad freezes. His lips parting, twisting slowly into a predator's smile. "Oh hell, the last thing in the world I wanted was something from that *woman*—but I was outta moves. What I *did* need is time. I ain't dumb enough to try to fleece something as hot as that necklace. But see, Angel *thought* I was. He gave me forty-eight hours to make it liquid—just enough time for me to play the float—let me disappear and pin it on Justin. See, I just needed to be good and dead, and that sparkler was as good a reason as any for people to think Justin had followed me onto the pier." He laughs and slaps the table. "The sheriff let it slip that fool thought it was that fucking mayor who planted the necklace at his place. Karma's a beautiful thing, ain't it?"

Ruth holds her breath as he talks, surprised that he's coming clean so freely. As it processes, she becomes more and more repulsed. "I still don't understand how you disappeared? There were gunshots—and I saw you on the pier?" Ruth reaches into her pocket, suddenly remembering the travel size hand lotion that had somehow made it through the metal detector. She takes it out. "How—" She looks at the officer in the corner. He is staring at the floor so she squeezes some hand cream into her palm before stealthy slipping it across the table to Thad.

Without missing a beat, her father takes the thick lotion and spreads it on his arms, his neck. The smell of lavender momentarily covering the stench of the room as he rambles on.

"All I really needed was a boat and a gun—Lord knows, Blue Compass got plenty of those. I anchored her out about a mile down the beach—deep enough no one would bother. I could do that swim in my sleep—"

Ruth offers him another squirt of lotion, and he closes his eyes as he rubs it in.

"Anyways, I'm not gonna lie—I was nervous as hell about how it was all gonna play out, but compared to what Angel had planned for me—it was a no brainer. Once I hopped that boat, I got as far from Blue Compass as two tanks of gas and a seventy-five Evinrude could take me."

"So, that's all of it—that's how it happened?" Ruth tucks away the hand creme. "And Justin and Mayor Bob were the two city councilmen taking a bribe—from Beaman Development? You're sure?"

"Yup—they were each getting buckets of cash—now listen, Ruth, I didn't mean for it to go so—"

"You can stop talking now, Thad—that's all I need." Ruth is already up from the table, wiping her hands on her pants. She's five steps from the door as her exit registers, and Thad's face drops.

"Ruth—wait a minute—" He's suddenly red "—Whad'ya mean *'need'*? Where you going—"

When she's almost to the door, she hesitates and turns back at him. "—I do want to know one more thing . . . was any of it real? It seemed like you wanted to be there—at the wedding . . . for me—" Her voice trails off. "It's just not something a person who cares—who loves another person does . . ."

Her father's face freezes and he snaps, "I care about you—of course. You're my daughter."

Ruth shrugs, unconvinced and is about to turn on her heels.

"Fine. You want more truth? I'll give it to you—then maybe we can sit back down and talk some more—help each other out—" He shifts in his chair and for a moment she's afraid he might get up, might try to come near her. Instead he says, "Ruth, some men are just different. Especially some fathers. We ain't mothers. We ain't these soft mushy rose petals—maybe that's why I been messed up so long, why I had my issues—I used to feel bad that I just ain't built that way—" He hesitates, "But the truth is . . . sure I care about you but—" He spits out a long exhale. "But hell, we all gotta love ourselves more—you know what I mean?"

"What you *mean*?" Ruth feels her mouth fall open. "You know what? Just *don't*—" For a second, she's angrier than she wants to be, then it hits her what comes next, what the last moment of this confrontation always was.

Ruth takes another step back and makes a big show about taking out her phone from her jacket pocket, turning the screen so her father can see it across the room. The recording app is still running. The timer reads forty-one minutes. As she clicks it off, she looks at him. "You know, you're old enough to understand that life doesn't always go how you expect it to either." She lifts her chin as she tucks her cell phone back into her pocket. "I think it *was* always about the necklace—I think you're a thief and a liar." She turns and spins on her heels. "And now they can prove it. Goodbye *Thad*. Thanks for the memories."

As a prison officer buzzes her through the door, he's on his feet, his voice a booming barrage of profanity that disappears as the latch slides closed behind her.

Chapter Forty Six

Kayla

～

Thad Hargrove was pleading out. Marcus just called with the news. It's a development that isn't completely unexpected after his daughter fed him to the wolves.

So her father is actually heading home early for once, and she's decided to cook dinner—or more specifically, Kayla is heating up a grocery store lasagna. As she sets the table, the whole scene feels a bit domestic. Even the table looks old fashioned, her mother's cloth napkins over a seashell tablecloth, her crystal sweet tea pitcher full at the center.

Marcus walks into the kitchen and takes a beer from the yellow fridge humming in the corner. The door groans as he opens it, and the awful hum amplifies into the room. It was the kind of thing that usually annoys her, but she's so glad to see him, to have him home for once that it doesn't bother her.

He takes a seat at the table in a pair of cargo shorts and a T-shirt. He'd showered at the station and changed for the first time in many weeks into his civvies. His jaw is unclenched, shoulders loose, but his face is a puzzle.

She picks up her glass and says, "Cheers to the bad guys going where bad guys go."

Her father presses his lips together and shakes his head. "I just got off the phone with Bay County—it's official, the department's been dissolved—" Her heart breaks as he takes another swig of beer like this isn't major news.

"What—I don't understand? After you handed them Thad Hargrove on a silver platter?"

He shrugs. "I was stupid to—" He huffs, "I guess budgets are budgets, and it sounds like everybody's getting bigger. Government's gonna bus the Blue Compass kids to new schools." He looks away. "Big schools, big departments—don't think there's anything anyone coulda done to change it."

Kayla's appetite is suddenly gone, but the timer goes off for the lasagna anyway. She takes the silver foil tray out of the oven and sets it on the counter, the top bubbling like molten lava in the growing silence.

"It's not as bad as it sounds—Davis Ray isn't as awful as I gave him credit for." Her dad breaks off a piece of garlic bread from the basket on the table and shoves it in his mouth. "I mean he's awful. Horrible. But Bay County's promised to take everyone from my department. All my guys' jobs are safe."

"That include you?"

"They offered to keep me on, but I think I'm done." He chews. "I know myself. I can't take orders—and I don't want to . . . don't have to." His voice trails off as he wrings the napkin in his lap. "Well on the bright side, I think the feds are gonna go after that quack internet doctor giving Justin all those ADD meds—though it may be a big waste of time considering all the booze that boy was drinking . . . it's gonna make both trials a mess . . ."

Kayla is speechless, thinking that Caroline Bancroft would be waiting that much longer to get her necklace back from evidence. She'd run into her the day she left town, the sight of Blue Compass's resident diva slumped over the town's only gas pump surreal. Her face buried in a brimmed hat and ridiculous sunglasses, her shiny BMW loaded down like a fugitive fleeing the country. Kayla had offered her a surprised half wave, and in response, Caroline had refused even eye contact, a snub which shouldn't have surprised her and shouldn't have stung. She was still annoyed with herself that it had done both.

"Who knows? All this change—maybe it's a good thing?" Kayla looks at her father. He seems younger, the weight of the town and its politicking off his back. Though a new ordinance vote had yet to happen, Mayor Bob's presumed guilt and chorus of denials meant the mayor would most certainly be voting no when the time came. She was pretty sure the town would make sure whoever replaced Justin would definitely be in that category too. At least the town felt safe for now.

They eat in silence for a few moments, the sound of chewing and the buzz of the fridge filling the space between them until finally she says, "Listen Dad, if I had known the wedding was gonna blow up—that the Bancroft girls would—" she swallows hard "—and all that press. I would never have put you in that position."

He takes another long swig of beer, the bottle nearly empty now, before he says, "Damn it Kayla, I make my own decisions— and I've got no problem with any of the ones I made."

Kayla stands and goes to the counter, cutting a second square of lasagna from the pan with the edge of a spatula. Her mother always said that the only two universal truths were that "navy blue looked good on everyone and old men don't change."

The day after Kayla had crashed her car with Sophia Bancroft, Marcus had come into her room where she'd been lying on her bed, still confused why she wasn't in a holding cell, a bump on her forehead and an awful hangover.

"It's taken care of—and that's all you need to know. I don't want to discuss this again."

And they never had. Not even when she'd taken on the Bancroft wedding or when she'd gone to Ruth and her sisters for protection from the media when she should have gone to her father. Not when it had jeopardized his job or her safety.

"This town . . . sometimes it's like living in arrested development." Kayla shoots a glance back at her father. He's peeling the label away from the body of the bottle. She shakes her head. "Maybe that's why I'm always changing my hair color." She spits out an uncomfortable laugh. "We all just want to feel *seen*—"

She waits for him to say something—to *hear* her, but he just picks up his fork and fiddles with it. The realization that her father never would washes over her. He loved her the only way he knew how. And she was lucky that the way he loved her meant she would never have to question how far he'd go to protect her, that he'd pick her over himself every time. That was something none of the Bancroft girls would ever have.

When she'd finally sat down and listened to Tania T's podcast with Sela, it had surprised her that the pair had not only mentioned Sophia's press conference, but pegged it to be the publicity stunt it was—although according to Sela, it was also a smart move made by a social media-savvy woman. The majority of the episode had been spent talking about Justin's unhinged attempt to confront Sela. (At one point, he had allegedly called Sela the c-word and blamed his career failures on her, saying that she should start paying his living expenses as reparations for destroying his life.)

Both hosts had been predictably appalled and though parts of the episode had been hard to swallow—especially as Tania T had ranted on, touting her journalistic integrity, it was the end of the episode that had given her hope. As the episode had wrapped, Sela had offered a convincing oration calling for women to band together to out the bad actors of the world. On some level, Kayla supposed she could be part of that group of women, for better or worse.

Kayla turns and brings him another beer from the fridge. They both knew that it was always a possibility things might come out later, that loyalties to her father might change or someone from the precinct might get loose-lipped, but soon it would hardly be front page news. For a retired police chief, the sting of the coverup would be more of a black eye than a gut punch.

For now, she wanted to spend her energy figuring out how to resuscitate Two Be Wed. Someday she still wanted to add on to it, maybe build a loft that looked out of Reid Street and move in. Her life was here, and once she was on Tania T's podcast next week—the highly promoted behind-the-scenes debriefing of what it was like to be in the eye of a storm and falsely accused of a crime—Kayla trusted business would pick up again. Maybe even double thanks to the visibility. Though it was something she never dreamed she might do, maybe things turned out alright if you could pivot, if you could weather the storm—at least that's what she hoped.

"You know—someday, the town's gonna need a new mayor . . ."

Marcus shakes his head and laughs, breaking the silence between them. "That's an awful idea. I worked at the department because I wanted to. I'm thinking it's time to get out of this rut . . . and maybe, I'd really just like to just go fishing."

"I guess that's not a terrible plan."

A second later, he puts down his fork. "I *was* thinking about something. It's about time we redecorate this place, don't you think? Ya know anyone with a good eye for fancy stuff like that?" He smiles. "Whad'ya think about bringing this place up—maybe, this guy up a few centuries closer to the one we're in?"

Epilogue

Ruth

Six months later

She can hardly believe it. They are sitting in thread-bare beach chairs, holding hands as the last bit of sun melts over the aqua waters of Aruba. The Caribbean island had not disappointed. Ruth and Teo watch as a young clergyman walks down the beach to the cathedral next to the resort. Turquoise ocean laps at the shore line, wetting the tip of the clergyman's white stole as he twists toward them, waving goodbye for the third time.

"That's the crunchiest priest I have ever seen." Teo mutters the words under his breath, his mouth carefully fixed as he adds, "I think he's a little starstruck by you." He waves again. "I still can't believe you managed to find the only Catholic priest in all of Aruba willing to marry us on the fly."

Ruth sighs, "Someday soon, no one will know me and I will just be your boring ol' wife making meatloaf and nagging you to pick up your socks." She threads her hand through his. "*I can't believe we're finally married.*"

"We couldn't have planned it any better."

She laughs, looking down at her bare feet. She's wearing a plain white sheath dress she'd bought in the gift shop. At the last minute, she'd pinned up her hair and thick tendrils spill out of the loose knot at the nape of her neck. Catching a glimpse of herself before the wedding she'd thought: *This is how it was always meant to be.*

Thirty-six hours earlier, they'd been sitting in their kitchen. A regular Thursday, drinking wine and making pasta. Teo was mapping out a run on his watch and had wondered out loud what to do with the long weekend. A second later, an email advertising a last-minute plane ticket sale had popped up on Ruth's phone. They'd both looked at each other and burst into giggles. From there, the details had somehow fallen into place.

Ruth looks down at her phone on the rickety metal table between them. It's sitting next to a pair of mai tais, the glasses sweating in the sun. She picks up her phone for a second then puts it face down before she looks around. The last-minute accommodations were simple, a two-room tiki-style bungalow, sparse and clean and most importantly—remote.

There'd been months of talking. To her sisters and Teo, to a therapist and the police. Hours and hours of interviews and depositions, some under oath. She just wanted quiet. Though some part of her wished her sisters had been there for the cere-mony, most of her was glad they wouldn't see another soul until they returned Tuesday.

Teo takes a sip of his drink and watches as Ruth eyes her phone again. "Go on and call—I know you're dying to . . ."

Ruth scoops it up and breaks out into a grin. "Well, maybe just Jo—"

Her sister answers on the first ring and there are squeals of congratulations. The promise to send pictures as Ruth closes her eyes and imagines Jo back in Savannah, a very overripe, very uncomfortable stuffed melon. She still had a few weeks to go before her due date but was already begging to be induced. The nursery done and JD's boat on "lockdown," there was talk of going back to the law firm part time after the new nanny moved in.

"Tell Auntie Sophia I will call her later, I know she's tied up with the move—and remind her that we said mums the word on all this." Sophia, firmly on the road to officially divorced, had recently sold her house and was in the process of moving into a rental in downtown Savannah. Though Ruth was glad she was getting on with her life, some things never changed. In a strange but not altogether surprising twist, Sophia was more famous than ever. In the aftermath, her Instagram following had tripled. The increased notoriety Sophia now claimed to use to highlight social issues—among them her continued stance against "big tech." Though Ruth really had no idea if she was following through or not. Nor did she care, she'd washed her hands of social media for good.

Of course, her sister's cone of silence about their ordeal had long ago gone to hell. There were murmurs of her starting a podcast with Sela Mason producing, *True Crime: It Happened to Me.* Big shock, sponsors were already lining up, and it was predicted to be a smashing success.

On one front, she was happy that Sophia had seemed to make some strides. After the coverage of the wedding had torpedoed Two Be Wed, her sister had stepped in to help Kayla Jennings. After the continued struggles of her boutique, Sophia had convinced the wedding planner to focus her talents on dress design. Somehow, they'd discovered that Tania T's rival blogger (who knew bloggers had rivals?) Rain the Rainbow Unicorn was documenting her struggle to find a "body positive" prom dress. With a little nudge from @sophiesez and some luck, the pair had created a viral photo of the blogger wearing a "Kayla Jennings's Couture" iridescent floor-length rainbow-colored gown. Now Kayla had more business than she could handle. Last week, *Panhandle Magazine* had just rated her one of the South's Top Ten New Designers to Watch.

Things seemed to be dying down for Teo and Ruth too. Justin had finally changed his plea to guilty, and his sentencing was scheduled for a few months from now. Her father's deal had included three years and restitution for the hundreds of thousands of dollars his search had cost. Though it was hard to find anyone among the various agencies who believed he'd pay back a single dollar.

Teo had heard that the Blue Compass rumor mill was also buzzing with news that the precinct had finally gotten to the bottom of the media leaks. It seems Jade Marshall's significant other had been selling information as fast as she could get it. Broke and perhaps hoping to sabotage her girlfriend's career prospects, the betrayal had become a sort of catalyst for Jade. Having sworn off both dating and pillow talk, she had already moved to Panama City and was working her way up the ladder of the Bay County Sheriff's Office. Now that the leaks weren't flowing so freely, the coverage of the story was waning too. Every day more shreds of normality snuck back into Teo's and her lives.

Ruth tells her sister that she loves her, that she can hardly wait to be an aunt again, then hangs up. She closes her eyes and hugs herself, staring out at the blue sky, the aquamarine waves rolling like a lullaby in front of her.

A moment later, she picks the phone up again and flips through it to the photo gallery. The first few shots are from today and were taken by a couple passing down the beach: the two of them holding hands and reciting their vows. Teo is beaming, dimples on full display, the breathtaking ocean behind them. They both looked relaxed, and most importantly, happy. Ruth scrolls some more and a picture from the night of the rehearsal dinner stops her. It's a group shot of herself, Teo, Maya, Caroline, and Thad.

She leans over to show the picture to Teo. "We all look so perfect." They are all huddled together under the tent—just moments before everything had gone sideways. Five sets of perfect white teeth, behind them an enormous flower arrangement, the slightest hint of Blue Compass's clear water beyond that.

Without realizing it, Ruth touches the screen, tracing the outline of her father's face then puts down her phone. The loss would always be there, like the ache in a phantom limb. She is quiet for a moment, watching the waves crash then ebb, a particularly large one reaching their bare feet before pulling quietly back to the sea.

"Do you think that someone—I mean a person who does things like . . . Do you think they must be all bad?"

"Your father?" Teo asks. "I guess it's probably not that uncommon to see functional addicts stop *functioning*." He stands up from his chair and picks up a rock, skipping it into the ocean. "I like to think that no one is truly *one* thing 100 percent of the time. Maybe there aren't any hard and fast rules when it comes to family." He pauses, "But I don't think you can save someone who doesn't want to be saved."

Ruth shrugs, feeling the weight of his words as a breeze whips through them. The wind catches the single white orchid she's pinned in her hair, lifting it out of the loose coil of curls. It swirls once in the air, losing a single petal before landing at their feet.

Acknowledgments

I have dreamt about writing a book like this one since I was a little girl whose favorite place was the library. I can still remember the magical textured feeling of running my fingers down the long lines of books on the shelves and being sure the answer to everything was in them. My gratitude is boundless, and I would like to acknowledge the extraordinary village of people who helped me make this book a reality.

First, a huge thank you to my agent, Ashley Lopez, and the Waxman Literary Agency. Ashley, you were the editor, champion, and hand-holder I needed at the exact moment I needed it. Your careful eye and wise input have shaped this book into what it is, and I am deeply grateful.

Thank you to Crooked Lane Books and to my editor, Tara Gavin. To Thai Perez, Rebecca Nelson, Dulce Botello, and Mikala Bender—you are all rockstars. Thank you to Crystal Patriarche, Hannah Lindsley and Leilani Fitzpatrick and all the talented people at BookSparks, and to Mackenzie Shaeffer (your voodoo behind the camera should be studied.)

Once upon a time, I had the good fortune of taking my first writing class with one of the world's greatest cheerleaders of women and authors, Amy Condon. Amy, thank you for taking a frightened wanna-be and giving her the courage to "vomit" on the page. Thank you to Carolyn Prusa, another amazing beta reader whose hilarious book, *None of This Would Have Happened if Prince Were Alive*, is a must read. To Pat Conroy, one of the greatest Southern writers in American literature, thank you for your beautiful body of work. Your achingly honest stories made me want to write and somehow believe I could. It's one of my greatest regrets that I never got to meet you.

I am blessed to have an amazing family (who bears no resemblance to the one in this story.) Thank you to my mother, who is always one of my first readers, and who knew I could do this long before I did. Thank you to my dad, who tells bad dad jokes and is the kindest, most hard working person I have ever met. Thank you to my brother, Jeff, and my two sisters, Kelly and Alexis, and to my chosen sisters, the Dutch Island girls, your love and encouragement throughout the years have kept me going. I am forever grateful to my husband, Travis, for his steadfast love and support (especially for putting up with me every time I jumped up in the middle of a really good movie, nap, or life moment because I absolutely had to write something down or I'd forget.) To my three boys, Austin, Alex, and Andrew, I hope you chase your own dreams because being your mom has been one of mine.

Last but certainly not least, thank you to God who is the source and inspiration for all good things.